D0837666

34-17

18

Don't miss Signature Select's exciting series:

The Fortunes of Texas: Reunion

**Starting in June 2005, get swept up in
twelve new stories from your favorite family!**

THE FORTUNES OF TEXAS:
Reunion

MYRNA MACKENZIE
Keeping Her Safe

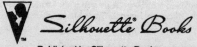

Silhouette Books

Published by Silhouette Books
America's Publisher of Contemporary Romance

Special thanks and acknowledgment are given
to Myrna Mackenzie for her contribution
to THE FORTUNES OF TEXAS: REUNION series.

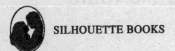

SILHOUETTE BOOKS

ISBN 0-373-38932-9

KEEPING HER SAFE

Visit Silhouette Books at www.eHarlequin.com

Printed in U.S.A.

Dear Reader,

For years I've been thinking that I'd like to write a book about a bodyguard, so I was delighted when I was asked to write *Keeping Her Safe* and tell Vincent Fortune's story. Vincent is the epitome of the protective hero, the type of hero that I love to write. Of course, the fact that he's big and handsome and tough and has a reluctant soft spot for Natalie McCabe, the heroine, only added to the joy of writing about him.

And Natalie is just the kind of heroine I can't resist, one who gives the hero a run for his money. Strong and feisty, Natalie is pretty sure she doesn't want a bodyguard, even though she realizes she might need one. And being a woman who likes to fight her own battles, she just can't help but end up thwarting Vincent at every turn, causing the sparks to fly and the heat to build, even as the outside danger threatens to end everything.

Writing Natalie and Vincent's story was an adventure, being able to continue Ryan Fortune's story made the experience even more exciting, and working with some of my favorite authors…well, I just couldn't have asked for a more agreeable task.

I hope you find abundant pleasure in reading this and all of the books in THE FORTUNES OF TEXAS: REUNION series!

Best wishes,

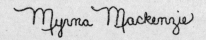

One

Natalie McCabe stared up at the massive dark-haired man standing in the doorway to her apartment and wondered what she had gotten herself into. The man blocked the light from the hallway. His intense gray eyes and sharp-edged jaw were practically predatory. He looked very much like trouble, and right now she already had enough trouble in her life.

"You're not Vincent Fortune, are you?" she asked, unable to hide her concern.

"None other," he answered in a lazy voice. "Is there a problem with that?" He glanced down at her and then beyond her into her apartment.

Yes, there's a major problem, Natalie wanted to say, even as she bit her tongue. When Daniel Fortune, San Antonio's assistant district attorney, had told her he was going to assign her a bodyguard, she supposed that she had expected someone big—just not someone whose eyes took in so much. Within two seconds of opening the door, she would swear the man had registered every aspect of her house and every inch of her person. A shiver of awareness ran through her. This was a man who was used to being in control.

If there was one thing Natalie couldn't deal with, it was having someone else trying to take her control away.

"Of course there's no problem," she finally said, trying to calm herself.

The man looked down, and Natalie realized that she had clenched one fist. "I've been hired to protect you," Vincent said more gently.

"Yes, I understand that it's a necessity. I'm okay with that," she finally said.

The man looked amused, as if sensing her lie. "Mind if I come in, then?"

Natalie thought about that for two whole seconds. There was no way she was letting Vincent Fortune into her apartment. It wasn't just that he was big, he was also handsome, with a killer smile and a low, sandy voice that promised carnal pleasure. Men like that were the kind that many women allowed favors. Women in those circumstances gave up more power than they should. Because they were lusting, not thinking.

Natalie was always thinking. Right now she was thinking that she had no business toying with the word *carnal*.

"Is it really necessary for you to come in?" she asked, desperately hoping the man couldn't read minds. "Aren't you just supposed to sit outside my house in a parked car watching for danger? Isn't that how it works?"

He raised one dark brow, not smiling. When he looked down at her, Natalie felt small and frail, even though she wasn't either of those things. At five-six, she wasn't short, and she visited a club regularly and had taken self-defense courses.

"You and I need to establish a working relationship and some basic ground rules before I can decide what the best course of action is, Ms. McCabe," the man said. "To do that, we need to sit down and talk, and you probably don't want to talk in a place where anyone can overhear us."

Okay, he had a point. Natalie took a deep breath, her options fading. Not for the first time she wished her situation were different. When she had been assigned to cover the party the governor had thrown to honor Ryan Fortune, noted philanthropist and head of the Fortune family, for his contributions to charity, it had been an ordinary day. Just as usual, her boss at the *San Antonio Express-News* had stuck her with the social circuit when she wanted the chance to cover hard news stories.

Then she had witnessed Jason Jamison murdering his wife, and everything had changed. She was no longer just a reporter but also a witness to a crime.

Not long ago, her tires had been slashed, and recently she had begun receiving threatening notes. She needed protection, and Daniel Fortune was convinced that his brother Vincent ran the best security firm available. Damn!

"I don't mean to be a pain, Mr. Fortune," Natalie said, still not inviting him in, "but exactly how do I know that you're who you say you are? Especially given my situation, I can't just invite a stranger into my house."

Vincent nodded slightly. His eyes crinkled at the corners in a way that made Natalie's stomach flutter. *Don't be stupid,* she told herself.

"You've just become my favorite client, Ms. McCabe," Vincent Fortune was saying. "Most people let me in without asking any tough questions. I'll show you my credentials, but I'd also advise that you call my brother just to make sure that I am who I am. That way you'll have some peace of mind."

That was such a joke. She hadn't had peace of mind since this whole Jason Jamison business had started. Moreover, she was currently involved in some sensitive sleuthing for an article she wanted—no, needed—to write, and having someone trailing her would be a decided disadvantage. Besides, this man, with his short dark hair, gray eyes and hard-muscled body, was not the kind to make any woman feel peaceful. Unless one counted the afterglow of a sexual encounter as peaceful....

"I'll call Daniel," she said, chasing her thoughts away as she pulled out her cell phone and dialed Daniel's number.

"Hi, Natalie," Daniel said when she had told him what she wanted. "Yes, that's definitely my big brother. He's a bit imposing, but I can assure you that he's highly effective."

Natalie looked up, and her eyes met Vincent's. For a minute, she couldn't look away, couldn't swallow. *Imposing* was a good word for the man. It was a word she didn't care for much.

"Are you okay with this, Natalie?" Daniel asked. "I don't mean to scare you, but until Jamison's case is complete, and with these notes circulating, you need to be protected. Vincent will do that. He's more dependable than anyone I know, and he's capable, as well. He'll get the job done. All right?"

No, she was not all right. For years, she had been treated as a cute but inept little doll by her family. Moreover, Joe Franklin, her good-ol' boy boss, felt that women should be happy just to write fluff pieces. Now Vincent Fortune would join the ranks of those who wanted to protect little Natalie McCabe from the world. He would smother her with his undeniable presence. But she had no choice. To change things, she had to remain healthy and alive.

"I'm fine with that, Daniel. Thank you." She hung up.

"All right, come in and let's get started, Mr. Fortune," she said, stepping back and letting the man in her doorway inside. "But I'm going to be honest. I'm really uncomfortable having a man following me around."

"Excuse me," he said, "but I have to ask. Is it just the prospect of having a bodyguard that bothers you or the fact that I'm a man?" His eyes turned dark and he didn't surge forward into her house as she would have expected. "Because," he continued, "you should understand that most people are uncomfortable having a shadow at first. They get used to it. If the discomfort goes deeper, though, I need to know."

She felt herself growing warm. "I just don't like feeling helpless. Having someone paid to keep me safe makes me feel hemmed in, frustrated. I have work to do, Mr. Fortune." It was important work, too. The story she was trying to uncover would not only help establish her as a respected reporter, but it would bring justice to many elderly people who had been wronged. She couldn't give that up.

Vincent gave her a curt nod. "I respect your work, Ms. McCabe. I hope *you* understand that while VF Securities is my business and I take pride in my work, this situation goes beyond that. I take the intimidation of innocent individuals very seriously. That's what I'm seeing here. You've been threatened. I've seen the notes that have been sent to you. Someone wants to frighten you. He or she wants you out of the picture. I don't intend to let that happen."

Suddenly the thing she had been avoiding thinking about came rushing back at her. *I'm watching you, Natalie. You're never alone, Natalie. Don't let down your guard, Natalie.* The notes had frightened her a great deal, it was true. Her hands had trembled just holding the bits of paper those notes had been written on, and she felt sick even remembering those moments. But giving in to that fear, letting someone else take away her choice to be strong and to be the one in charge…it just made the fear worse, in a way. She had struggled all her life for the chance to follow her own path. This was too much like admitting that her family had been right all along, like conceding that she really was weak, parasitically helpless.

The thought threatened to overwhelm her, suffocate her. She gave herself a mental shake and tried to stand taller. "Mr. Fortune, I grew up with parents and three older brothers who felt I was incapable of even walking across the street without assistance. I *do* understand the need for your expertise and your protection, and I *am* grateful for all you and Daniel are trying to do for me. But I have to be able to live my life and do my job without interference. I have to be able to have some semblance of normalcy."

"All right," he said in his dark, sexy voice as he entered her home and shut the door behind him. "I'll do all I can to make that possible. I'm here to watch your back, and I'll do my best to make it easy for you."

But as he brushed past her, and she caught a whiff of his aftershave, a fragrance that only emphasized his masculinity, she couldn't imagine it ever being easy to have this man watching her every move. Already she felt as if she were walking around in her underwear. His eyes were everywhere. She could see him assessing every nook and cranny of her living room, noting the locks on the windows, the open curtains that let in the sunshine.

She could almost hear her parents clucking every time she took a risk. She could remember her three brothers' frowns if a boy so much as glanced below her neck. This kind of scrutiny was not new to her. The old, familiar sense of beating her head against the wall crept right back in, only this time she couldn't pretend the scrutiny was unjustified, that she could handle everything on her own. Like it or not, someone really was threatening her.

"I appreciate your candor and your promises, but my life *is* going to change, isn't it?" she asked softly.

"Yes," he said, turning to face her. "It already has. You were at the wrong place at the wrong time, and because of that everything will be different from here on out."

"Some people would say I was in the right place at the right time. Jason Jamison is behind bars."

He gave a slight nod. "Yes."

But Natalie had to admit that his first comment had been right, in a way. Because she was a valued witness whose safety was in question, she was going to be spending a lot of time with a man she wouldn't ordinarily have ever met, one she would never have chosen to meet.

Natalie sighed and nodded. "All right, keep me safe, Mr. Fortune."

"It will be my primary goal."

And hers would be to keep her life as normal as possible, to make sure that Vincent Fortune remained a shadow, one she could shed once this mess with Jason Jamison was over.

Vincent sat down at Natalie McCabe's fussy little kitchen table and did his best to look a little less formidable. In his line of work, having a little brawn was usually good, but it was never a good idea to make a client uneasy.

Natalie McCabe, with her soft, husky voice that couldn't quite hide her nervousness no matter how hard she tried, was clearly uncomfortable where he was concerned.

"All right, Ms. McCabe, we'll need to go over all that's happened to you since you attended that party, and I'll need to have an idea what your daily schedule is."

"I can tell you everything that's happened," she said.

"Great. And the schedule?"

She looked to the side. "I'm a reporter, Mr. Fortune."

"Vincent. We're going to be spending a lot of time together and, really, I'm just not a 'Mr. Fortune' kind of guy."

She blinked those light green eyes of hers. Eyes he would have been attracted to if she were not a client. But she was.

"Vincent, then," she said, her tone reluctant. "I'm a reporter, Vincent. I interview people. If I tell you my schedule, you'll follow me around, won't you?"

He smiled. "That's generally the idea of a bodyguard, yes."

"Exactly. That's going to be a problem."

"In what way?"

Natalie looked at him dead-on. "Vincent, I don't know if you've noticed, but you are a…well, you're a rather big man."

He raised one brow.

She raised one right back.

"It comes up now and then," he admitted, trying not to grin.

"Yes, well…my contacts might be intimidated by a man with linebacker shoulders. How am I supposed to get people to open up and tell me their secrets if they're looking over their shoulders wondering what you're doing?" She threw her hands out in apparent exasperation, and then she frowned. "I'm sorry, I know you have to look forbidding to do your job. I really didn't mean to insult you." She glanced up and he couldn't believe it, but she really did look as if she thought she might have hurt his feelings.

"Don't worry about it. Any of it. I promise you, Natalie, that I can stay out of your way when it's necessary. There are times, though, that I'll need to be a presence. If someone is threatening you, that someone needs to know that you're not to be messed with. So yes, intimidation helps in those instances."

Although he understood her concerns, his size had always been a bit of a problem, and not just for others. Vincent was all too aware of the fact that he was physically powerful and that his power needed to be tempered. People got hurt when a big man didn't control his emotions. He knew that from personal experience, but he really didn't want to think about that.

If he could help it, he wouldn't let Natalie experience anything of that nature.

"I'll keep my distance when I can," he repeated.

She smiled warmly, and something moved deep inside him. *Forget it,* he told himself. *She's not for you.* Not that any woman was. He dated women. He was, after all, a normal, healthy male. He just didn't have relationships, not the kind where a man lost it over the color of a woman's eyes, anyway. As far as he was concerned, the only things he needed to notice about Natalie were those related to this case.

"Now, tell me about the party," he prompted.

She nodded, her lips suddenly tight. He could almost see her pulling herself together, straightening her spine, breathing more deeply, tightening every muscle as she prepared to relive what had to have been a damned terrifying experience.

"Take all the time you need," he said gently, prepared to wait all day if necessary.

She lifted her chin high. "I don't need time, Vincent. I remember that day perfectly. I had been asked to cover the party because it was considered an important social event." Natalie frowned slightly.

"You didn't consider it important?" Vincent asked.

She looked up, directly into his eyes. He could see that she would be an effective reporter. One look into those expressive eyes and a subject might give up every secret he possessed. Good thing he wasn't a subject.

"I didn't say it wasn't important. It's always an event when the Fortune family gets together, but this time it was the governor himself who was honoring Ryan Fortune for his charitable works. It was a very notable gathering."

Vincent sensed that there was a huge *but* about to follow, but Natalie surprised him by stopping at that.

"And where did Jamison fit in?"

She frowned. "I thought that Daniel told you all of this."

"He did. He's not the one I'm guarding. I need to see things through your eyes."

Natalie firmed her lips slightly, obviously reluctant, but then she nodded, her dark, shoulder-length hair swishing with her movement. "All right. I'd been assigned to cover the social scene but I was also planning my own story on Ryan's effect on Fortune, TX, Ltd. in his role as an advisor. I wanted to interview Jamison, and I went upstairs looking for him, but when I got there I heard arguing. I didn't know what it was, but I...well, I was curious. A reporter's nose for news, I suppose."

She looked to the side suddenly, swallowing hard. For a minute, Vincent worried about her.

"The words were ugly," she said, "but when I got to the door, the arguing had stopped. At first I thought I'd caught a couple embracing. The man had his back to me and his arms seemed to be around the woman, tipping her back in that way you see in movies. I'm not sure exactly what I thought then. Maybe that they were one of those couples that likes to argue and then make up, I guess. At any rate, it was clear that this wasn't a scene I wanted to witness, and so I turned away and even moved partly down the hall. Then I heard a strange choking sound, and things clicked—the fact that the embrace might not have been all that it seemed. I ran back and I heard a thud. Jamison was standing over the woman. 'Good riddance. You were more trouble than you were worth,' he said."

Natalie turned back toward Vincent. "I've thought about that day over and over," she whispered. "If I had only known what was going on—"

"Natalie, you know it wasn't your fault."

She shook her head and sat up even straighter. "I know." But she didn't sound completely convinced. Vincent couldn't imagine what she'd gone through since that day. "Anyway," she said, her voice regaining strength, "I stood there, frozen, until he looked up to me. Everything seemed to be so unreal. Then, he actually smiled. 'Take a good look, honey. Because you'll be next,' he said. I knew for sure that she was dead, then. I didn't even think. I just ran and I kept running until I realized that he would get away with murder if I didn't come back. That was it. I turned around and drove back to the party. They arrested him, and he's awaiting trial now."

"The letters?"

"I saved copies if you need to look at them again."

He didn't ask why she had saved copies. He would have done the same. And she was a reporter, a person who lived by facts and evidence. But he shook his head. "The experts have gone over them thoroughly. There's no way of telling who sent them or even if the person who mailed them was working alone."

"I know. It seems hard to believe that a man accused of murder and under constant guard would be able to sneak messages out."

"He's been allowed visitors. Maybe he didn't write the messages."

"Yes. It could be someone on the outside," she said. "An accomplice of his." Vincent thought he saw her tremble, but she didn't allow her voice to break. She didn't show any other sign of being nervous.

He sat forward suddenly and leaned nearer, moving into her space, her soft floral scent filling his senses. "I don't mean to be immodest, Natalie, but I make a point of being good at what I do. No one—absolutely no one—is going to get to you without going straight through me."

Finally she smiled, her pretty pink lips curving upward in a way that made his breath hitch in his chest. "You're a little cocky, Vincent."

"It goes with the territory. A bodyguard has to be willing to go through walls and step on a few toes to make sure his client is safe."

She glanced down at her toes.

"Not yours," he said, grinning slightly.

"Don't be so sure," she said. "My parents and my brothers thought I was a hellion. They've spent years trying to get me to behave, and even though they're normally sane, calm people, they've been known to go to extremes in their quest to keep up with me."

"Is that a warning, Natalie?"

"It's a sad truth, Vincent. I have been told that I'm unmanageable. Consider yourself warned. Now, do you have everything that you need to know?"

"I know enough to get started."

"Good." She rose to her feet. "Because I have an appointment."

He nodded and stood. "All right, let's go."

Those green eyes suddenly flashed dark. "You told me that you would be discreet, but where I'm going…well, you just can't."

He gave her a slow, lazy smile. "Watch me, Natalie. Your welfare is on my head now. Where you go, I follow."

"I'm not going anywhere important. Nowhere anyone else would be interested. Just to a neighbor's house."

"Well, then, let's go meet the neighbors," he drawled.

She blinked. "What am I going to tell them about you? How am I going to explain you away?"

Vincent placed both palms on the table and leaned closer. "You're the reporter. You know how to relate a story. Tell them the facts…or make something up. Tell them I'm your lover, for all I care. But understand this, Natalie. Your safety is my concern, and I am not letting you out of my sight."

She blinked and frowned.

"It's for your own good," he promised.

She frowned harder. "I know. I hate that. I hate that it's for my own good. It would be so much easier to argue about it if it weren't. All right, come on, lover boy."

With that, Natalie turned and headed for the door. Vincent had watched any number of women's backs over the years. Most of the women had been infatuated with the thought of having a man following them around, their own personal paid protector. But Natalie McCabe was royally pissed off. In spite of admitting to the necessity of having him here, she didn't want her neighbors to meet him.

What was that about?

Already his new client was a total pain in the ass who was going to make his job hell. Too bad she had a sweet, slender body and pretty eyes that were hard to ignore.

She was merely a client, and that was all she could be. He couldn't wait for this assignment to be over.

KAREN WHIDDON

At most, her hair was barely mussed, a few strands
pulled free. No, that wasn't it. If only she had a way to wipe
it. No drop seemed to move on its own.

One was sunken into a bit? And then around the front by her
peripheral vision, she found herself...

Two

Natalie had been living in this apartment complex for several years. She was one of the youngest people in the building. Most of the inhabitants were well into their senior years.
Yet, she had never felt self-conscious or out of place until she
walked down the hall with Vincent two paces behind her.

The man was just so hard to ignore. His aftershave drifted
to her, and she could almost feel his warmth at her back. She
was so incredibly aware of his presence that her own breathing kicked up a bit.

Damn the man. Why couldn't he be a bit less noticeable? But
she knew it was her own fault. For some reason, she was having trouble blocking Vincent Fortune from her mind. No doubt
she'd simply been rattled by those threatening notes and the fact
that she had to have a bodyguard at all. Well, that was about to
stop. She had important work to do, Natalie told herself as she
rapped on an apartment door near the back of the first floor.

Long seconds passed. Natalie turned to look at Vincent.

"Mrs. Morgensen uses a walker. It takes a while. You can go if you like."

He grinned. "Nice try, Natalie, but I've got nothing but time. I'm all yours."

Natalie suddenly felt warm. Surely that wasn't a blush creeping up her cheeks. She never blushed.

Gritting her teeth, she forced a big smile and turned to him. "That's very generous, Vincent, but I'm not sure I'm equipped to handle all of you."

To her delight, Vincent looked as if he was going to choke, although she wasn't quite sure whether it was with shock or laughter. And since the door opened at that moment, she couldn't ask.

"Natalie? I'm so glad you could come." Mrs. Morgensen's voice quavered a bit, but her eyes were bright and shiny. She glanced past Natalie. "Oh, you brought your young man."

"No, I— He's not my—" Natalie began to say, but she needn't have bothered.

"Vincent Fortune. I'm delighted to meet you, Mrs. Morgensen," Vincent said, stepping forward and touching the elderly woman's hand.

The lady smiled and looked at Natalie. "Good choice, Natalie. He's a looker."

Natalie blinked. She refused to look at Vincent, and she didn't answer. After all, what could she say? If she told Mrs. Morgensen that Vincent was her bodyguard, she would have some explaining to do. She might frighten the woman, and that just wasn't acceptable. Moreover, Mrs. Morgensen might no longer feel comfortable telling her story to Natalie, and without her story and those of her other neighbors, Natalie had no hope of digging deeper and getting the information she needed to reveal the misdeeds of Starson Investments.

"He's very pretty," Natalie agreed, which was a total lie. Vincent was masculine, sexy, handsome in a decidedly rugged way. *Pretty* was a word that no one would ever apply to the man. "Adorable, actually."

She couldn't resist turning to Vincent, who looked as if he wanted to squirm. Natalie smiled and allowed Mrs. Morgensen to usher them inside.

"I think we've embarrassed him," Natalie confided to her neighbor in a stage whisper.

"Men," Mrs. Morgensen agreed with a wink and a shake of her head. "They just don't know how to take a compliment."

Natalie's heart warmed at the older woman's smile. She looked around her at the modest surroundings. There was a nearly threadbare couch, a small chair and table, and one tiny bookcase, as well as numerous inexpensive knickknacks.

"It's almost all I've got left," Mrs. Morgensen whispered. "I've been so stupid." And now the lady's eyes didn't twinkle anymore.

Natalie's heart almost broke. She cast one frantic look at Vincent and he nodded. "I'll just sit outside and leave you two alone," he said as if he'd read her mind.

Mrs. Morgensen pulled her shoulders back and gave him a stern look. "I may not have much, but I can still entertain a guest or two and I do not leave my guests sitting in the hallway. You'll sit in the kitchen, have a cup of coffee and read the newspaper. I still splurge on the newspaper," she said stubbornly as if expecting Vincent to criticize her for spending too much money. "Does he know?" she asked Natalie.

"Nothing," Natalie told her truthfully. "I apologize for bringing someone along without asking."

"I insisted on coming," Vincent volunteered.

Mrs. Morgensen smiled again. "I don't blame you. She's a love. Don't want to be apart from her, do you?"

"Not a minute."

Natalie sent him a warning glance. Vincent ignored her.

"But thank you for not volunteering my circumstances," the

lady said to Natalie. "I know the story has to come out, but until you catch them, I'd prefer people not know all the embarrassing details," she told Natalie as if Vincent weren't there.

Vincent studied a bookcase as if it held the secrets of the universe rather than a few dozen copies of old condensed novels. Natalie wondered how many times in the past Vincent had had to pretend he was a piece of the furniture. In his line of work, it must have happened often.

"This is just between you and me for now," Natalie agreed.

Mrs. Morgensen gave her a grateful look. "But we should tell him something, so that he doesn't think I'm a criminal with all this secrecy and whispering."

"Anyone with an ounce of sense can see that you're not," Vincent told her. "Don't worry about it. Mind if I show myself to the kitchen?"

"Through the hall," Mrs. Morgensen told him. "The coffee's on the counter. And thank you. For the record, I've fallen on hard times."

"Happens to everyone."

It didn't, Natalie thought, but she was grateful that Vincent was doing so much to make her neighbor feel comfortable. "We won't be long," she promised him.

"I follow your schedule, not the other way around," he said as he left the room. Natalie couldn't help noting that he looked just as good from the back as he did from the front and immediately berated herself for even thinking such a thing. What was wrong with her, anyway?

As soon as he was gone, Mrs. Morgensen grasped both of her hands. "Ooh, latch on to that one, love. A man who wants to accommodate your schedule instead of his own is a rarity indeed. And what a great butt, don't you think?"

Instantly heat and confusion climbed through Natalie. "I—" She held her hands out helplessly.

"Oh, I've embarrassed you, haven't I? I do that now that

I'm old, more often all the time. And here you just came to get some information." Mrs. Morgensen sounded so sad that Natalie wished she had been able to set aside her reservations about Vincent and enter into the spirit of things.

"No, you haven't done a thing wrong. It's just that Vincent and I don't know each other very well yet."

"Oh, I understand. And you can't be too careful with strangers. I've learned that the hard way. Now, why don't you sit down and I'll tell you my story. I understand you've already talked to Mr. Jackson in 2B and Mr. Darby in 1F."

"Yes, just the other day. They said that you lost more than they did."

That heartbroken look returned to the old lady's eyes. "Yes, through my own stupidity. I won't have anything to leave to my grandchildren now."

"I'm so sorry. Tell me what exactly happened."

"I don't really know. I only know that I decided to invest a little of my money. Not much, just a little. So I contacted a broker, a man from Starson Investments. You've heard his name before," she said as Natalie started to nod.

She had, from some of her other neighbors. "I don't really know anything about him," Natalie confessed, "except that he is, indeed, a broker."

"I didn't even talk to him all that long," Mrs. Morgensen said, "and I made sure he knew that I didn't want to invest much money. Then one day I got a bill for thousands of dollars. I really don't understand what happened. I just know that my money's gone," she finished sadly, a lost look in her eyes. "I wanted to buy my grandson a bicycle for Christmas," she said. "Now I can't do that."

Natalie felt the tears filling her throat. She patted Mrs. Morgensen's hand. "We'll figure it out. We'll find out what happened. Whatever it is, it wasn't right. I'll do my best to make sure people know."

For a second, hope flared in the old woman's eyes. "I don't suppose you can get my money back, but…"

Natalie wanted to scream, because no, she didn't have the wherewithal to turn back time and save this gentle woman from what had happened to her. "Do you have the paperwork?"

"Just the canceled check. I sent the bill back with the check."

"All right," Natalie said. "We'll at least start there." Which was more or less like starting with nothing at all. That meant she had to go to Plan B. As soon as she thought the words, she remembered the man in the kitchen.

Vincent was not going to like Plan B, because it meant that she was going to have to ditch him. Somehow.

Vincent waited until they were back in Natalie's car before he spoke.

"For a reporter, you have a soft side."

She gave him the look, the one that said, "Get real." He couldn't keep from smiling. "I'll bet you want to be hard-edged and no-nonsense, the reporter who'll stop at nothing to get a story. If that's the case, you shouldn't have asked Mrs. Morgensen for her recipe for oatmeal raisin cookies."

Natalie looked away. "They're good cookies. Besides, she's so proud of them. She makes them for her family."

"And you wanted to give her back a little of her dignity because someone has taken it away."

"Is that so wrong?"

"No. It's very right. It's just…surprising. I thought you were all about the story."

"I am."

He shrugged. He didn't doubt that she wanted to be a good reporter and that she would do a great deal to make sure that happened, but she wouldn't hurt an old lady's feelings. She wasn't the type to go for the jugular. Not that it should make any difference to him. It didn't. No matter how enticing she looked with those long lashes and those lush curves, he wasn't going to allow himself to be interested. But it was nice to know that he was at least guarding a real person. He'd guarded plenty of the plastic types. No matter what, he did his best, but he would enjoy protecting this woman.

Just don't let yourself enjoy it too much, he told himself. He wouldn't. He had rules and they were rock solid.

As long as he remembered that, there should be no problems. His only job was to keep Natalie safe, and he intended to do that, and that alone. Anyone who got to her would have to take him down first—and that just wasn't going to happen.

"I don't belong here." Jason Jamison said the words out loud. He must have said them at least fifty times today already, but he still liked hearing the sound of them. The words were true, anyway. He might have been calling himself Jason Wilkes lately, because it was convenient to do so, but in truth he was a Jamison, and the Jamisons came from fine stock. What's more, his grandfather had been Kingston Fortune's lost half brother, which meant Jason was also related to the Fortunes.

"And jail's not for the likes of the Jamisons and Fortunes." Besides, Melissa, the woman he had killed had had it coming to her, anyway, hadn't she? She'd been willing to pretend she was his wife, but in the end she'd gotten greedy and had tried to mess in things that hadn't concerned her. He'd thought she loved him; he'd spent tons of money on her and then she'd tried to work her own con and blackmail him in the bargain.

She'd laughed at him, and nobody laughed at Jason Jamison. No one messed with him. Soon enough, everyone would know that. Especially that little bitch that had blown the whistle on him. If it weren't for her, he would still be living the good life.

Jason let out a long string of expletives.

"Yeah, McCabe and the high-and-mighty Ryan Fortune, they're the ones who put me in here."

And they would be the ones who had to pay.

Jason chuckled. A guard stopped by his cell.

"Something especially funny, Jamison? You remembering what it used to be like before you turned killer and ended up behind bars?"

"None of your damn business."

"Ah, but we know it is, don't we?" the guard asked.

Yeah, they did. Even prison guards had their uses. This one would be more useful still in the near future.

"You like your temporary home here? You better be grateful for the treatment you get. Because this ain't nothin' like it's going to be. Once you stand trial and end up in maximum security, you might not meet guards as friendly as me."

"And you might not meet prisoners who can do as much for you as I can."

The guard shrugged. "You got a point. I definitely prefer guarding a man who at least has some money and a few rich connections. Makes this job more bearable." The man raked his nose with his sleeve. Jason wanted to sneer, but instead he smiled.

"I can make the job more bearable if you like."

The guard looked to the side, as if to see if anyone was listening. "What do you mean?"

So Jason told him. Yes, he definitely had a plan, but not everyone was going to like it.

The very thought made Jason smile. He was going to relish getting even.

But first he was going to relish getting free.

Three

"Lock every door, lock every window and stay away from them. Don't let yourself be silhouetted in the light," Vincent ordered Natalie as he prepared to leave her at her door.

She nodded. "And where will you be while I'm making myself invisible?" Even though she hadn't meant to, Natalie asked the question out loud. The truth was she was dreadfully afraid that if she didn't know exactly where Vincent was, she would be peeking out the window trying to spot him just like a star-struck teenage girl.

And then there was the other concern. She needed to get out of the house, and she needed to make sure that Vincent couldn't follow her.

"I'll be nearby," he assured her.

"Don't you have a family? A wife? Kids?"

"I don't do the wife-and-kids stuff. It's not for me." His voice was hoarse. There was clearly a story behind that comment, one he obviously didn't want to share.

"Okay, but don't you ever go to bed?" She tried not to imagine him in a bed. She really did her best not to think about what he might wear or not wear…and what kind of woman he might sleep with.

"Sure, I sleep," he assured her. "But I'll never leave you unprotected. When I'm off-duty, I'll put my best man on your case. Derek Seefer. If anything should happen, Derek knows what to do and he knows how to reach me."

"Nothing will happen," she said too quickly.

Vincent cocked his head, but he simply nodded. "Derek and I will see to it. Sleep well, Natalie."

She looked up at him then, into those concerned dark gray eyes, and she wished she didn't have to deceive him. She wished she could tell him what she had planned, but of course there was no way she could ever do that. If she did, he would follow her. Vincent certainly wasn't the kind of man who would stay or go just because a woman told him to.

No, she would have to be sneaky. Too much was at stake here.

"I'll be careful, Vincent," she promised, even though she realized he couldn't understand what she was talking about. "I promise. And thank you. I *will* sleep well." Just as soon as she was back from her mission, she would sleep very well.

Vincent had encountered a lot of guilty looks in his days. He wondered if Natalie knew that she played with her hair when she was being evasive. Those pretty green eyes couldn't quite focus on him, even though in all other ways she looked perfectly calm and in control.

"If I were a betting man," he murmured, "I'd say that Natalie isn't going to lock all her doors and sit tight. She's going to run."

He wondered why. She really appeared to be in danger, and it was clear from her reaction to the memory of those notes that she didn't take the threats lightly. Yet she chafed at having a keeper. Not that he blamed her. Even if a bodyguard was for her own safety, the lack of privacy, the sense of being watched and treated like a child was bound to rankle with a woman who had been on her own for as long as Natalie had. She was twenty-nine, an independent woman with a career, and now she had a keeper.

No, he'd just bet he wasn't on Natalie's list of favorite people right now. He wondered who was. What man topped her list of those she wanted to spend time with?

"Whoa, don't go there, buddy. None of your concern. This lady is just a client. That puts her off-limits for everything."

Right now the lady was slipping out some back entrance if the slight screech of wood against wood was any indication. Opening a window?

"Maybe, and maybe it's someone else opening the window to climb inside, you dolt," he told himself, sprinting around the corner.

He was just in time to see a pair of shapely legs emerging from the window. He frowned. She was wearing beige sandals that displayed pretty pink toes. When she started to slide out of the window, her narrow skirt caught on the frame and stuck, sliding up to reveal a pair of thighs that could make a man beg to touch.

Vincent breathed in deeply, ordering himself to ignore the lady's thighs and just concentrate on the task at hand.

"Need a hand?" he asked, stepping forward and reaching up for her.

Her head came up and her eyes met his. To her credit, she didn't shriek, something she certainly had a right to do. Instead, she stared down at his hands and at her own exposed flesh. If he lowered his hands, he could cup his palms around those rounded thighs.

Natalie gave a frustrated sigh. "Yes, thank you," she said primly. "I could use a hand."

"And a lift? You appear to be going out."

"Yes. I have work to do."

"All right, let's go." He reached up and she squirmed, but it was clear that if he let her continue her downward slide, he'd be seeing a lot more than just her thighs. Right now Vincent didn't think he could handle viewing Natalie's nearly naked and undoubtedly lovely little ass. A man only had so much self-control and while he had more than most men, while he had spent a lifetime teaching himself to ignore the dictates of his mind and his emotions, the urge to slide his palms across Natalie's bare skin would still be there. He couldn't have indiscreet thoughts about his client interfering with his job.

Carefully, Vincent placed his hands on Natalie's waist and lifted her from the window. "You were going to walk?"

She shrugged. "It seemed best. If I took my car—"

"I'd see you and follow. I'll drive you."

Suddenly, she placed her hand on his sleeve and heat filled him. "Vincent, you more than anyone should understand what undercover work is like."

He nodded. "Go on."

"I have a job. I'm trying to help people like Mrs. Morgensen. In order to do that, I need information. I have things I need to do, but I need to be able to fit in without causing a stir of any sort."

"You want me to be scarce," he finished for her.

"If that's possible." For a minute, he thought she was studying his body, as if she were deciding if he might fit behind a potted plant. "You're a very large man, Vincent," she pointed out again.

He tried to blank out his thoughts, to remember that she was just being practical, not speaking in sexual innuendos.

"I know how to become a part of the furniture, Natalie. Believe me. It's my job."

She nodded. "All right, then."

She turned to go. He turned to follow her. Suddenly she whirled and he was closer than he had intended. "One more thing," she said. Her eyes looked dark and worried.

"Tell me."

"I might make mistakes, but I won't be in any danger. Even if I do err and things look as if they're falling apart, don't help me. I have to learn."

"Natalie?"

"What?"

"You've been a reporter for a while, haven't you?"

"Yes, but I've never had to play a part. When you're interviewing Beep-Beep the Clown and the owners of The Party Hat Store, subterfuge isn't really necessary."

"You're telling me you've never played a part? You've never gone undercover?"

"That's right."

"The people you're mingling with tonight, tell me what type we're talking about. Dangerous?"

"Not really. Accountants, that type."

He relaxed. "All right. I won't worry, then. Will you be pretending to be an accountant?"

She hugged her arms. "Natalie?" he prodded.

"I'll be pretending to be a woman."

He chuckled.

"A woman in search of a man," she said, raising her chin. "Maybe more than one man."

"And you want me to take you to meet your dates?"

"You don't have to."

But if he didn't, she'd try to go on her own again. Well, what difference did it make? She wasn't his to order around. He just had to guard her.

"Vincent, if anyone thinks you're with me, they probably won't come near."

He wasn't so sure of that. She had an earnest look on her face that made a man want to find out what put that expression there. And she had those long, delicious legs that could make a man fight for the chance to have them wrapped around him.

Vincent almost swore. "I'll let you go in first, but I won't be far behind you," he finally conceded.

"It's the best I could hope for, I guess," she agreed. "All right, let's go to The Ladder."

"The Ladder?"

"It's—"

"I know what it is. It's a major pickup place."

"You've been there? Did you get lucky?"

He glared down at her and she gave him an impish grin.

"I'm sure you did. Women probably swarm all over you when you walk into a bar."

But she had asked him to make himself scarce. Now why did that rankle so much?

Natalie had been to The Ladder before, but only as an observer, as a researcher. Those had only been preliminary runs to make sure this was the place where she would be most likely to meet up with employees of Starson Investments and to locate Brad Herron, Mrs. Morgensen's broker. Now she was going to have to wade in and actually become a part of things. The very thought made her quake inside. The fact that Vincent had come inside, seated himself at a small table in the shadows and was watching her every move only heightened her nervousness. She was going to have to attempt to come on to a man while Vincent watched. She had a feeling that Vincent was an expert at enticing women. The fact that she had little experience at luring men was bound to show.

Why should it bother her that Vincent should think her inexperienced and naive? "It shouldn't," she murmured.

"What shouldn't, sweetheart? Brad Herron," the man sitting at the next table said by way of introduction, holding out his hand. Natalie looked up at the man she had observed here before, one she had deliberately seated herself near tonight. He was in his early forties, divorced, handsome and very aware of how handsome he was.

She took his hand, then fought a spate of nerves when he held on to her longer than was really necessary. She had to be smart here. Tonight was just to get the lay of the land.

Beating back the urge to yank away, she disentangled herself from his grip as casually as possible. The man was a player, she reminded herself. She'd known that when she came here. In fact, knowing that gave her a decided advantage in this game. Natalie took a deep breath. "What I meant was that age shouldn't matter when choosing new friends," she carefully replied to the man almost fifteen years her senior. Somehow, she even managed a small smile.

"Oh yeah, I couldn't agree more. You have exceptionally beautiful eyes, honey, do you know that?" he asked. Except Natalie couldn't help noticing that it wasn't her eyes he was looking at but her breasts. She felt slightly sick. Even worse, she had an awful urge to get up and go sit next to Vincent. She wondered what he was thinking of this whole scenario. Because even though he couldn't possibly hear what was being said, the fact that Brad was practically salivating on her had to be obvious. And if she was going to make this subterfuge work, she had to pretend that she didn't mind Brad's attitude.

"Why, thank you, Brad. I'm Natalie," she said, holding on to her fake smile. "Do you come here often?" Not thrilling conversation, but she needed some way to get him to lead into his Starson connections.

"Two or three times a week," Brad said. "A lot of the people I work with hang out here. But you're not a regular. I've never seen you here before."

That was because the few times she had ventured here in the past week or two, she had been wearing a wig, enveloping clothes and sunglasses. More importantly, Brad had been busy hitting on other women. His modus operandi seemed to be stake out the nearest free female, which was why she had seated herself within range of his radar. Her ploy appeared to be working.

Except she looked up right then and couldn't avoid seeing Vincent, who was watching her closely. He was frowning, his dark eyes narrowed. For some reason, her heartbeat kicked up in a way it hadn't when Brad had given her the once-over. She hastily looked away.

"No, I don't get out that much," Natalie said.

"Well, we'll have to change that," Brad said, sliding closer. He smelled heavily of cologne. Natalie fought the urge to inch away…or to slam her fist into his nose.

"Are you here with friends?" she asked.

Brad laughed and winked at her. "If you mean, am I with a woman, not tonight. If you want me to be alone, then I'm alone. Just you and me, babe."

Okay, it was difficult to fight her gag reflex after a line like that. Brad's shoulder was rubbing up against hers now. Out of the corner of her eye, she could see Vincent rising. Was her panic that evident? Clearly it was time to effect a change, both in her demeanor and in Brad's attitude.

"Oh, I'm not in the mood for alone tonight," she simpered. "Not yet. I came here looking for the thrill of a crowd, and if you're a regular here, then you must know at least some of the people here." Besides, she needed to locate other people at Starson who might talk to her.

"Sure do know some people, sweetheart. You could say that I'm a man with connections," Brad boasted. "I'm a broker at

Starson Investments, a damn fine one, and being charming and making lots of friends is part of the game. Not many I don't know here tonight. Come on, I'll introduce you around, show everybody what a sweet, pretty thing I've found."

Grasping her hand, Brad pulled her to her feet and made his way through the crowd, his grip clamping down tight.

If things went suddenly south and she had to change her mind, breaking that grip was going to take some serious work. She wondered what Vincent would think if she suddenly resorted to kicking her new buddy in the groin. For some reason, she had an urge to do just that, to show Vincent that she really wasn't helpless. It was all Natalie could do not to look Vincent's way.

She was sure his eyes were following her, but then, that was what he was paid to do, wasn't it? There was nothing more to it than that. Which was good, she reminded herself.

Try to forget about Vincent and concentrate on Brad and the task at hand, she ordered herself. Just find out whatever you can about who might know what at Starson. Natalie studied the other people to whom Brad was introducing her.

"This is Sheila. She's the receptionist."

Natalie smiled and said hello. Judging by the frigid look Sheila gave her, the woman had either slept with Brad at one time or wanted to. Not a woman who looked as if she would talk to another woman she viewed as competition. She filed that information away for later and turned to the next group. Alicia Summersby, an administrative assistant too scared to do more than squeak; Lon Warren, who worked in the mail room and might very well be a misogynist judging from the disgusted look he gave Natalie; Neil Gerard, an account manager.

An account manager? Natalie smiled at Neil. He mumbled a shy hello, shifting awkwardly from foot to foot.

"I'm pleased to meet you," she said.

He shrugged. "Me, too. Um, have you known Brad long?"

He shifted again, and she knew what he was getting at. Brad probably didn't date anyone for very long. He was in it for the skin and when that palled, he moved on to the next conquest.

"Actually, we just met."

A look of interest lit Neil's face. He seemed pleased, even though he didn't say anything. He struck her as the shy, polite guy that every woman should want but seldom did.

Brad chuckled. "Natalie and I have just met, but I intend to get to know her much better, Neil, my man. Isn't she hot?"

Neil fidgeted again, and Natalie felt sorry for him, but not so sorry that she wouldn't come back and talk to him later.

"I don't know that much about investments," she said, even though she'd already done plenty of research on the Internet. "What exactly do account managers do?"

Neil opened his mouth to speak, but Brad pulled her away. "Oh no, none of that work talk. This one's mine, and we've got other ground to cover, Gerard."

Natalie felt the heat of anger rising within her. She wondered how much of this conversation Vincent had heard. Brad was drinking, and he was getting louder by the minute. "Come on, babe," he told her. "You've met everyone. Now let's go somewhere and…talk."

Four

Vincent felt like grinding his teeth. The good-looking predator had Natalie in his sights, and he wasn't about to let her get away.

"I don't even have to hear what they're saying to see that," Vincent mumbled. Because the man was practically draping his body around Natalie. She didn't look especially comfortable, either. Especially when the guy led her to a table in the corner of the room.

For a second, Vincent thought he saw Natalie glance his way, but she turned around just as quickly. Not that it mattered. As a man, he knew all too well what this guy had in mind, and it just wasn't going to happen. At least not on his watch, Vincent thought, rising and heading back toward that dark corner. Within seconds, he was within hearing range.

"Here," the man was saying. "Right here." He sat down heavily on a stool pulled up to a tall table and dragged another stool close to his. "I'm not really into group togetherness.

You're much too tasty to share." He smiled at Natalie with that pretty-boy face, his voice slightly slurred. He was urging Natalie toward the stool, which would put her practically right on his lap.

Fiery anger rolled through Vincent. He hated men who tried to use a physical advantage to coerce a woman. He'd had far too much experience of that kind of thing, and it still hit him right in the gut.

Fueled by that thought, Vincent took the few steps necessary to reach the small, intimate table. Pretending to be looking elsewhere, he blundered into the stool the guy was trying to muscle Natalie into, bumping it aside.

"Hey buddy, watch it!" The guy's voice was that of an on-the-edge drunk. Vincent knew that routine all too well. He'd lived it far too often when he had been growing up, and it wasn't the indignant lush that concerned him. Instead he turned his attention to Natalie, who had to have been surprised by this turn of events as he had approached the table from behind. Her pretty eyes were big and green and startled. He remembered telling her that he would make himself scarce. Damn.

"Excuse me, must have been my mistake," he said to the jerk attempting to seduce Natalie. "I apologize if I created any problems for you," Vincent added, turning to Natalie. He motioned to the stool that he had somehow knocked two feet away from where the lech had placed it. "Please, be seated," Vincent said, nodding to Natalie.

"Yeah, sit here, babe," the drunkard said and he started to move the stool again.

Quickly Natalie sat, the stool still a good twelve inches from where the guy had first placed it. Vincent wanted to wink at Natalie but refrained.

"Thank you," she said to him softly, "but it really wasn't necessary."

Maybe not to her, but to him? Guys like this one brought

out his worst side. But he only shrugged and smiled at her before he started to walk away. For half a second, he thought she smiled back, and warmth spiraled through his body.

Idiot, he told himself. This woman was a job. That was all she was to him. And as far as she was concerned, he was a necessary nuisance, one she was eager to shed. He'd better do his best to remember that.

"At last, we got rid of him. Now it's just us," Brad said, scooting closer to Natalie. Somehow she held back a sigh and wondered if she was going to get anything at all out of this encounter other than a headache. Immediately, a vision of Vincent glaring at Brad and apologizing to her, his eyes dark and fierce, slipped into her thoughts. Her heartbeat skittered, and she cursed herself. She was here to get information, not start acting ridiculous about a man, especially a man she had no business even thinking about.

Reluctantly, she turned to Brad. "Tell me about your work," she coaxed.

"Work?" he asked, smiling slyly. He slid his hand toward her knee.

She moved slightly, and he missed. He nearly toppled from his stool. "Sorry," she said, not sorry at all.

"No problem. Let's not even mention work, though," Brad said. "Like I told Gerard, this night isn't for work." He attempted to touch her knee again.

She evaded him. Again.

Natalie wanted to scream. Was this night going to be a total bust? "Oh, but I'm fascinated by the word *broker*. It's such a powerful term, so masculine." She leaned forward on her elbows so that her knees were inaccessible. Of course, her breasts were more exposed, but she had fists and she knew how to use them. Not that she wanted to use them. Sooner or later, she wanted this man to either confirm or disprove her suspicions about what was happening to her friends. That wouldn't happen if she sent him flying. "Tell me about yourself," she said, hoping that those were the magic words that would get him to stop leering and start talking.

Brad grinned, leaned back and began to talk. "You're right, brokering *is* a very powerful profession. Gets me respect, power, money. Practically everything I want. What I want right now is to see more of you, especially those pretty legs," he said with a knowing smile. "Come home with me tonight, and I'll tell you all about the life of a broker, some of my conquests."

Somehow, Brad found her knee and squeezed. He started to walk his fingers higher.

Natalie fought the urge to strike out. Instead, she scooted back and away from his roving hands. She was obviously not going to get any information from Brad Herron tonight. "Whoa, it's really getting late," she said, looking at her watch. "I didn't realize so much time had passed. And tomorrow's a working day. I have to get home and get some sleep."

Brad's brows nearly touched, he was frowning so hard. But then he almost visibly pulled himself together and smiled. "You'll be back, won't you?" It was almost a command rather than a question, the comment of a man who was used to getting his way with women.

"I might be." She *would* be, but it wouldn't do to appear too eager. It was information she wanted, nothing more. Next time she would come prepared with a better plan.

He laughed, reaching out quickly as if to grab her again. She dodged as he laughed again. "You're a fascinating woman. I'll bet you look great naked."

Natalie refrained from decking the guy. Instead she gave him a fake and fleeting smile, said goodbye and did her best to walk calmly toward the door. Just as she was leaving, she saw Neil Gerard from the corner of her eye.

He smiled shyly in a little-boy kind of way.

"It was nice to meet you," she said, and he tugged at his collar self-consciously. "Next time we'll play pool," she added, motioning to the cue he held.

He nodded jerkily and she moved toward the door.

"Watch yourself, Gerard. I've got first dibs," Brad called, but Natalie could tell he was just making fun of the shyer man. "You wouldn't know how to handle those legs, anyway."

Natalie didn't look back, but quickly exited the building, letting herself out onto the cool, dark street and heading toward home.

She was halfway down the block when she heard the noise pick up again, and she guessed that Vincent had left the bar. Immediately she felt an urge to tug on her skirt. Which was completely ridiculous. Her skirt wasn't even revealing. It wasn't tight.

But she could feel Vincent's eyes on her and she felt suddenly naked, as if he were aware that she was wearing white bikini underpants beneath her clothing. It was a bizarre and unsettling feeling for her. She was used to being in control, the one who called the shots, the one who dictated how things were going to be. Now she felt as if she were spinning in circles, completely off balance, unable to control anything. Her body felt flushed and hot in a way it hadn't when Brad was trying to grab her.

Bad sign if she was lusting after her bodyguard. She didn't like men, or people for that matter, who hovered.

She heard a car door slam, an engine rev, and soon Vincent pulled up beside her. "Get in," he said.

Oh, that would be such a completely bad idea. Just moments ago, she had been thinking lusty thoughts about him. Closing herself up in the small space of a car wouldn't help anyone. She shrugged and tried to look nonchalant. "It's a nice night. I'd like to walk."

He rubbed one hand over his eyes. "It is, but I don't feel

like having to beat anyone to a pulp tonight. That greasy idiot in the bar was bad enough, but those guys behind you could be dangerous."

Natalie turned and saw that there were three men following her down the street. They eyed her with interest.

"Get rid of that guy, lady. We can pay you more."

"Or you can pay us," the second one said, making kissing sounds at her.

Natalie's heart started to drum. It was obvious that, lost in her thoughts, she had been careless. And Vincent was right. Brad she could take down if need be. Three guys who looked as if they fed on fear were something else entirely. And from their vantage point, they couldn't see Vincent's size. They weren't slowing down. She thought one of them might be holding a knife.

She turned toward the car, but heard rushing footsteps behind her.

"Not another step," Vincent ordered the men as he climbed from the car, rolling those impressive shoulders of his and turning to face the men in the street.

The men hesitated, but they didn't stop.

"You want to fight for her, let's do it," Vincent said, his voice eerily quiet and deadly. He looked like a man who could kill with his bare hands, and he was twice as big as any of the men he was facing.

"You think you're scary?" the guy with the knife asked. "Not a chance. Get her," he ordered his friends. He ran straight at Vincent, while the other two men headed for Natalie.

Vincent ignored the guy hurtling his way. Instead, he kicked out at one of Natalie's pursuers, and there was a crunching sound as his foot connected with bone. Then he whirled, leaving the guy screaming, kicking the man with the knife in the stomach while he brought his elbow up and caught the third man in the neck. Both men fell.

"Are we done?" Vincent asked, and Natalie wasn't sure if he was talking to her or to the men. She didn't wait to see. Instead, she got into the car.

Vincent followed her, leaving the three men struggling to rise. He drove the car in silence for the first few blocks.

"Have fun back there?" he finally asked.

"Not especially, no." She tried not to shiver with revulsion as she thought about Brad grabbing at her or about the three who had awaited her outside.

"Good. I'm assuming you're done with the octopus."

She breathed in deeply and the scent of Vincent's aftershave, the scent of man, drifted to her. Natalie closed her eyes and tried to ignore her reaction, which was very definitely female. She hated having those kinds of reactions. It was a weakness, and in her line of work and with her background, she couldn't afford to be weak. All her life, weakness had been the enemy. She couldn't let it creep in.

"I have to go back and see the octopus again. I need information."

Vincent swore beneath his breath. "That guy isn't looking to hand out information. He's looking to get laid."

"I know that. I'm not planning on getting that close."

"Is this so important?"

Was it? Natalie examined what had happened tonight. She had been propositioned, nearly pawed in a sickening and degrading kind of way. She hated that. Frankly, she wanted to do as Vincent asked and turn her back on the whole thing. But then she thought of Mrs. Morgensen and she knew that this job had become more than a job for her. It was much more than a ticket to a hot story and a byline. Her family had never trusted her to get through an entire day on her own. But Mrs. Morgensen and the others trusted her to help them, to salve their wounds, to see that justice was done, to save them. No one had ever needed her in that way. For that alone she cared about her frightened neighbors. She felt such an overwhelming sense of responsibility for each and every one of them. And while she didn't know if she could save them, she had to try. That was all there was to it. If she didn't do it, who would? And if she *couldn't* do it, then maybe her family had been right all along. No, this was more than a story, more than a career path. Helping her friends was a necessity.

"Natalie?" Vincent urged.

She sighed. "These are elderly people, people with very little money to lose, and they've had their life savings taken away. I think someone is cheating them."

"Then leave it to the police."

"The police know about it, but there isn't any proof whatsoever. Old people lose their money every day. They get taken advantage of. No one can do anything about it if there isn't any proof."

"And you intend to get that proof. You want to stop covering Beep-Beep the Clown."

She glared at him. "Actually, Beep-Beep was a pretty nice guy in his way, but yes, I'd like to do something more meaningful."

"And you're willing to put yourself in danger for a story."

She refused to explain about her bonds with Mrs. Morgensen and the details of her problems with her family. That wasn't anyone's business but her own. Besides, she didn't want anyone thinking she was soft in any way.

"That's what reporters do," she said, trying to sound as hard-boiled as possible.

"And to hell with the risks? To hell with everything? Including your own feelings about being some man's toy?"

No, that was part of her problem. She couldn't seem to put the emotional aspects of this case aside. She was already too personally involved with this story, but Mrs. Morgensen and her other neighbors were real people who hurt and dreamed and cried. She was supposed to be able to turn the emotion off and just write, but she couldn't. It wasn't good for a reporter to get entangled with her subjects. She knew that.

"Natalie?"

"I can handle my feelings," she lied.

"Can you deal with what's going to happen if those two men both decide they have to have you? Can you handle the fallout and the risks?"

"I'm not going to lead anyone on. I'll keep it light."

"What if you can't? Men can be animals." He practically growled the words, his voice deep and husky. Natalie shivered. Anger and passion were so closely related. She couldn't help wondering what that voice would sound like in a bed in the dark of night.

"It's not going to get that far," she insisted. "I know how to protect myself and how to call a halt to things."

"Some men get ugly when a woman calls a halt to things. Don't do this, Natalie. I'm trying to keep you safe. Don't make it harder. You're already getting threatening notes. Don't add another element by pursuing these men. The story would be just as compelling if you simply wrote Mrs. Morgensen's story."

He was probably right. "But there wouldn't be any chance of justice. I want her to have justice. Do you understand?"

When she turned to him, his eyes were like dark flames. "I understand the desire for justice. Very much so." His voice was a promise, harsh and full of pain she didn't understand. She felt a sudden urge to touch him, to soothe him.

She opened her mouth to ask him what he meant, what his personal stake in justice was.

But he reached out and touched one finger to her lips, startling her. Her body reacted and she almost leaned forward to get closer and feel more as he pulled away. "You need some sleep," he growled, and she knew that he wasn't going to give up any secrets to her. Maybe he didn't trust her not to turn him into another feature story, or maybe he just didn't like her all that much. She was, after all, a client his brother had foisted on him.

A slow, disappointing ache slipped through her. That was too darn bad. Because Vincent Fortune was exactly the macho type of man she needed to stay away from.

"Don't worry, I won't ask about your personal life."

He gave her a slow smile. "And you'll be more careful than you were tonight?"

She nodded.

"Good. I didn't like that guy."

She didn't have to ask what guy he was talking about. Neil had barely said a word. "I didn't like him much myself."

Vincent chuckled. "He did get one thing right, though. Nice legs," he said as he pulled up in front of her house and came around to open her door. "I'd be more careful slipping out of windows if I were you."

Her eyes opened wide and she blinked. Vincent laughed again. "Ah, not as hard-boiled as you like to pretend, are you, Natalie?"

She managed a challenging smile as she got out of the car and stood beside him. "I'm many things, Vincent, and hard-boiled is just one of them. Nice biceps," she said, reaching out to squeeze his arm. "I'd be more careful knocking the stuffing out the bad guys. Your muscles show." She took a deep breath and dared to wink at him.

Vincent's eyes turned dark, but then he laughed. "All right, one for you," he admitted with a touch of admiration in his voice as she turned and walked to her door, the sound of Vincent's heels on the pavement close behind her.

All the time that Natalie was moving down the hall to her apartment, opening her door, letting herself in, and saying goodnight and locking the door behind her, she was incredibly aware that Vincent was watching her every move. She might be his client, but she remembered that look in his eyes and realized that he didn't think of her as just a job. He also saw her as a woman.

And that made her feel like a woman, soft and desirable and...frustrated, because she couldn't ever touch or be touched by Vincent Fortune.

"No, one for you, Vincent," she admitted with a sigh once she was safely inside. One of them was going to go sleepless tonight, and it wasn't Vincent. Derek Seefer would be taking over his duties in an hour. Vincent would go home and sleep like all men slept, like her fathers and brothers had slept. No matter what happened, they managed to sleep soundly.

While she would toss and turn in her bed and wonder why on earth Daniel Fortune had had to send her a man like Vincent.

A man who reminded her that no matter how much progress she had made over the years, she still had weaknesses. Ah well, no matter; by morning she would have those weaknesses harnessed.

Vincent wasn't going to get under her skin again. And he'd probably soon be gone. Those notes were most likely written in the heat of the moment and would soon stop.

Reporters got them all the time. There was no real danger other than Vincent's masculine appeal.

Vincent spent a long time staring up at the ceiling that night. He had half a mind to call Derek and ask him if everything was all right. The other half of his mind wanted to drive to Natalie's house and tell Derek that he would take care of things from here on out.

Which was stupid and wrong. Derek was a good guard. He knew how to do his job.

Even if Natalie tried to give him the slip? Vincent wondered, and he almost smiled at that. He remembered her climbing from that window, remembered her giving him that knowing smile and tossing his own words back at him. She was sassy and determined and she cared about her subjects. He had to admire that about her. Her green eyes were alive with intelligence and indignation at the injustice done to her friends. She was a beautiful woman on a mission, and she was determined to do her job no matter what. Could Derek handle that?

"The better question is, can you handle that?" Vincent asked himself. He was attracted to her, and he never allowed that to happen on a job.

But he would handle it this time.

Somehow.

"This is so difficult to handle," Blake Jamison said two days later in a conversation with Ryan Fortune, head of the Fortune family and empire and now a new friend and relative whom Blake cherished. "I don't really understand how all of this can have happened. In the years since we've been married, Darcy and I have led a dull but mostly contented existence. My family has had its problems, but this…this is so…I don't know how to handle this. How is it that one of my sons—"

His voice broke. "I'm sorry," he said.

"You don't have to explain anything to us," Patrick Fortune, Ryan's cousin, said. Patrick's banking business had led to a life in New York but he was spending more time in Texas these days and planned to retire here soon. His opinion carried weight. "I'm sure you know that the Fortunes have had their own history of family problems over the years."

"Yes, but for one of my sons to kill his own brother!" Blake practically yelled the words. "How does a man deal with that?"

"I don't think he does, Blake," Ryan said quietly. "I don't think you'll ever be able to reconcile the fact that Jason was able to kill not once, but twice, and that one of those he murdered was his own brother."

Blake ran one hand through his hair, mussing it. Not that it mattered. Did anything matter anymore?

"I spent years trying to locate Jason. I don't know what else Darcy and I could have done. We tried so many things. We tried to reach him, to change him. He was always difficult, but still, he was mine. I thought he would change as he grew up. I thought he was still mine. I understand that he seemed to be an exemplary employee while he was working for you." Blake raised his eyes questioningly, hopefully, to Ryan.

"He seemed to be. But there's a lot we still don't know. Like the woman he killed. He passed her off as his wife. It appears that she wasn't. The police said that her real name was Melissa Anderson, not Melissa Wilkes."

"If that reporter, Natalie McCabe, hadn't seen what happened and reported it, he might still be on the loose."

Ryan shook his head. "They would have found him in time. Family members always get questioned. The fact that he claimed to be married to her and wasn't would have only made the authorities more suspicious. Natalie's witnessing the act only speeded up the process."

Blake nodded. "I'm glad she turned him in. That's a terrible thing for a father to say." Tears filled his throat, and he paused, searching for words. "There's a sickness in him, I think. He has to be sick." But sickness implied that no one was to blame. That wasn't what he meant to say.

Blake held up his hand as if to add something, but he didn't know what was left to say. He had fathered three sons. Emmett was missing, Christopher was dead, and Jason might as well be dead.

"You can't change what has happened, Blake," Ryan was saying softly. "Don't even try to make sense of it. It's impossible. You'll drive yourself crazy."

"I know. I have to learn to live with this."

"You have to learn that you're not to blame for Jason being

in prison for murder," Patrick said. "Don't go down that road. As Ryan said, this isn't your doing."

"Christopher was a good man," Blake said, barely able to even mouth the words. "I can't forgive Jason."

"You don't have to," Ryan said tersely. "Not unless you want to."

Blake shook his head. "I can't, but I have to see him. I have to try to understand. I have to learn to deal with all of this somehow."

In his heart, Blake knew that he had to learn to deal with his own part in what had happened. Despite what Patrick and Ryan had said, Blake knew that he was not blameless in all of this. Not by a long shot.

Jason had been a problem child, and Blake had let it pass. He had ignored Darcy's pleas to keep his children away from their grandfather, Farley. Farley had been half-crazy and jealous of the Fortune family, telling his grandson, Jason, about how Kingston Fortune had been fathered by a Jamison and how some of Kingston's money and power should have belonged to the Jamisons. Never mind that Kingston's father hadn't even known he'd had a son, or that Kingston had been raised by the Fortune family. Farley ranted and raved to Jason, and Jason, already a troubled young man who idolized his grandfather, had listened to his grandfather's demented ravings of injustice for years.

Deep down inside, Blake knew that he was to blame. He should have paid more attention to Jason, loved his son enough to try harder to save him from himself. If he had done that, maybe Jason's idolization of Farley wouldn't have happened. Farley had been a dangerous man.

Now Blake couldn't help wondering just how dangerous and depraved Jason really was, and what he would do now that he was trapped.

"I have to try to do something," Blake said.

Five

The next morning, Vincent peered down at the report on Jason Jamison. He tried to think about what it had been like for Natalie in that moment when she had realized that Jason had murdered Melissa, when Natalie's eyes had met his.

Jason was a man who had killed twice. He was a man without scruples, and Vincent didn't doubt that he would kill again if killing suited his purposes.

"Is he the one?" Vincent whispered. "And if he is, what kind of connections does he have? Have I done all I can to make sure that Natalie is safe?"

Against his will, a memory arose of himself as a young boy swearing to protect his mother from his father's fists. Yet he had come home from school time and time again to find her battered and bloody. The impotence had almost driven him crazy. It was what drove him to do what he did for a living, and most of the time he was damn proud of his accomplishments. He was no longer assailed by those doubts or that feeling of being helpless in the face of circumstances.

Jason might have connections, ways and means Vincent was unaware of. Most likely he did, since he had been able to work his way up so far in Fortune, TX, Ltd. But Vincent had resources, too, and he could supply Natalie with round-the-clock surveillance.

"Heaven help Jason Jamison if he gets through my boundaries. He won't touch her. I swear I won't let him," he said beneath his breath.

Blake watched as Jason was led in cuffs toward the table where he waited. It was now or never, he thought. Jason was under heavy guard, but once he was moved to a maximum-security prison, communication would be even more difficult. At least it would be more stilted, if that were possible. If they were ever going to begin to talk, to unravel the twisted threads of their relationship that had contributed at least in part to Jason's downward spiral into darkness, then let them do it here. Today.

"Son." Blake barely got the word out, his throat was so tight.

Jason smiled. "'Son?' How touching, but inappropriate. Farley was my father, more than he was yours."

The knife sliced through Blake. "Farley was your grandfather. He was not a sane man, not near the end and not for many years before that."

Jason narrowed his eyes. Blake almost could envision his son doing to him what he'd done to Melissa if Jason hadn't been cuffed. "The Fortunes made Farley that way," Jason said.

Blake shook his head. "The Fortunes didn't have anything to do with that. They owe our family nothing."

"They owe us everything. Kingston Fortune was sired by a Jamison. He built an empire, one that should have stayed in the Jamison family."

"Kingston's father didn't even know he existed. Kingston was raised by Dora and Hobart Fortune. He was theirs."

Jason growled. "The money and the power should have been ours. Farley tried to tell Kingston that, but Kingston wouldn't have anything to do with him. I would have made the Fortune family pay for their indifference. I had plans."

"Is that—" Blake felt tears clog his throat. "Did Christopher's death have anything to do with your plans?"

Jason stared his father full in the face. "Christopher was a pain in the ass. He tried to spoil things for me."

If he hadn't been seated, Blake was sure he would have fallen. Christopher had been good and kind. Of all the Jamisons, he was the one who saw the way clearly, who always chose the path of least destruction. He was the one who cared.

"You killed your own brother."

Jason laughed. It was an oily, ugly sound. "You should have seen him. He actually wanted us to try to be a family. What an idiot."

Rage boiled within Blake's chest. Bile filled his throat, but he fought it back. "You don't even care that you killed him."

Jason smiled again. "On the contrary, it was one of the finest moments of my life. He was always the good one, but where did all that goodness actually get him? Facedown and bloated, floating with the fishes in Lake Mondo. And you know what the best part of all this is?"

Blake felt the blood draining away from his face. He braced himself for what was to come.

"It hurts you that he's dead. I love that," Jason said. He licked his lips slowly. "I really do love that."

"And the woman?"

"The bitch? She was going to betray me. Too bad she didn't get a chance. Melissa was an opportunist. She might have changed her mind and decided to stick with me if she'd had a chance. But—" he leaned forward slightly "—she was having trouble talking at the end. Her eyes were bulging out. She wasn't nearly as pretty then as she had been."

Blake fought for air, for words, for sanity. "You don't even care, do you? Not about Chris or the woman or anything."

Slowly Jason shook his head and smiled. "I care about one thing." He paused as if for dramatic effect.

Blake refused to ask the question. It was obvious that Jason couldn't wait to tell him the rest, anyway.

"I care about revenge," Jason said. "I want revenge, and I'll have it. Don't worry about that, father." He drawled the last word, sneered it. "I'll have my revenge, on everyone who deserves it."

Blake's heart broke completely then. Jason was going the way of Farley. He had no laudable goals, no future, no conscience. It would be so easy to walk away. He wanted to walk away. No, to run, as fast and as far as he could, to pretend that this son had never been born.

But that was where the problems had started, wasn't it? He had turned away from Jason's childhood problems, pretended they didn't exist. Two people, one his beloved child, were dead as a result. His conscience would never allow him to live in peace for the rest of his life. Especially if he turned away again.

Rebelling against all that came naturally, Blake watched the guard take Jason away, and he vowed one thing. He would do all that he could to fulfill Christopher's goals and the goals that should have been his own.

He would reach Jason somehow if it was the last thing he did.

Natalie felt like a tightly strung wire. Nearly a week had passed. Vincent was everywhere she went, and knowing he was always behind her made her aware of herself in a way that she never had been before. That was all too clear this morning, she noted, staring at the mess on her bed.

Clothes were tossed everywhere, taken from her closet, studied and discarded.

"Agh!" she yelled. "The man is making me crazy. I've never paid that much attention to what I wear. For the past few years, all my efforts have gone into my work. And I'm not going to let the fact that some man is constantly staring at my butt make a difference now."

So saying, she picked up the closest article of clothing at hand and marched into the bathroom. Once there, she applied only as much makeup as was necessary to look professional. She donned the slim leaf-green dress, ran a comb through her hair and prepared to leave the house.

Almost without thought, she checked every window lock, the back door, swished every curtain into place so that no one could peek inside and closed the door behind her. Just as Vincent had advised her.

Exiting her apartment building, she couldn't help but look for Vincent sitting in his black sedan across the street. That little move was fast becoming a ritual, even if it rankled that she couldn't stop herself from looking each day.

But to her surprise, Vincent wasn't there today. Derek, her nighttime shadow, was still sitting in his SUV. He waved to her as she moved out.

Vincent never waved. He just looked dark and brooding and determined. Ever since that day when he had traded words with Brad, he had kept his distance, ever watchful but not interfering with her life in any way. In spite of the space he maintained between them, she could never seem to ditch her awareness of him. Not just as a bodyguard, but as a man.

She hated that. So this was a good thing that Derek was here today, wasn't it?

"Absolutely," Natalie whispered. Besides, Vincent had assured her that Derek was very good at his job. She would be just as safe with him as she was with Vincent, wouldn't she?

The fact that her back felt naked and exposed today was just ridiculous. She didn't need Vincent to feel safe, did she?

Besides, she hadn't received any new threats lately. Any day now, Vincent would tell her that he was being pulled off her case. The danger was over.

Vincent would drop out of her life just as fast as he had dropped in. She supposed that was a good thing. It meant that she was safe, and she didn't really need Vincent. In any way.

Jason glanced out the window of the transport van. He stole a look at the guard driving the van. The man was nervous, his jaw tense with a nervous tic, his back ramrod straight. His hands were clenched on the wheel. Jason liked that. It felt good to scare someone after the long days of enforced confinement and humiliation.

It had been all he could do to contain himself these past few days. His head had been pounding and he had almost messed up badly when he had lost his temper with one of the scumbags who was housed in the same jail.

Small-time scumbags. Riffraff. Brainless thieves and drunks. Not a brain among them. No one who could manipulate the way he could. The temptation to try the blade he had bribed out of a guard had been almost overwhelming. Not that there was anything special about the knife. It had a serrated blade that would work well enough and would cause some extra pain. There was that, but he had been forced to pay an exorbitant sum and work too hard, convincing a Fortune TX, Ltd. underling that he had debts of honor he wanted to pay while he was locked up and helpless. The dolt had believed him and had sent him the money. The guard had come through with the knife.

As for the idiot guard, he knew which side his bread was buttered on now. When Jason had lost control with the convenience-store thief who had gotten too close and nearly caught Jason looking for a hiding place for his treasure, Jason had savaged him with his fists, feet and teeth, ignoring the temptation to try the evil blade. The knife was for later, and anyway, in the end the guard had been more than willing to make more easy money by hiding the knife for him. The idiot was probably sorry that his charge was being transported to maximum security, because now the gravy train would end.

Jason wanted to laugh. If only the guy knew the whole story about how things would end…

Well, he would soon enough. In fact, right now would be a pretty good time. The van was out in the middle of nowhere and there was plenty of forest for cover.

Jason slid his hand down beside the seat. The cuffs hurt like hell and made it tough, but then his whole life had been tough. Tough was the thought of facing a lifetime behind bars or a shortened life by getting juiced. Pain was nothing.

Finally he grasped the hidden blade and held it in his clenched hands.

When he looked up, he was staring into the eyes of the guard, the one who had placed the blade in just the right place.

"Just like you told me," the man said. "I'll take my money now."

Yeah, like that was going to happen. Once the guards had transported him to max, the guy would have no incentive to stay quiet anymore. He might figure he could get more money by lying to the authorities and squealing, suggesting that things had happened differently than they had. Jason knew the type. Heck, Jason *was* the type, only much, much smarter.

"The money," the guard said.

"What the hell is going on?" the driver said.

"Nothing. I got this guy some first-class food while he was in the slammer and he hasn't paid me yet. That's all," the guard said. "But you will now, won't you?" he said to Jason. "Because I can make your case much worse when it actually goes to trial."

"I don't like this," the driver said, his body going even stiffer.

"Just drive. Don't worry," the greedy guard told him. He shifted as if he would reach out and touch Jason.

Jason smiled. Without so much as a blink, he looped his cuffed wrists over the driver's head and slit the man's throat.

"What the hell?" the guard yelled as blood poured from the driver's throat and the van skidded wildly around on the road.

"Better hit the brakes," Jason suggested.

The man's eyes were wild, but he did as he was told. "You didn't have to kill him. He wouldn't have said nothin'. He didn't know nothin'. Hell, the man has a wife and kids. What's wrong with you?"

The car skidded to a stop. The guard started to exit the door.

He would tell. He would lead them to him, Jason thought. All the money in the world wouldn't stop a terrified man from telling.

"What's wrong? You want to know what's wrong with me? Try this," Jason yelled, grabbing for the back of the man's shirt and plunging the knife in.

The guard let out a scream.

"Oh yeah, you thought you could manipulate me, didn't you?" Jason sneered as he climbed over into the front seat, heading for the open door.

The guard was in his path and Jason elbowed him out of his way. He looked at the man who was gasping for air. Oh yeah, he loved looking into their eyes as they died, as they realized who really held the power. "You wanted to know what was wrong with me. Well, how about I'm a killer, remember?"

The guy didn't answer. Didn't look. Probably dead already. Damn, he had been robbed of that last look of fear. He hated that.

Better make sure he was really dead, stab him again if he wasn't.

The sound of a car approaching filled his ears. The guy was coming fast. Real fast.

"Shit!" Jason said. He shoved the door open and slipped out of the car and into the trees. Good thing he knew a thing or two about survival. Farley had taught him.

Good old Farley, and to hell with the rest of them. He wished they were all dead, and if he had his way—and he always did—some of them would be soon.

Six

"Okay, this isn't working," Vincent muttered to himself. He had kept watch over Natalie last night, intending to sleep today and switch shifts with Derek.

But sleep wasn't coming, and his plan wasn't working. It had been all too obvious to him these past few days that his interest in Natalie was more than the interest a bodyguard had in a client. She was tough and spunky and sassy, and he saw her as a woman, and that wasn't good. It made a man sloppy.

He had figured that Derek would be the better choice for daytime guard. Derek had a wife whom he adored. He would be impervious to Natalie, and Vincent would take the night-time shift when he would be less likely to run into her.

"But the damned woman isn't going to let me sleep, is she?" he asked, rolling out of bed and hunting for his pants. Just when sleep drew near, he would imagine her walking ahead of him, that gentle sway of her hips, or she would turn around and give him that lazy, insolent grin that dared him to call her soft. She liked being able to take care of herself. She hated having a guard, but she had been pretty good about the whole thing. She knew the necessity.

He was the one with the problem. Right now, his problem was that, in spite of his respect for Derek, he wasn't sure the man was up to keeping up with Natalie.

Maybe he would just check in…

"Stop it," he ordered himself. "Derek is the best. He's perfectly capable of doing everything that you would do." And more. Derek would keep things impersonal. As they should be.

The sound of his phone ringing ended the dilemma. Vincent picked up the receiver.

"Vince here."

"Vince, it's Daniel. We've got a problem."

Something dark and frightening swirled through Vincent's gut. Daniel wouldn't say that if it weren't so. "Shoot," he told his brother.

"You're going to need to increase your surveillance on Natalie. Jamison skipped."

Vincent's heart began to pound. Anger surged through him. "What the hell do you mean?"

"Exactly what I said. He somehow managed to get a knife. When he was being transported to maximum security, he slit the driver's throat. Stabbed the other guard in the back. Ran."

"Where the hell did a guy like that get a knife? He's a killer."

"I don't know anything yet. The driver's dead. The other guy's critical. Lost a lot of blood. When he comes to—make that *if* he comes to and is still functional—maybe we'll know. For now we've got one dead guy, one severely wounded and a knife. And Natalie is a woman Jamison has plenty of reason to hate. Vince, do what you can. Watch your back. Watch hers."

He'd do better than that. He was going to make sure Natalie didn't take a breath without him knowing it.

"It's taken care of. Thanks, Daniel." Vincent hung up the phone. Now to find Natalie and tell her the bad news without scaring her to death or ticking her off.

Either way, she wasn't going to be happy.

Neither was he because, like it or not, smart or not, he didn't intend to let Natalie more than an arm's length away from him from now on.

"You're going to do what?" Natalie tried to breathe normally, but it was nearly impossible. She looked at Vincent and hoped that he was joking.

"I'm moving into your apartment."

Deep breaths, she told herself. Take deep breaths. One. Two. Three. Her tension climbed higher. This wasn't working. Deep breathing was a bust.

"No," she said, her voice coming out too wispy. Damn, she hated sounding weak. "You can't do that. Can't you see what problems that would cause?"

Vincent's jaw went rigid. His eyes were dark, darker than usual. "I don't blame you for fighting this, Natalie. You're an independent woman and you've already given up a fair amount of your freedom, but…" He hesitated.

"But what?"

Vincent stepped closer. "Jason Jamison has escaped from custody."

She took a step back as if he had tried to hit her. "How?"

He shook his head. "The details aren't clear yet, but he's out, Natalie, and it looks like he's killed again. You can't stay alone. It wouldn't be wise."

"We don't know that it was him sending the notes." She wished her voice didn't sound so frightened. She took a deep breath.

"That's true. We don't know much yet, but for now, let me stay. Let me do what I need to do to keep you safe."

His voice was deep and low and reassuring, but when she looked up into his eyes, she could see that he was worried. Maybe he thought that she would fight him on this. She wanted to. She hated Jason Jamison for being what he was, for hurting people and for making her a prisoner in her own home, but she could see the necessity of having Vincent close.

"You're asking me?" She studied him.

He looked away.

She crossed her arms. "You're pretending to ask me, but in truth you're telling me. You have to keep the witness alive."

"Damn it, Natalie, you're more than just a witness. If you don't value your own life, at least consider my sanity. I don't want to be responsible for letting you get hurt."

"You wouldn't be. That would be Jason who would be hurting me."

But his eyes were anguished. His jaw was firm. "I'm not giving you a choice. I'm sorry."

Natalie signed. "No, *I'm* sorry," she said. "I know this isn't a game, and I know how seriously you take your commitments. Of course you need to be close to protect me. I'll do whatever I can to cooperate. Just give me a few minutes to make a place for you." As if he was a new piece of furniture she was buying. For a minute, the whole concept sounded so ridiculous. Then Natalie smiled just a little.

"What?" Vincent crossed his arms and glowered at her.

She shrugged. "I was just thinking that finding a place to put someone as big as you will be a lot more difficult than finding a space for a new floor lamp."

Almost as if she had waved a magic wand, he relaxed. He smiled, and her heart did that crazy flip thing she was beginning to think of as her Vincent mode. Probably girls had been experiencing that sensation all of his life. "I'll try not to require too much space," he told her. "The couch will be fine."

"Oh no. If I get up in the middle of the night for a glass of water or because an idea hits me and I need to get at my computer, I don't want to be stumbling across a half-naked man. I'll move my desk out here. You take the spare room."

He shrugged. "It's your place. I'll honor your arrangements."

"Do you have to do this often?" she couldn't help asking.

"What?"

"Move in with women?"

Vincent grinned. "You're my first."

He might have been talking about sex. What a ridiculous thought, she told herself. A man like him had no doubt had any woman he wanted.

But she definitely didn't want to examine that thought. "I'll try to be gentle with you," she said.

"Thank you." He gave her a mock bow. "I'll try to stay out of your way as much as possible."

"No wet towels on the floor," she lectured, trying to look stern.

"Never."

"And no belching or scratching or any of those disgusting man things."

He chuckled. "I'll try to contain myself. You seem to know a lot about the bad habits of some men." His raised brow suggested that he was wondering what kind of personal experiences she had had.

"I do. My three brothers taught me to arm-wrestle, swear with the best of them, and play a pretty mean game of rock, paper, scissors. And I can hold my own in a fight. Most men find me a bit pushy or unfeminine."

Vincent held up his hands palm out, begging off. "Hey, I have nothing but respect for a woman who can best me at rock, paper, scissors. And for the record, I don't think Brad Herron found you unfeminine. He seemed to be determined to have you."

She shrugged. "I don't think he's very discriminating. I'm

not normally a very soft woman, Vincent. You won't have to worry about finding any frilly undies hanging in the bathroom."

"Good to know," he said, a trace of amusement in his eyes.

"Are you mocking me, Vincent?"

"Not a chance, Natalie. You're a client and I would never mock a client. Besides, I respect your right to eschew frilly undies. Plain white is just fine." Something about the husky tone of his voice made Natalie want to squirm. She had always been a plain white kind of woman, and she had never considered that remotely erotic. She didn't want to be erotic, had hated the role she had taken on at The Ladder the other day, but just the way Vincent said *plain white* made her feel hot and bothered. She could imagine Vincent removing a woman's white cotton bikinis with his teeth. She suddenly felt as if the room temperature were soaring, the air disappearing.

"Well," she said with an attempt at breeziness. "I'm glad we understand each other. I'll do my best to play it safe and help you do your job. And you'll do your best not to interfere in my daily existence. Shouldn't be a problem at all. Piece of cake. Nothing to it." She held out her arms in a show of nonchalance.

Vincent tilted his head and studied her. "All right, spill it."

"What?"

"Whatever's bothering you. You hate having me here, and you're not going to be able to hide it. I need to know why if we're going to make this work. Is it the sex thing?"

She felt as if she were glowing like a tomato. "The sex thing?" Her voice came out on a croak.

"The fact that you're a woman and I'm a man and I'm attracted to you."

"You are?" She hated the fact that her voice squeaked. She was not a squeaky-voice kind of woman and never had been.

Vincent gave her one of those you've-got-to-be-kidding looks. "Look, you're an attractive woman, and I'm still very much alive. You've got great legs and great eyes and some other pretty good parts, too. I couldn't help but notice, but believe this. I don't attack my clients. I'm here to protect you, not jump you."

Natalie's breathing kicked up even higher. The fact that Vincent could have made hunk of the month in any women's magazine was an issue with her. It made her aware of herself as a woman, and she didn't like that at all. She hated feeling all feminine and helpless and gooey. But the sex thing wasn't the main thing.

"You're right. I'm not used to sharing my space with an attractive, virile male, but it's more than that."

He waited. She tried to think of the right words to make it very clear what she needed and didn't need because he was right. If this had to go on for any time at all they would both be screaming if they didn't set some ground rules.

"As I mentioned, I grew up with three brothers and two parents who all were very protective. I was the only girl, the fragile one, the one who needed to be coddled. At least that seemed to be the general opinion of my family. If I sneezed, it was a major crisis. If a boy said something negative to me, my brothers were ready to break all his bones even if I deserved the negative comment. When I went on a date, everyone wanted a play-by-play. They were sure that someone was going to try to take advantage of me and that I wouldn't be able to defend myself or speak up for myself. I had to sneak around a lot just to do the things that other normal girls did."

"So having a bodyguard is like a continuation of your childhood." He was studying her carefully.

"Well, you're not related to me, and this time there is a real possible threat to me, so no, it's not exactly the same."

"I sense the word *but* coming on."

Natalie nodded. "I just want you to understand that I can

sometimes be a bit stubborn about certain things. I had to be to survive in my family, but I'll try to watch myself around you."

"Don't."

She frowned. "Don't what? Don't be stubborn?"

"Don't watch yourself around me. It's your life. You're the client. I'll do my best to adapt."

A warm feeling slipped through Natalie. "You're telling me you won't restrict me?"

"Well, I won't set you a curfew and I won't dictate who you date."

She hadn't dated much in the past year, but there was no point in mentioning that. A girl had some pride, after all.

"But I might interrogate your dates if I think there's a reason to. Don't hesitate to cuss me out if you feel like it. I'm not a brother or a father. I won't get offended if you yell. And I'll do my best not to underestimate you. I figure any woman who had the chance to run away after staring into Jamison's eyes immediately after he had killed a woman and who had the guts to turn around and come back so that he wouldn't go free is a woman who is pretty gutsy and smart."

Natalie was left speechless. All of her brothers and both of her parents had yelled at her for coming back to the party where she had known there was a killer waiting.

Vincent understood. He would have done the same.

"Thank you," she said, the word coming out a bit choked. "I just couldn't leave it alone."

He smiled. "Isn't that the mark of a good reporter?"

"Well, I wish you would tell that to my boss. He doesn't believe Mrs. Morgensen's story is anything special. I'm covering the cotton candy festival tomorrow."

"So you're dropping Mrs. Morgensen's story?"

"Not a chance. I'm going to nail whoever it was that took advantage of her and bilked her out of her money, even if she signed papers giving them permission to take every penny."

"I believe you will," he said, and he reached out and brushed her cheek with one finger. Heat seared through her. She wanted to lean closer, have him touch more.

Ignore that, she told herself. "Do you…need to get something? Some clothes or something?"

"Got everything in my car. I'm ready."

The truth came crashing down on Natalie. Vincent Fortune was going to be moving into her already tight apartment. She was going to be living with a man, one who made her aware of herself as a woman in ways she hated to acknowledge.

"Natalie? I'll be back in a minute, all right?"

She took a deep breath. "Go get your stuff. I'm ready." As if anything could ever prepare her for the reality of living with a man like Vincent.

Natalie was like a puppy who had been cornered and didn't know what to expect next, Vincent couldn't help thinking a few hours later. She jumped if he got too close. She kept eyeing him as if she expected him to do something naughty. She was working at her computer, but he didn't hear any keys tapping.

"Agh! This is not working," she finally said. "I need to get out of here."

He put down the case files he was studying and rose to his feet.

She grimaced. "You have to go with me, don't you?"

"'Fraid so, Natalie. That's the way this works. You go places and I go with you. I do my best to fade into the woodwork."

"I can see you're trying," she said, looking at his pile of work. "I'm just not used to having a roommate."

"That makes two of us."

She raised her eyebrows. "I remember. You said you didn't believe in marriage."

"No, I said marriage wasn't for me. And for the record, that's not a sexist thing. It's just that in my life and line of work, I've seen the worst that marriage can provide, and it can be unbelievably ugly. I'm not willing to risk that route."

Natalie nodded. "I'm not judging. Marriage doesn't hold any appeal for me, either."

She didn't explain, but that was okay, because he wouldn't ask her to give up her secrets when he was keeping his. Early in life, he had known that he would be a loner. He had grown up being the only real thing standing between his father and his siblings, given the fact that his mother was usually too beaten and bruised to be an effective shield. Living like that had set him apart; it had kept him from social opportunities. In time, he realized that being alone came naturally to him. He was good at it. Besides, living by himself made it easy to keep his worst fears at bay, and he liked it that way.

"Well then, here we are. Together. We might as well see how we can make this work."

Natalie nodded. She frowned, and her brows bunched together in concentration. "Do you cook?"

Vincent did a double take. "I get by. Why?"

"What's 'I get by' mean?" she asked with a laugh. "What can you cook?"

He twisted his mouth in concentration. "Burgers, steaks, pancakes, that kind of thing."

"Pancakes? You make pancakes?"

"Occasionally," Vince admitted. He was getting a bad feeling about this.

"Great!" She gave him a wide grin, and her green eyes sparkled with what looked like delight. "That's perfect. I never make pancakes."

"So what do you make?" He studied her closely.

"Canned soup, frozen meals, maybe salad or an omelet if I'm feeling creative. But you make the tough stuff. Come on." She held out her hand.

He looked at what she was offering. Long, slender fingers,

nails buffed and pretty without polish. Her skin looked soft. He wanted to touch. Probably a bad idea to do that. He could tell that she wasn't thinking of him as a man in this moment, but as something lighter. A friend, a fellow cook, perhaps. At any rate, she wasn't arguing with him or looking worried.

Vincent took Natalie's hand.

Instant awareness shifted through him. Her pretty body became not just something that looked good, but something that felt good. He wanted to slide his hand up her arm, to touch his thumb to her lips, to taste her mouth. He wanted to know what lay beneath her blue jeans and white T-shirt.

And he had no business thinking such thoughts.

"Where are we going?" he asked, and his voice came out just a touch too harsh.

"We're going shopping," she whispered conspiratorially.

Vincent almost cringed. "Shopping?"

She chuckled. "For food, so you can make some of that hearty man stuff you like to eat. I like to eat it, too, and it only seems fair that if I'm sharing my house with you, you could share some of your steak with me."

He couldn't help laughing. "I think you're a witch, Natalie. No woman has ever insisted I go shopping with her, and yet, somehow I think this is an experience I'm never going to forget."

"I'll try to make it memorable," she promised.

He'd just bet she would, Vincent thought as they left the house together.

Seven

Natalie's hand felt small in Vincent's grasp, and she wondered if she had been stark raving mad to reach out to him this way. His skin was warm, his touch made her too aware of herself as a woman. She couldn't stop thinking about what it would be like to have his entire body pressing against hers.

Stop it, she wanted to say, but she couldn't because Vincent was right here with her. And she'd never been more aware of a man in her life.

The only relief was when he let go of her hand to open his car door for her. But that provided only short-term relief because Vincent's car was sinful, with black, butter-soft leather seats that reminded Natalie of a cushy bed. The errant thought made her squirm.

She forced herself to sit still until Vincent had pulled up in front of the grocery store, and then she hopped out before he could help her. This time, she didn't hold out her hand.

"What first?" she asked as they entered the store. She waited for him to come up beside her.

"*You* first," he told her. "I walk behind."

Of course. How could she have forgotten? This was going to be awkward, but darn it, somehow she was going to make it work. If she and Vincent were going to be joined at the hip for a while, she intended to make the best of it.

"How far behind?" she asked. "Does it have to be real far, because talking is going to be difficult if I have to yell."

"Don't yell," he said softly. "I'll stay close." She felt him at her back, at her elbow. He was definitely close. He leaned forward and placed his mouth near her ear. "I just need to watch your back, that's all," he told her.

But it was clear from the looks people were giving them that the other shoppers thought he was doing a lot more than watching her back. They thought he was sleeping with her.

Warmth stole through Natalie. She looked down. They were in the produce aisle, which was draped with Christmas tinsel and red and green bells, and she hadn't even noticed. "Onion?" she asked.

He blinked. "Why not?"

She put one in her basket. They walked on together. Like a couple. He handed her mangoes and bananas.

"Energy drink in the morning," he told her. Of course, a man who made his living physically placing his life between others and harm had to stay fit.

When anyone got too close, Vincent shifted subtly—too subtly for anyone else to notice, most likely, but Natalie noticed. Every time.

"How far does it go?" she finally asked, her voice choked.

"How far does what go?"

She looked up at him and wondered if he had ever had to get between a client and a bully or a bullet. And suddenly her throat closed up. He was a man of honor. She was almost sure that he would place the life of his client above even his own safety, but in the end she didn't want to know. She didn't want to wonder about whether he had ever chosen someone else's life over his own, about whether he had ever been wounded. For sure she didn't want to worry about the fact that he could get hurt guarding her.

"I mean, is there anything else you need?" she asked.

"Just one thing." His voice was low and husky.

"What?" Did she want to know this?

"Chocolate." He practically breathed the word, and she could almost feel his sly smile, but feeling wasn't enough.

She turned suddenly, catching him off guard, and found that she was right. He was grinning.

"Don't you like chocolate?" he asked.

Natalie raised one brow. She grasped Vincent's arm and smiled up at him. "Chocolate? Something gooey that melts in the mouth? Downfall of half the women I know? And I thought you were such a hard man."

He smiled. "I am. I just have a weakness. I like sweet things."

For a minute, their eyes met and held. Natalie almost wished she was soft and sweet, but she wasn't.

"Well then, let's go find some chocolate. I'll race you." And she laughed as he swooped in behind her and kept pace.

Vincent closed all the shades. He made a swift check of all the doors and windows. Jamison was out there somewhere, and he was a smart guy. He probably knew where Natalie lived.

"Do you think he's looking for me?"

Vincent turned. Natalie was standing there in the doorway all covered up in a fluffy pink bathrobe that covered her from neck to toes. Not that it mattered. No amount of covering up could mess with his overactive imagination. He had a pretty good idea of what that sweet little curvy body looked like beneath all that pink fluff. He'd been living here for days, trying not to envision her naked for just as long. But he couldn't dwell on that now. Her clear green eyes were filled with concern.

"He's had some time to get away. Maybe he's just running as far and fast as he can," he said.

She nodded. "I should want that, I guess, but I don't. If he keeps running, he'll eventually run into someone. Another someone he might hurt when he's already hurt too many."

"Then maybe he's not running. But if he's around here, he won't get to you. I'll take care of you."

"But then you might get hurt." She licked her lips, grave concern in her eyes. "And…"

She looked up, tilted her chin just a bit too high. He was beginning to recognize that look. "And you want to tell me that you can take care of yourself," he said.

"It sounds childish."

"No. It just sounds like what anyone would say if they'd never been allowed to get hurt or to try when there was a risk. The world is full of risks. It's healthy to take a few. Just…"

She frowned at him. "Say it."

"Just not this time. Not with this man," he said. "You have to let me keep watch over you."

"Because you're bigger and stronger."

"Because I'm trained to defend and protect, and I won't hesitate to do anything that is necessary to keep him from getting to you. I won't waver. You would, because it's human nature to give other humans a second chance. That would be a mistake. Could you shoot if you had to, maim if you had to, or even kill?"

She studied him, her chin still lifted. "I've never had to find that out. Have you?"

He slowly nodded, but he offered no details. He didn't like remembering what it had been like the night a deranged madman had thrown himself at one of Vincent's clients, then came at Vincent with a knife. The crazed man had lived, but just barely. And Vincent had had to go to sleep every night remembering the taste of blood and the look in the madman's eyes as his own knife was plunged into him. What had happened had been necessary but it had also been ugly, and Vincent didn't want Natalie to ever have to experience something like that.

"Do you resent having me here so much?" he asked, wondering what the hell he was doing. This wasn't the tack he normally took. He didn't discuss his clients' reservations with them, but then his reaction to this woman wasn't like his reaction to any other client.

"No, I don't resent you," she said. "I'm grateful. I just resent the fact that I can't do what you do. I want to be that strong. I want to be invincible, to control everything it's possible to control. I don't want to have anyone else running my life."

He smiled then. "No one can do everything. We all do what we're good at in life. You're going to help Mrs. Morgensen. That counts just as much or more as any contribution I'm making here."

She stared at him, questions in her eyes. Vincent felt as if she were searching his soul, as if he were the subject of one of her articles. It wasn't something he was used to, being the object of attention this way. In his job, he stayed in the background as much as possible; if he was in the foreground, his sole purpose was to intimidate the bad guys. No one ever wondered what he was thinking, what made him tick. He was pretty sure that Natalie was trying to figure him out, and the very thought made him want to move, to move *to* her, to touch her in order to distract her from her thoughts. Or hell, maybe he just wanted to touch her, and there was no good reason other than the fact that she was a beautiful woman with eyes that did him in.

He studied her, and some of what he was thinking must have shown in his face, because she blinked then and shifted.

"About Mrs. Morgensen," she said. "Thank you for understanding."

"It was a no-brainer. She's a really nice lady, and she's been hurt. You're going to do something about it, make the bad guys pay. That's admirable."

All traces of concern left Natalie's face. She smiled, and damn him, his breathing kicked up, hard. It was all he could do to keep himself from going to her, unwinding her from that frothy pink thing she was wearing so that he could see all of her.

As if she knew just where his errant thoughts were headed, she suddenly wrapped her arms more tightly around herself. Her lashes drifted down. "Well, I guess I should be getting to bed. Is there anything you need?"

You in my bed, he wanted to say. But instead he said nothing. He shook his head, said good-night and settled in to try to sleep. He hoped he didn't dream of Natalie tonight, with or without her bathrobe.

The days were settling into a routine, Natalie was surprised to admit. Not that she would ever get used to having Vincent so near all the time. He just wasn't the kind of man a woman ever forgot was around. But he had done his best to make her comfortable. He had joined in with household chores without being asked and he was a surprisingly good cook.

"You could give lessons," she told him, savoring a taste of pork tenderloin that Vincent had served her. "Did your mother teach you to do this?"

He laughed. "Necessity taught me how to do this. I didn't feel like starving, and I figured I'd starve if I couldn't cook a decent meal."

"I can't cook much, and I haven't starved," she pointed out.

He looked at her as if checking to make sure she was still in the world of the living.

"No, you certainly haven't," he finally said in a deep, husky voice.

Natalie blinked. "Are you telling me I'm fat?"

Vincent laughed. "Hardly. Why do women worry so much about being fat?"

"Because it's unhealthy?" she suggested.

He shrugged. "True, but a few curves are…nice, don't you think?" He looked at her in a way that made her aware that yes, she had a few curves.

"I—I guess so. But we weren't talking about curves. We were talking about how you learned to cook."

"Yes, we were, and no, my mother didn't teach me. She was a wonderful cook, but my father had very strict beliefs about what men and women did. Men didn't cook. Women didn't work."

"I thought those rules went out a long time ago."

"They did. In most places." Vincent's voice was tight, his expression unreadable. It was clear that he didn't like talking about his family, and that this conversation was becoming too serious.

"Well," she said with a smile. "He probably wouldn't have liked me at all, then."

Vincent took a step closer. He touched her cheek. "No," he said in a harsh but gentle voice. "He wouldn't have liked you, but the flaw wouldn't be yours."

Natalie swallowed hard. Vincent's fingers were warm, and he was close. He was clearly not happy but was being so gentle with her. At the moment, stupid as it was, she wanted to lean into him, to place her fingers on him, as well.

And then what? she thought. Natalie, you're living with this man, she reminded herself. He's a protector. Once the need for protection is over, he's gone. And could you ever really get involved with a man whose whole life is built on calling the shots, a man who doesn't believe in relationships?

She swallowed hard and backed away. "I'd better get ready

to go. I have to interview a man who has been running a holiday party for a local day-care center for twenty-five years."

"All right. Let's go."

Natalie's heart sank. She had seen Mr. Felsmith, another wronged neighbor, in the hall last night. He was worrying about not being able to buy Christmas presents for his grandchildren this year. She hadn't had any more contact with Brad Herron or Neil Gerard since that day at The Ladder. With the holidays coming, the paper had been sending her on every human interest story in San Antonio, and at this time of year there were plenty. She hadn't done a thing to help Mr. Felsmith or Mrs. Morgensen, and that just wasn't right.

Whenever Vincent was around, she felt too aware of him. She didn't act the right way or do the right things to get the answers she needed. And asking him to let her slip out alone just wasn't going to cut it with him, even though there hadn't been a peep out of Jason Jamison since he had made his escape. If she pointed that out to him, as she already had, he would only smile at her indulgently and continue to tail her, to protect her.

What she needed was a plan.

"Well, we'd better get moving," she muttered, but she knew that her directions were more for herself than for Vincent. He, of course, needed no further encouragement. The man was tireless, and he was always at her side.

The only problem was she was beginning to like having him there.

"Oh, hello, Vincent." Mrs. Morgensen came out of her door just as Vincent and Natalie were heading down the hall.

"Hello, Mrs. Morgensen," he said. "You're looking lovely this morning."

"Oh, Natalie, he's a flirtatious one. Does he do that with you, too? I'll bet he does a lot more than flirt." Mrs. Morgensen gave Vincent a sly wink.

He almost blushed.

"Oh, Vincent definitely does a lot more than flirt," Natalie said.

Vincent nearly choked. "Excuse me?"

"Men," Mrs. Morgensen said. "They like to make wild, passionate love, but they don't want anyone to talk about it. My husband, Bernard, never did like me to compliment him publicly about what we did in bed. I don't know why. He was an excellent lover."

Vincent saw Natalie's shoulders shaking. Was she actually laughing?

"Natalie?"

"I'll bet he's a tiger," Mrs. Morgensen said.

"I'll bet he is, too," Natalie said, "but Mrs. Morgensen, Vincent and I aren't— Well, I'm sorry if I somehow misled you, but we aren't— That is, we don't—"

Vincent began to grin.

"Help me here," Natalie said, turning to him.

"Oh, you're doing just fine, love," he told her in a low drawl.

She wrinkled her nose at him and turned back to Mrs. Morgensen. "Vincent and I are just friends," she said in a clipped voice, "and that's all we'll ever be."

Mrs. Morgensen rolled her eyes and gave Vincent a long, hard look. "Really? But you two are shacking up, aren't you? That's the right way to say it, isn't it?"

"Yes, we are, but only as friends," Natalie insisted.

"Hmm, just friends. I have to say I'm a bit disappointed in you, Natalie."

Vincent chuckled.

Natalie turned and glared at him.

"And you told me he could do a lot more than flirt," Mrs. Morgensen said with a smile. Vince could see that she still didn't believe that he and Natalie weren't lovers.

"I meant that he could cook."

"Ah." Mrs. Morgensen nodded. "Well then, I'd keep him. I hate cooking, don't you? And a man who can cook is almost as good as one who knows how to make love. Not quite, you understand, Vincent. If I were you, I would get someone to give you some lessons. You can't expect Natalie here to stay with you without some extra benefits. I'm sure she has men lined up wanting to kiss her."

He leaned around Natalie just in time to see her open her mouth in surprise. Gently, he touched her chin with his thumb, closing her mouth.

"I'll be sure and get some lessons, Mrs. Morgensen. Is there anything we can do for you?"

All at once Mrs. Morgensen's eyes turned sad. "Well, if you could talk to the landlord. I think I may get evicted if I can't come up with some more money soon." Her voice seemed to shrink. Even her body looked smaller as she hunched into herself. "If you could just tell him that I'm a nice person, that I'm saving every penny I can and I really will pay him as soon as my next check comes."

Suddenly Vincent's good mood was gone. "Don't worry, Mrs. Morgensen. No one is throwing you out on the street while I'm living here. I'll talk to him."

He knew it would take more than that. Landlords had rights, and one of them was the right to expect payment, but there was no way Vince was going to let this sweet lady get evicted.

Mrs. Morgensen nodded, but her usual cheery mood had been obliterated. Vincent knew she was still expecting to find herself out on the street. A sense of injustice railed at him, anger coiled inside him, and he fought it. He clenched his fists and battled the awful urge to hit someone.

Minutes later, he and Natalie said their goodbyes to Mrs. Morgensen and exited the building. Just before they got into the car, Natalie touched his arm.

He turned to her.

"Thank you," she said softly.

He shook his head. "For what?"

"For caring what happens to her." Her voice broke a little at the end, and he couldn't help himself. He hooked one hand around the nape of her neck, staring into those pretty, troubled eyes.

"I hope you nail whoever it is that took advantage of her. Take them to the cleaners, Natalie. I'll be right there with you."

But of course, that might not be true. As soon as Natalie was out of danger, he would no longer be needed. He had to find out if there were any leads at all. Just how long would he and Natalie be a pair?

Eight

True to his word, Vincent had actually gone and talked to the landlord when they returned to the building. Or what passed for a landlord. Natalie wasn't sure if Mrs. Morgensen realized that Terrence Mason was only the building manager and that the building was actually owned by a corporation. At any rate, Vincent and Terrence engaged in a lot of low-pitched discussion and then Terrence shook Vincent's hand before he left.

"That seemed to go well," she said as they walked back to the apartment. "Want to tell me about it?"

"No."

"Are they kicking her out?"

"No." He gave her the smallest of smiles.

"Vincent, why aren't they kicking her out? Terrence is an okay guy, but I'm sure he has a few unbendable rules. Did you offer to pay her rent or something like that?"

"Drop it, Natalie. This isn't a story."

She whirled on him. "I wouldn't make it one. I'm just worried about her, and I'm also impressed."

He stopped in his tracks. "At what?"

"You, taking an interest in a total stranger."

"I don't think Mrs. Morgensen has ever met a stranger. And she's a woman alone. If what you're telling me is true, then she's been abused. Maybe not in the traditional sense, but I'm sure being cheated out of all that you have by someone you trusted is a type of abuse. That's just wrong."

His jaw was set, his eyes were cold. He looked like the hardest man in the world, like a rock that would never move, steel that could never bend. Yet she'd seen him smile at the children when they'd visited the preschool today. A little girl had asked him for a story and he had allowed the child to climb on his lap while he'd read her *Harold and the Purple Crayon*. She suspected that Vince had some soft spots, especially where females were concerned.

Natalie's eyes started to mist. She blinked to clear them. *Don't think that way,* she told herself. *Don't start getting any ideas. Besides, no matter what his feelings are about women, you aren't going to talk him into letting you go out alone.*

And she had to go alone. Today had been a wake-up call. She was failing her friends by not pursuing her story. Brad Herron or Neil Gerard might have the answers that would be a permanent fix for Mrs. Morgensen and Mr. Felsmith. Somehow, she had to find a way to shed Vincent temporarily.

She wondered why that made her feel so lonely.

No one had heard a thing about Jamison. Vincent had spoken to Daniel to bring him up to speed on Natalie's situation.

"We can't lose her, Vincent. She's an eyewitness."

"She's more than that, Daniel."

"Yes, I know. It's just that sometimes it's easier not to make things too personal. Frankly, I'm worried about her. I think Ryan is, too. He's been looking tired lately. I think he feels partially responsible for Natalie's dilemma, since Jason was his protégé. I know you assured him that you would keep Natalie safe, and I know you'll do your best, but I hope you realize what you're up against. Jamison's crazy. He doesn't like to be crossed, and she crossed him. So watch your back, and keep her safe, Vince."

"Try to stop me, Daniel. And let me know anything you hear."

"You'll be the first person I call."

Vincent clicked off the connection, tension filling his soul. He remembered Natalie with those kids today. In spite of her desire to write hard news stories, she had leapt in there in the midst of fifty three-, four- and five-year-olds, gotten down on her hands and knees and played board games, told stories and made animal noises with the best of them. She had been electric. She had sparkled.

At one point, she had looked up at him, her hair mussed, a huge smile on her face.

"Aren't they great?" she had asked. "I want about five hundred of my own."

His heart had stalled in his throat. The image of Natalie joyously, beautifully pregnant had slipped in and refused to let go. He longed for the idyllic picture she had painted.

But the picture he got was of a man threatening his wife and children, hitting them, throwing them against walls. Idyllic pictures were fantasies. Reality always changed things.

He and Natalie were oil and water. He was a bit old-school; she was ultramodern. They would clash, and things wouldn't be picture-postcard pretty anymore. Wasn't that the way of things? And when the good stuff failed, the bad stuff crept in. He'd seen the worst in his own family, but he'd seen other examples, as well. Anthony Bannister, one of his finest agents, was going through an ugly divorce that left their kids screaming in their sleep, and Anthony and Lisa had been the most perfect couple Vincent could ever have imagined.

So get Natalie out of your mind, he ordered himself. *Go do something.*

He stepped into the next room. She was working at her laptop at the kitchen table, wearing a pair of jeans and a white T-shirt. Nothing fancy, nothing special, nothing out of the ordinary. He had seen thousands of women dressed the same way.

But he looked at her and all he could see was the way the jeans fit her legs, the way the scoop of the shirt made him imagine what lay underneath.

He nearly groaned. "I think I'll take a shower," he told her. Not his usual way. He always hit the shower in the morning, but tonight he wanted Natalie. With every cell in his body, he wanted to hold her body against his, flesh to flesh, and that just couldn't happen.

"A shower? Okay," she said. "That's a good idea."

He frowned.

"That is, it's good to get it out of the way now," she explained. "I've got an early interview with a snake house worker at the zoo tomorrow. We might be pressed for time."

"Okay, then, I'll see you in a few minutes," he said.

He stepped into the bathroom, turned the spray full force on Cold and stayed under there long enough to drive his heated thoughts of Natalie from his mind.

When he returned to the living room, she was gone. There was a note on the refrigerator door. "Be back soon. Don't worry."

"Like hell," he said and headed for the door.

Guilt could be a crushing thing, Natalie thought as she drove toward The Ladder. No time to change, no time to think, but she still couldn't get Vincent out of her mind.

He had been protecting her for days now. He took his job seriously. She knew that he genuinely worried about her, especially now that Jason was at large. And she had seen from Vincent's interactions with Mrs. Morgensen and the kids at the preschool that he was just naturally protective with those who were unable to protect themselves.

When he found out that she was gone, he would be frantic with worry. And he would be angry. She didn't know which concerned her more.

Either way, it couldn't matter. She had to find Brad Herron or Neil Gerard and glean some information from them. Vincent couldn't keep paying Mrs. Morgensen's way and he couldn't protect all of the elderly people in her building who had been swindled. He couldn't help those who would be swindled in the future if someone didn't do something. She had to find the key, dig out the facts. So for now, even though, yes, she *was* aware that she might be in some danger, she had to do what she could to help. There was no one else.

She hated the thought of getting near slimy Brad again, but at the same time she hoped he would be at The Ladder tonight. She wanted to get what she needed, get it over with and get back home. To Vincent.

The deeper implications of that last thought nearly made her stumble. "Don't think, McCabe," she ordered herself. "Just do what you have to do."

She opened the door of the bar and stepped inside to the sound of pounding music. The dark wooden rafters were decorated with white lights, a concession to the season, but the season wasn't what Natalie was interested in.

Almost immediately, she located Brad, who was hitting on a young blond woman swaying drunkenly on her stool.

"Nice choice, Brad," Natalie whispered to herself. The woman clearly had left sound judgment behind several drinks ago. She would be easy to bed if she managed not to pass out.

But to Natalie's surprise, Brad turned around at that moment and, seeing her near the door, said something to the blonde and left her there. He made his way through the sparse crowd toward Natalie.

"I thought you were never going to return. It's been a long time," he said with a smile that looked as if he practiced it in front of the mirror.

It hadn't been all that long. "What can I say?" Natalie asked. "Sometimes life collides with our plans. I couldn't get away."

"But you're here now. You came back just as I said you would." He gave her a sly grin. Natalie wondered if it worked on most women.

"Why me?" she asked, nodding toward the blonde.

Brad shrugged. "You're more interesting."

Natalie frowned. "How so? You don't even know me."

"Well, you're not drunk, for one thing," he said, conveniently forgetting his own drunken actions the last time they met. "And I remember that you asked me about my work. She just wants to get laid. I can get laid anytime. Not that many women take an interest in my business. You intrigue me."

Okay, so this might be a little dangerous. She didn't want to seem too much like a reporter, but it was still a darn sight better than having to battle his sexual advances all night.

Natalie shrugged and smiled at him, hoping she looked sincere. "I'm always interested in what men do. Their world is so much different from a woman's world. It's the differences between the sexes that make life intriguing. Besides, I've never known a broker before. Your world is a bit of a mystery to me." Especially the part about how a broker stole old people's savings without explaining how it had happened.

"Well, I'll have to tell you all the secrets of my mysterious world," he said, dropping his voice. "But maybe someplace else. Too many of my fellow employees are here tonight. How about the coffee shop three blocks over?"

"You mean Mocha Matters?"

"That's the one. How about it? We'll take my Jag."

It figured that he drove a Jaguar. But she wasn't getting into any car with this guy. "I'll meet you there."

Brad gave her a practiced chuckle. "Scared of me?"

She hadn't been, but his comment made her think twice. Should she be scared? "Just careful," she told him. "And I'm kind of attached to my car."

"Must be some car."

It was a bit of a beater, to tell the truth, but it was the first item she had bought when she got out of college. It was a symbol of her independence. She and The Blue Thing, as she affectionately called it, went way back. They were a team. She trusted it, despite its age and ailing parts. She did not trust Brad Herron. "Ten minutes," she promised.

He opened his mouth, probably to object, and she smiled to head off his words. Behind him, she could see Neil Gerard staring. He was playing darts with a small group of people. He gave her a wistful look, and this time her smile was more genuine. But for now Brad was her target. "Don't be late," she said, figuring that would seal the deal. She headed for the door, praying that Brad would follow her and this time give her some small hint of what she needed to know.

Ten minutes later, she entered Mocha Matters with Brad right behind her. "The usual spot," he told the waitress.

Natalie felt a twinge of foreboding at that. Obviously Brad was a regular, but this was a coffee shop. How bad could things get?

Pretty bad, she thought, when the waitress showed them to a dark corner near the back. "So what do you like best about being a broker?" she asked, hoping to head off any groping Brad planned on doing.

He smiled and shook his head. "Natalie, Natalie, you know

we didn't really come here to talk about work, so why are you playing around? I know how the game goes. So do you."

"Game?" she asked, steam rising inside her.

"Oh, come on, honey," he said, sliding closer to her on the vinyl seat of the booth. "I can see you're a class act. You didn't want to be like the drunk blonde. You didn't want to look cheap in front of the crowd at The Ladder, but here? We're alone, or as good as alone."

He was right. The booths in this place were made for private conversation, for working on a laptop, for reading. Brad had obviously found another use for the privacy of this little corner of the shop. He placed a hand on her thigh.

With great restraint, Natalie kept herself from planting a fist in his solar plexus. She pushed his hand away. "Alone is good," she said. "It makes for pleasant conversation. I don't believe in fooling around with a man until I get to know him, so tell me about yourself."

"Hard to get, huh? I like that. At least for a short time. Makes the anticipation of what's to come even sweeter. I tell you, you are totally hot, honey. You want to talk? All right, let's talk before we do it." And he proceeded to tell her his life story. "My old man didn't think I could ever be anything," he said, sneering, "but I showed him. I could buy every stick he owns and not even notice. I put him in a nice home last year. Real exclusive." Brad chuckled. "He hates it. Good. Because I don't care. I've got money and I get the babes. I can buy you things, whatever you want, and I know how to make a woman feel good, babe. You know enough about me yet?"

Natalie was feeling rather ill. "Not yet. How did you manage to do so well businesswise?"

"I get people to talk about themselves, you know? They like that. People will do anything if you find their weaknesses and get them started talking. Like you, I'd say you look smart.

Damn smart, classy smart. Tell me, are you one of those really intelligent women? I'll just bet you are."

Uh-oh, this wasn't the way she wanted the conversation to turn. No questions about herself. And to tell the truth, she was beginning to doubt her own intelligence. She was, after all, seated in a secluded corner with a total stranger who wanted to hustle her into bed.

"I have a degree," she said noncommittally. "Nothing special."

"Oh, yeah? What do you do?"

Think fast, she thought. "I'm an accountant. Going to school part-time to get my master's." Maybe that would put him off.

He gave her a slow smile and placed his hand even higher on her thigh, squeezing hard. "An accountant? Delicious. Accountants spend their days with numbers, so by nighttime they're crazy and ready to be wild. This will be good."

That was it. Natalie grasped his hand hard to keep him from groping her any further, then squeezed a button on her watch beneath the table. It gave off a high-pitched beep.

"Oh, man. I am so late," she said, practically pushing Brad off the booth and climbing out. "If I'm not back home in twenty minutes, my roommate will call the cops."

He frowned. "Roommate?"

"Fred," she said. "My brother. Big guy with an itchy fist."

Brad laughed. "You're lying, but I like that. Makes things more fun when we finally get to it. All right, run away tonight. Another time. I'll talk to you until you think you know me well enough."

Then, as if he were done with her, he gave a whistle. The waitress slithered over, and Brad patted the seat beside him. Natalie didn't know if he was trying to make a point or if he really was that shallow.

At any rate, it was clear that she wasn't going to find out anything of value tonight. Other than the fact that Brad got his clients to do what he wanted by getting them to talk about themselves. But wasn't that true of almost every salesman in the world? And wasn't a broker a salesperson of sorts?

She sighed and climbed back into her car, starting toward home. But no. She still hadn't learned a thing, and if she went home she would have to deal with the fact that she was attracted to Vincent. She wondered what she would have done if Vincent had put *his* hand on her thigh.

Her heart began to thud hard.

"Oh, great, I can't even *think* about the man touching me without acting like a teenage girl with a crush. He probably knows I feel this way. It probably happens all the time, women he's protecting wanting him to kiss them." How humiliating. She hated feeling stupid and inadequate, and she hated the fact that she had done nothing at all to help her friends.

Reluctantly, Natalie turned her car back toward The Ladder. With Brad at Mocha Matters, she would be stupid to pass up an opportunity like this.

The Ladder was somewhat quiet by the time she got back, but Neil was still there. He gave her a tight nod, and she walked up to him. "Hi," she said. "Mind if I join you?"

He hesitated. "What— I mean, what about Brad?" he finally asked.

"We had a cup of coffee. I had to leave. He found a new friend." She figured she didn't have to say more. Anyone who worked with Brad must know what he was like.

"Okay. I'm glad you came back," Neil said. "Want to play pool or darts?"

She wanted to talk, but she didn't want a repeat of the Brad scene. Activity was safer. "Darts," she offered. She took the darts from him. Their fingers brushed, and he quickly moved away.

"You come here all the time," she noted, trying to make

him feel at ease. She threw her three darts and made a creditable showing.

"It's something to do after work," he said noncommittally. She smiled at him and he blushed again. He turned toward the dartboard and narrowed his eyes as he prepared to throw. He flubbed the first shot.

His skin turned a fiery red and he didn't look Natalie's way. He narrowed his eyes again and repositioned himself. His next two shots were near bull's-eyes. Interesting.

"That was great!" she said.

He shifted from foot to foot in that awkward way he had. "Your turn." She noticed that he was careful not to touch her when he handed her the darts.

"So coming here and playing darts is a form of release? Working for a brokerage firm must be pretty high-pressure," she prompted.

"It is."

"Do you like it?" She turned to look at him, still holding her three darts.

He studied her, his look intense. "It's a job. I'm not in love with it. Are you just playing darts with me because you're bored? We could do something else." He frowned.

She turned and threw a dart. "No. This is nice. Why do you ask?"

"I don't know. Your questions are the kinds of polite things you ask when there's not much else to say."

He was right, but she had just been trying to lead in slowly. She couldn't very well ask him if he thought his company could possibly be involved in dirty games. Although maybe she was asking the wrong guy. She had been here twice and she had yet to see him laugh, although they were surrounded by laughing people. Maybe the other employees didn't confide in him that much. On the other hand, he was just the unassuming type who might get people to talk to him.

"I'm interested in a lot of things," she said. "And I like darts."

"Yeah," he said as she finished up and gave him all three. He missed the first two but gave a vicious but straight throw and made a bull's-eye on the third. For a second, she got a glimpse of his face, and he looked like a man who had just had an unusually satisfying orgasm. It was the most expressive she had seen him thus far, almost out of proportion to the deed. Crazy thought. Why shouldn't he be pleased?

She managed a smile. "You're good. You could give lessons."

He shrugged. "Want to sit down for a while? I could buy you a beer."

"That would be nice." She sat down and waited while Neil tried to get the waitress's attention. Twice the girl passed by and didn't see him, even though he was waving one bony arm around.

Natalie almost wanted to call the girl over herself, but she could see the trace of red around Neil's collar. He probably wouldn't appreciate being shown up by a woman. Men got funny that way.

At last he procured the beer and started to hand it to her as if he were offering her a glass of gold.

Natalie couldn't say why she looked up at that moment. People had been coming and going at The Ladder ever since she had arrived, but something compelled her to gaze at the door just then. It was as if she could feel Vincent's presence when he opened the door and walked in. She turned to look and stared straight into dark gray eyes filled with anger.

He sat down at a table near the door.

She picked up her beer and took a gulp, choking as she swallowed.

"Are you okay? Is something wrong?" Neil asked, looking as if he wanted to pat her on the back but not sure how to go about it. "Maybe you came back because you and Brad had a fight? Yeah, that could be it. Brad is always dumping girls.

Sometimes they follow him around afterward. Sometimes they even hit on other guys trying to make him jealous."

Natalie blinked. She could barely concentrate on what he was saying. Vincent was watching her every move. He was like a predator waiting for her to dodge and bolt. She wanted to run. Actually, she wanted to go to him and try to explain, as if there were any explanation he would want to hear. She had abused his trust. He wasn't likely to forgive or forget that very quickly. Guilt assailed her. What had Neil said? That she was trying to make Brad jealous?

"Brad isn't here," she said, not completely paying attention to her own words.

"But people here would report back to him that you were here with me."

He looked at her intensely, leaned a bit closer, uncertainty and a trace of something—anger?—in his eyes.

Natalie knew the minute Vincent got up and moved to a closer table. Because he thought Neil might hurt her or because he wanted to have a word with her himself?

"I'm not interested in Brad in that way." She said the words louder than she had intended…or maybe not. Had she meant them for Neil or for Vincent?

An uncertain smile played across Neil's lips. "Do you want another beer?"

Natalie looked down and saw that she had drained her glass. She hadn't even noticed it. Every cell of her being was concentrated on Vincent. He was one big bundle of male rage, dark and mysterious and completely tuned in to her every move.

She was as aware of him as she had ever been aware of anything, and heaven help her if she didn't want to go over to him and touch him, ask him to understand, ask him to kiss her.

Natalie took a long, deep breath. "I'm afraid I may have had too much to drink already," she blurted out. "I'm feeling kind of crazy. I have to go."

"Yeah, that always happens," Neil said.

She looked down. "I'll be back," she said, but he didn't look convinced. She didn't have time to convince him because she had gathered up her courage and looked at Vincent again. Really looked.

His dark gray eyes bore into her. She felt as if her soul were being sucked from her body, as if she were some helpless puppet, because all she wanted to do right now was to go to Vincent, to feel his warm, solid skin beneath her fingertips and ask him to forgive her.

The very thought scared her to death. She was losing control where this man was concerned, and control was what she had fought for all her life.

With one deep breath, she turned and walked to the door, letting herself out.

And then she ran.

Nine

Vincent waited until Natalie had left The Ladder. Already he had called Derek and asked him to follow Natalie home. Now he simply sat here trying not to think of her with that guy, who had clearly been besotted with her. She had the right to socialize with the men of her choice. He couldn't go there. It wasn't his right, and given the fact that he couldn't get involved with her himself, it couldn't be his business. But the other thing—the danger—was different. He gave her enough time so that he wouldn't blow her cover, even though rage was flaying him alive. He wanted to go to her immediately, to grab her by the arm, spin her around and demand to know what kind of foolish, dangerous game she was playing. But doing that might only put her in more danger. The last thing she needed was a scene where her name might get mentioned in the papers.

So he waited. He counted to ten. To twenty. To fifty. To five hundred. Then he did it again. He ordered a drink so that he wouldn't look suspicious. He even took one swallow so he wouldn't look even more suspicious. Then he carefully got up and left the bar.

He drove like a madman back to Natalie's apartment. He didn't bother knocking but used the key she had given him. And when he was sure that all the doors and windows were locked up tight and the house was secure, he turned to her. She was waiting on the far side of the room.

"Go ahead. Say it," she said.

He advanced on her.

She flinched but she didn't back away. He hated that, that he was looking daggers, that he was clearly in a dangerous mood, but she refused to run. If she had run, he might have been able to break away from this anger that was like a wild thing inside him. The thought that someone might have gotten to her tonight and killed her made him crazy.

He had seen death, seen what people could do to each other. The thought that anyone might hurt her, cut her, shoot her or take her life senselessly made him insane. The thought that anyone could terrorize her or frighten her all but killed him. He wanted to hit things, throw things, yell out his rage.

And there she stood, just waiting as if nothing at all had happened.

"Were you completely out of your mind?" he asked, his voice much louder than he had intended. But nothing could stop him now that the words were flowing. "What on earth were you thinking? Or were you even thinking at all?"

She stood her ground, even though he thought he saw her tremble. The image of another dark, shadowy man intimidating her with deadly intent consumed him. Someone had sent her threatening notes, and she was acting as if that had never happened.

"Were you?" he demanded.

She blinked and two rosy stains blossomed on the beautiful planes of her cheeks. "I—" she began.

"Of course, you weren't thinking. You were acting on drive alone," he said, his voice cold and deadly. He swooped across the room so that he was standing directly in front of her.

"Is this so important, then?" he demanded. "Is a byline in a newspaper more important than your life? Is the story all that matters? That's it, isn't it?"

He glared down at her.

"No," she said.

"Yes." The word was like a shot. He took one step closer and then he was right up against her. She had to tilt her head back to look at him, and she did it. She continued to defy him.

"You don't understand."

"I understand that you think having a bodyguard is an inconvenience in your life, an interference. I understand that you refuse to see the seriousness of the situation. And I know darn well that you used deception to go out and meet your friends at the bar."

"I didn't." But her voice wavered. She dropped her eyes slightly.

"Damn it to hell, this isn't a game, Natalie. There's a killer out there, and I don't know where he is. Right now I don't even have a clue. The only way I can protect you is to be there with you so that if something happens, I can do *my* job, which is saving your rear end. So don't even consider running out on me again. I'm warning you, don't even think about it unless you really do have a death wish, Natalie, because I will tie you up and lock you in if I have to. I will do whatever is necessary to keep your pretty little butt alive, and you can tell all your buddies at The Ladder that they need to get through me to talk to you."

He leaned closer.

She blinked but she did her best to raise her chin. Her eyes flashed fire. "Don't even try to order me around, Vincent. I won't be ordered around. I've had enough of that to last me forever. Is this how you get your way? By physical intimidation? Because don't worry. I'm well aware that you're bigger and stronger than I am. You don't have to threaten me. I know who would win in a physical fight. And if you left a few bruises, you could just tell everyone that Jason did it. They would probably believe you. You're a Fortune, after all, and Fortunes don't ever do stupid things, do they?" Her voice was small, but she stood her ground.

All the air fled Vincent's lungs. He looked down and saw that his hands were balled into fists. He was nearly knocking Natalie over with his body. He had raised his voice, lost all sense of reason. He had wanted to hit something, and she had been there, an easy target.

Spinning on his heel, Vincent left the room. He came to the far wall in the guest room and stood there staring sightlessly out the window, his forearm resting on the window frame.

He had lost control, and not only that, he had lost it with a woman. With Natalie.

Who knew what he might have done if she hadn't brought him back to reality? He had been a bully of the worst kind, just like his old man. Using his size to threaten, not even noticing what he was doing when the heat of anger consumed him. Dark revulsion for his actions filled his soul, but it was done, and he couldn't take back his words. He wondered if she would ever trust him again.

And if she did, would he ever trust himself?

Regret slipped through Natalie like a constant trickle of ice water, chilling her. She sat down on the couch and closed her eyes, bowing her head.

She had accused Vincent of terrible things when she knew he had just been reacting out of concern for her. He was spending day and night trying to keep her alive, adjusting his schedule to hers, and she had acted as if he were simply an annoying inconvenience in her life.

All of her life people had tried to stop her from doing what she wanted, and she had resented them because all too often their fears were built on the assumption that she was incapable. Vincent had never inferred that she was incapable. He merely thought she was being threatened, and she was.

Standing up, her feet dragging, Natalie wandered into the guest room where Vincent had gone. A big bed sat in the corner of the room covered with a light blue spread edged in white lace. The carpeting was light blue, the trim around the doors and windows white. It was a woman's room, soft and pale, and Vincent, standing with his back to her, staring out the window, was big and male and hard. He seemed to fill the space. He became the focus of the room. She had come to apologize, to say her lines and leave, but she was drawn to him and, almost against her will, she crossed the room.

"I'm so sorry, Vincent," she said.

He whirled, pain in his eyes. "Don't say that."

"But I am." She touched his arm. "I wasn't fair. I took advantage of the situation when you told me that you were going to take a shower. I didn't even stop to think about how you would feel. I was only thinking that I had to help Mrs. Morgensen." Her throat ached with the need to take back what must have been some terrifying moments for him. Even if she was only a client to him, she knew that Vincent took pride in his work. Daniel had told her how hard Vincent had worked to build his business. To be tricked by a client would scald his pride.

"You were trying to do a good thing," he said, correcting her. "And you were right. I had absolutely no right to use my size to intimidate you."

"You were upset."

"That's absolutely no excuse. Natalie—" He looked across the room, shaking his head as if he didn't know where to go from here. "A man my size has an obligation to always be aware, to use his body responsibly. In my line of work I do sometimes have to use physical force, but only if it's absolutely necessary. I'm never to use it against a client, especially not against a woman."

"You didn't do anything, Vincent." She placed her hand on his chest, and he sucked in a deep, audible breath. She felt the rise and fall of his muscles beneath her fingertips.

"Don't make excuses for me, Natalie. I know my business, and I don't intimidate my clients."

"Even when they're wrong?"

"Especially then. Anger toward a client is never an option. Force against a woman is never okay. I could have hurt you."

She shook her head slowly. "I know you wouldn't have hurt me. I wasn't afraid of you. I was just angry and resentful that you were berating me, even though I knew I deserved it."

"Hell, no woman deserves to have a man looking at her like that."

"Like what?"

He shook his head and frowned. "As if he wants to throttle her." He groaned and she couldn't help herself. She placed her other hand on his chest.

"Did you really want to throttle me? If you did, I don't believe for a moment that you would. You've got some code, like the knights had. You're an honorable man." She looked up at him earnestly, both palms planted against the warm, solid wall of his chest.

He closed his eyes and groaned. "Damn it, I'm not that honorable, Natalie." And as if to prove it, he leaned down and covered her mouth with his own.

The world flew away. All sense of time disappeared. All

Natalie recognized was this moment, this man and his touch. She leaned into him, and he deepened the kiss, his hands coming up to cradle her face.

Natalie had never felt anything like this, nothing so all-consuming. She wanted the moment to go on forever, wanted to explore the hunger that was rising within her.

Vincent's touch was gentle, even though she knew that he considered himself a hard man. She could see the physical strength within him, could sense the leashed power in his touch. No matter what he said, he was being careful with her.

She moaned deep in her throat, and almost immediately Vincent pulled back. His eyes were troubled. "That was not supposed to happen," he said, his voice thick.

Natalie shook her head. "You were still angry. I shouldn't have touched you. Anyone might have lost control under the circumstances," she whispered. Meaning the same might have happened had she been any other woman under the same circumstances. She tried not to allow herself to think of that.

"I'm not anyone. I'm a man who knows his limits and lives by them. You're a client. I don't touch my clients."

She bit her lip, then asked the question his comment called up. "You haven't done this before?"

He ran one hand through his short, dark hair. "Damn it, Natalie."

Her throat felt as if her heart had risen up and lodged there. "You *have* done this before?" Of course, he was an undeniably handsome man. Women would throw themselves at him. Cast into the role of protector, he would have women begging him to make love with them.

"Of course it hasn't happened. What kind of man do you think I am?"

A sexy one, she thought. A good one.

She nodded curtly. "I wasn't implying that you weren't professional."

"*I* was implying that," he said. "I'm supposed to keep you safe. I'm not supposed to touch you."

"I upset you."

"That's no excuse." He paced away from her, and she wanted to reach out one hand and ask him to come back and kiss her again. Stupid, stupid, stupid. She felt out of control. Worse, she was letting a man have control over her. She hated that. It went against everything she had fought for all her life. But he was blaming himself for what had just happened, and if Natalie was anything, she was honest. She had provoked him.

"I pushed you," she said. "I'll bet you're not used to having female clients who run toward danger instead of away from it. I sneaked out on you when you weren't expecting it. I made your job more difficult. You probably weren't thinking straight. You probably didn't even know what you were doing."

Vincent's laugh was a rough bark. "I might have behaved irresponsibly, Natalie, but I knew exactly what I was doing when I kissed you. I knew I was touching forbidden fruit. So you don't have to make excuses for me. I'm not allowed to blame my clients for my own bad behavior."

So he wouldn't touch her again. An amazingly strong stirring of loss and disappointment welled up in Natalie. She knew what those women who had thrown themselves at him must have been feeling. It was one of the few times in her life when she had felt in tune with her own sex.

It was a disturbing feeling, a helpless feeling. She didn't like it one bit. No doubt about it. Kissing Vincent Fortune wasn't a good idea.

She probably shouldn't hope he would change his mind and do it again.

But somewhere deep inside, she knew that she wanted to have him kiss her one more time. Just to see if she had been mistaken about how powerful his touch had been, she told herself. That was the only reason.

"Vincent, I'm sorry," she said.

"I suppose you had your reasons for running to The Ladder tonight," he said.

But that wasn't what she had meant. She wasn't sorry about The Ladder. That had been one of the necessary parts of her job. What she was sorry about was that now the two of them would be wary around each other. The memory of that kiss would linger in the air whenever they were together.

And Vincent wasn't going to like that one little bit, she thought with a trace of sadness. He didn't like the fact that he had kissed her.

No doubt he was sorry he had ever met her.

"They'll be sorry," Jason said, clipping out the snippets of text from a magazine and then gluing them onto the cheap paper he had purchased. That he had been reduced to this—hiding, using inferior materials and out-of-date methods—was unforgivable.

He was Jason Jamison, not some beggar, not some nobody. His prison break had taken so much of his time and attention, he hadn't been able to send notes lately, but now he was back…in so many ways.

Those who had wronged his grandfather and wronged him would see that what goes around comes around. Jason Jamison would get what he deserved.

And so would anyone who attempted to harm him.

He eyed the cheap room with its soiled bed. "What a dump. It's all their fault, but that's okay. The tables will be turned soon enough."

And until that day came, he thought, eyeing his handiwork, he would make sure that those who were responsible for his predicament never had a good night's sleep.

A slow chuckle welled up in his chest. He took a long, satisfied drag on his cigarette. "Oh yeah, this is good," he said, looking down at the crude note on the table.

In spite of the poor workmanship, they would know the source of this missive, and they would be forever looking over their shoulders.

Waiting, waiting, for something to happen. Something very bad.

In time it would.

And that would be very good. For him.

Jason laughed again, took out a new sheet of paper and began again. The clock was ticking.

The clock was his friend.

Time was running out, Ryan Fortune thought the next day. The headaches were getting worse. The pain of not being able to tell his beloved Lily what was happening to him was like a sword in his gut. He loved her so much. He had kept so many secrets from her.

Would she ever be able to forgive him? Would he ever be able to tell her everything?

Yes. Yes, he had to. In time. But they had just gotten over the hurdle of her finding out about Linda Faraday, the young woman Cameron Fortune had impregnated and nearly killed when he'd gotten drunk and wrecked his car, killing himself. Linda had been in a semi-conscious state for years, had even given birth in that state, and was just now getting her life back. During all that time Ryan had been forced to move heaven and earth to keep her secret and keep the public and the press from finding out. After all, she was the mother of his irresponsible brother's son. As the head of the family, Ryan had owed her that much. He had even kept Lily in the dark about Linda and her son, Ricky. And in the end, after Linda had regained consciousness and was trying to get her life back together, when

Lily had seen him with Linda, it had nearly broken his wife's heart. It had nearly cost him everything he loved most in life. He might have lost Lily over that one. Thank heaven he had her back, and she still loved him.

He wanted more years of loving her, of just reveling in what they meant to each other. So damn it, it was just too soon to tell her the truth about these headaches. It would hurt her so much. It would change things. It would mean the end of so many things for him and Lily. If they were to only have a short while, he wanted that time to be spent loving, not worrying and regretting. That meant keeping one more thing from Lily. He hated that, hated himself for doing this to her, and yet...

Ryan ran a hand over his forehead. He cursed fate for forcing him to this point.

"You're not well," his cousin Patrick said, and Ryan looked up, startled. When had Patrick come into the room?

"I'm fine," Ryan said, but he knew his voice lacked conviction. Patrick had always known him too well. It was good to be that close to someone you trusted.

Patrick shook his head. "It's no use, Ryan. You hide your condition in front of Lily, but I'm not your wife. You don't have to protect me. I know how much pressure is on you as the head of the Fortune family and empire, and I can see what a toll keeping things to yourself takes on you. I've known you all our lives, and I know that if you're keeping this a secret from everyone, it's bad—and it's private. So you can trust me. Tell me."

Ryan blew out a long breath. He looked to the side. "It's time you knew, anyway. Decisions have to be made."

Patrick shook his head and frowned. "Explain."

Throwing out his hand, Ryan chose the blunt path. He explained everything. When he was done, Patrick let out a low, shaky whistle. "That's rough, Ryan. I'm sorry. More sorry than I can tell you."

"It means a lot just to have you here to listen. I would have told you sooner, but I'm only just now starting to come to grips with the news myself and…well, it's time to start getting things in order."

"You'll tell Lily?"

"Not yet, please, not just yet. But could you get Blake? I think the three of us have some business to tend to."

"I'll do anything you want or need." Patrick grasped his cousin's hand, and it was all Ryan could do to keep his grateful tears from falling.

When Blake entered the room a short time later, it was with a confused look on his face. "Patrick told me that you had business to discuss with me. I don't quite understand."

Ryan stood and shook Blake's hand. "It's family business, and it's private. You qualify. You have the right to be here. In fact, I need you to be here. Have a seat."

The three men sat. Patrick rubbed one hand over his jaw as Ryan tried to find the words once again.

"I've recently found out that I have an inoperable brain tumor," Ryan told Blake.

Blake stared as if Ryan had struck him. "You're dying?"

Ryan nodded. "I've been checked out by two doctors. They both concur. There's nothing they can do to save me. Anything I do, I have to do soon."

Pain filled Blake's eyes and he closed them. "I'm so sorry. I— Damn it, all these years gone. I wish I had gotten to know you sooner."

Ryan managed to smile. "That makes two of us. You've become a good friend, Blake. Lately I realize just how important family is. I count both you and Patrick as not only family but as the best friends a man can know, and I'll need to be able to rely on the two of you to see that things go right when I'm gone. To make sure that Lily doesn't have to handle everything alone."

"You know you can count on us." Patrick's voice wobbled a bit.

"Of course. Anything," Blake said. "Are you…in pain?"

Ryan nodded. "Yes. Although I'm taking medication for that, it never really goes away. But I'm coping."

"The family reunion scheduled for May," Blake began. "I know a lot of work has already gone into that. I'll take care of canceling things for you so you won't have to concentrate on that. It's the least I can do."

Ryan put out his hand and touched Blake's sleeve. "No, I still want to go through with it."

"Ryan," Patrick drawled. "Are you sure?"

Ryan looked at the two men before him, strong men who had dealt with their own blows in life. Men who knew about difficulties and pain and endurance. His friends, his cousins, his brothers in life.

"I've never been more sure of anything," he said. "There have been so many bad things happening lately—to all of us. I want to bring us all together, the young and the old, in a good setting this time. The Fortunes need to stay together, and they will have a reunion. Help me to make that possible. Please."

Patrick and Blake put out their hands, covering Ryan's.

"Whatever you want," Patrick said.

"Whatever you need, it's yours," Blake said. "We'll help you. That's a solemn promise."

What more could a man ask for than that? Ryan wondered.

Ten

Maybe she was asking too much of herself, Natalie thought a day later as Vincent emerged from the bathroom and a shower, his hair wet, his body smelling of soap. She shivered. Since when had the smell of soap made her tingle? Since when had wet hair made it difficult to breathe?

Living with Vincent was doing odd, impossible things to her system, and she kept beating up on herself about it. But maybe that was just unfair. What woman wouldn't react to a man who looked like a promise of paradise in bed and who had sworn his life to protect her from both the bad guys and his own natural sexual impulses?

A woman with frozen slush for brains? Natalie wondered. A woman with no vital signs? Of course, she was attracted. It was okay to be attracted. Any woman would be. Best to just accept that so she could get beyond it and get back to her life and her business.

All she needed to do was stop acting like an idiot, wishing

Vincent would kiss her again, and start acting like any normal, intelligent, indifferent person.

She pasted a smile on her face and breezed past Vincent, heading for the coffeepot. His warmth hit her like an overwhelming wave of testosterone. She swallowed hard, nearly swayed.

"Natalie, are you okay?"

She turned to him and looked up into his eyes. Those fierce gray eyes studied her carefully. He looked angry.

"Am I okay? Of course," she said, her voice a hoarse whisper. She cleared her throat. "I'm as good as it gets." Somehow this time, she managed to make her voice come out normal.

"Yeah," Vincent said. And he moved on, but he hadn't looked any happier. She wondered if he still regretted kissing her.

What a humiliating thought. A man kissed her and then spent days kicking himself about it. Unexpected pain trickled through her. Which was just too bad, because Vincent was right. It would be so wrong for the two of them to even think of getting involved on any level. She needed to concentrate on the things that mattered.

Vincent couldn't matter to her.

The ringing doorbell pulled her out of her thoughts. She glanced up and saw Vincent headed for the door. It had come to this. She couldn't even open her own door. But she knew better than to argue. Vincent was just doing what he had to do.

"Is she in?" Natalie heard a small, soft voice that she recognized. Marjorie Redmond was her downstairs neighbor, a retired teacher and the first person Natalie had met when she had moved in here. Marjorie hadn't lost her money the way many of their neighbors had, but she worried about them like a mother tending her chicks, just as Natalie did.

"Hi, Nat," she said. "The neighbors have planned a little pre-holiday get together, and they've asked me to come escort the guest of honor, so…here I am." Marjorie smiled.

"Guest of honor?" Natalie asked.

"You, you goose," her friend said. "Look at her," Marjorie said to Vincent. "She doesn't even get it."

"Get what?" Natalie looked at Vincent. "Do you know what she's talking about?"

Vincent grinned. "I might."

"How do you know, and I don't?"

Vincent gave Natalie a sexy smile. "When I took the garbage out the other day, Mr. Felsmith might have mentioned something to me about a small gathering."

"And you just said yes."

Marjorie laughed out loud. "Oh sure, he said yes, after he made Mr. Felsmith show him where the party would be located and gave everyone a set of instructions about safety."

"Vincent," Natalie said.

"Natalie," Marjorie admonished. "Nobody minded, hon. We all know that you saw that dreadful man kill that woman, and we want to keep you safe, too. Vincent is doing you and us a favor. Heck, this building has probably never been so safe with a bodyguard roaming the premises. Besides, sweetie," she whispered, pulling Natalie aside, "the man is to die for. If I had that parading through my shower every day, I'd be one happy woman. You've got some serious male muscle there, and he's charming as well. No one is offended that he's doing his darnedest to guard you."

Natalie's breathing had kicked up when Marjorie had mentioned the part about Vincent in the shower. She turned concerned eyes on her friend. "Mrs. Morgensen thinks he's my boyfriend."

Marjorie raised one brow. "No harm in letting her think that. It takes her mind off other things. You don't mind, do you?" Marjorie said, turning and raising her voice so that Vincent would hear.

Vincent raised one brow. "Mind what?"

Natalie pulled on Marjorie's arm trying to stop her, but to no avail. "Letting the neighbors think that you and Natalie are an item. It makes the whole situation less sinister, and it gives them something to think about other than their troubles."

Natalie crossed her arms. "You don't have to go along with this, Vincent. You've already done enough."

"I'm fine with that, Natalie," he said in that low, sexy voice. "You and I know the truth. There's no harm in giving everyone else some peace of mind."

Marjorie beamed. "Good. Then you'll come, too?" she asked Vincent.

"I would have come, anyway."

"Oh yes, of course," Marjorie said. "Are you always by her side?"

"Every second of every day," he answered in that low, commanding, shivery voice of his. Natalie thought that Marjorie was going to swoon.

"Nat, you lucky girl," she said before swinging about to head back down the stairs. "Five minutes," she called out to them, her voice floating out behind her.

"Every second of every day?" Natalie said to Vincent once the door was closed again.

He grinned. "They want to know you're protected around the clock, Natalie. I'm just giving them what they want."

She barely suppressed a smile. "You're going to give them heart palpitations imagining what we might be doing together every second of every day." Not that the thought of Vincent skin to skin with her every second of every day didn't give her palpitations, as well.

"They love you, Natalie. This will relieve their minds."

"I don't think relieving my neighbors' minds is part of your duties, though," she said softly. "So thank you for thinking of them and going along with the playacting."

He shook his head. "Pretending to be attracted to you isn't

a hardship, Natalie. It's coming back here and keeping my hands off you that's the difficult part."

And with that vision in her mind, Vincent took her hand and led her down to the party.

"Honey, this is for you. Just a little something. Not much," an elderly woman said, shoving a small tissue-paper-wrapped package into Natalie's arms. "We're just so grateful to have you."

"Thank you." Natalie blinked back tears, and Vincent turned her and wiped her eyes with his handkerchief.

"You keep taking good care of her," the lady said.

"Her life is golden," Vincent promised the woman. "No one is going to touch her."

"Except you," the lady said with a smile.

Natalie sucked in a breath, but she didn't refute the woman's words. By then, Mrs. Morgensen, the last of the neighbors, was filing past. "Just a little nothing," she said to Natalie, pushing a small leather-bound book into Natalie's hands.

"Mrs. Morgensen, I can't take this. Your husband gave it to you."

"He gave it to me in love, and I'm passing it on in the same spirit," Mrs. Morgensen said. "Bernard would have approved. You're a love for trying to help us."

And Natalie knew in that moment that no one actually believed that she would be able to help them. They simply appreciated the fact that she wanted to. Even though many of them had lost their life savings, they had all brought her some token of affection. They had given what they had.

Thick tears clogged Natalie's throat. She watched as Vincent moved forward to help Mr. Jorge back into his wheelchair for the ride down the hall, and she felt such a moment of affection for her neighbors and such gratitude to have Vincent helping her take care of them. A moment of absolute despair followed immediately. What if they were right, and she couldn't do a darned thing to help them? What would happen to all of them?

When they had returned to the apartment, she turned to him. "You see now why I'm doing this, don't you?"

"Because they're your family, and you care about them. Yes, Natalie, I see that."

It hadn't been what she was going to say. She did care, but the family part— She had never phrased it that way. "I...already have a family," she said, confusion in her voice.

"I know, but this family—Mrs. Morgensen and Mr. Felsmith and the others—trusts you to work miracles. They believe in you implicitly. That makes them extra special."

She swallowed hard. He was right...and he understood.

"It's part of why I have to get that story, Vincent. Do you see?"

He gave a tight nod. "I don't like what you're forced to do, but yes, I do see."

"And I'm not succeeding very well lately." Anguish filled her soul. She hated the thought of not coming through for these good people whom she loved.

"You will. I'll help you."

Natalie looked up at Vincent. He was gazing at her with a fire she hadn't seen in his eyes before. "How?" She whispered the word.

"I'll stop fighting you so much. Just let me be there. I can't let you walk into danger and not go crazy. We'll work this out some way. I have faith."

Something bright and sunny and good sprang forth within Natalie. "Thank you," she said softly. She wished she could kiss him, but she couldn't. Because if she touched him, she would want to go on touching him. She would want him to take her to his bed, and that just wasn't fair to him when he was fighting so hard against it.

"I'll set something up, and I'll do all I can to accommodate you," she told him. "And Vincent?"

"Yes."

"Thank you for watching my back."

He smiled. "Watching you isn't a hardship, Natalie. Not at all."

With that, he turned around and left.

Natalie couldn't help wondering what Vincent saw when he looked at her, when he watched her. But thinking that way would drive her crazy. Because when she looked at him, she saw a caring person, one who had helped Mr. Jorge with his wheelchair. And she remembered his mouth on hers, his hands on her. Heaven help her, she wanted him to kiss her and touch her again.

When Vincent handed Natalie the newspaper the next day and she pulled it from its plastic wrapper, a piece of paper fluttered to the ground.

She growled. "Darned annoying inserts."

Vincent chuckled. "You need coffee. I'll get you some." He turned to go, but then he swung back.

She reached down to pick up the piece of paper.

"Don't," Vincent said.

Natalie looked up at him from her bent over position, her hand still outstretched, but he was pulling a handkerchief from his pocket, reaching past her.

Her heart started to thud, slowly at first, but then more rapidly. "Let me see."

Vincent ignored her.

"Vincent."

He looked at her, worry lines knitting his forehead. He didn't hold out the paper.

"I have the right," she said, even though her voice shook.

"The man's an animal," he told her. "He doesn't matter." But he held out the paper so that she could read it.

You see, I know where you live, it said, *I know how to get to you, and when I'm ready I will.*

Natalie's body went cold. She struggled for breath and closed her eyes.

"He's not getting in," Vincent promised her. But they both knew that he had gotten close enough to insert this note in her newspaper.

Vincent's arm came around her. He led her to the couch and eased her down on it. She felt the shift of the cushions as his big, warm body came down next to her.

"Natalie, look at me," he said.

She kept her eyes closed, fighting the fear, searching for courage, for whatever she needed to get through this.

"Please." Vincent's voice was harsh, rough. She turned and looked into his worried eyes…and found what she needed. Calm, steady strength. She saw a man who would go to any lengths to keep her from harm, a man of unswerving conviction. She continued to gaze into those eyes.

"You okay?" he asked, reaching out to brush her cheek with his hand.

She nodded and leaned into his touch, never looking away from him. "Yes. I'm…better now. In fact, I'm—that letter— how dare someone sully my morning paper? That's the news, that's my personal paper, my morning relaxation, what I read with my first cup of coffee. That newspaper should never be sullied," she said, knowing she sounded irrational but also knowing that she needed to whip herself into a frenzy. "In fact, I'm so appalled that anyone would have the nerve to touch my stuff this way that—darn, I'm getting angry."

"Good. You're far better than him. The guy isn't fit to touch anything you own," Vincent agreed. "He's slime."

"And I'm not going to let him scare me into huddling inside waiting for him to strike," she said. "I swear to you that I'm not. Nothing is going to stop me from living the way I want to."

No answer followed.

"Vincent?"

He stroked one thumb over her bottom lip. Her anger faded a little. She fought to keep from trembling from fear and from gratitude that Vincent was here with her at one of the worst moments she could remember.

"I'm not going to lie," she said. "I'm scared."

"I know."

"But it's—I can't explain. It's important to me that I fight him."

"Yes, I guess I know that, too." He sounded sad and resigned.

"Will you help me?"

He turned on the couch, cupped both of his big hands around her face. "I promise you, Natalie, that I will do anything and everything I can to help you. He's not going to win. I swear to you that he isn't."

A tear threatened to roll down her cheek, but she fought it off and smiled.

"I'm glad you're the one protecting me," she said.

He gently traced his index finger down her cheek, but he didn't answer her. Not that she could blame him. Despite her brave words, she was scared out of her wits and she was pretty sure he knew that, but her way of dealing with fear had always been to run toward it, not away. She needed to make it seem smaller by pretending that it didn't matter, so trying to protect someone like her had to be a frustrating affair.

And things had just gotten worse.

Sitting at the bar of The Ladder that night, Vincent was starting to get edgy. Natalie had been talking to Brad Herron for several minutes already, and today the guy actually seemed to be sober and reasonably serious. A good thing from her perspective, Vincent figured. He did hope she at least got some good information, but Vincent couldn't help noticing that the guy paid way too much attention to Natalie's breasts and lips. He wanted to go over there and belt the guy, except he hadn't been hired to protect her from men who admired her beauty, only from people who wanted to hurt her.

Brad wanted to do something with her, but it definitely didn't involve abuse or death. What Herron wanted was to get Natalie naked, and it appeared he was beginning to realize that that was never going to happen as long as he acted like a lech.

Today, he wasn't acting like a lech. Natalie was listening to the guy with what looked like interest.

A low growl erupted from Vincent's throat.

Fortunately, a loud group of Starson employees entered the bar at that time, and Natalie got up and excused herself. Herron said something to her, but she shook her head politely. She headed toward the ladies' room, and as she passed him, she gave Vincent the briefest of looks, just a tiny smile. He knew what she was doing. She was telling him that she was all in one piece and he didn't have to worry.

As if she didn't know that Herron would try to hit on her again the next time he saw her. A slow burn began in Vincent's chest, but Herron's cell phone rang at that moment, and he headed for the door. The fact that he looked toward the door of the ladies' room before he left did nothing to ease Vincent's mind.

"Don't go poaching on my territory," Brad said as he saw Neil Gerard walking toward The Ladder. "The lady is marked as mine, and I mean to have her." Brad tapped Neil on the shoulder to make his point.

"Don't touch me, Herron. And don't think you know so much. There's a whole heck of a lot you don't know."

Herron snorted. "About women? You've got to be kidding. I've been tossing women's skirts since the day I was old enough to realize that their anatomy was different from mine.

Not much I don't know. Someday, I'll teach you a thing or two if you ask nicely." He grinned and patted Gerard on the back.

Neil swung around and punched Brad's arm away. "I told you I don't like to be touched, Herron, especially by idiots."

Brad frowned. "You're calling me an idiot? I might remind you—"

"Don't bother reminding me of anything. I know all I need to know. More than you realize. And if I want to talk to Natalie McCabe, that's my affair."

"Why? You interested in getting lucky with her?"

"I'm interested in her brain."

"Not her boobs?"

Neil flushed a rich, dark red. Brad gave him a slow smile. "Yeah, you're just interested in her brain, all right. Good luck." Not that he meant it, not that it mattered. Gerard wasn't the type that women dreamed about in their beds. He had arms like string beans, he had zero conversation skills and he blushed like a kid. Brad started to move on when Gerard shoved his face up against Brad's nose.

"You're going to do something stupid, and then there'll be trouble," Neil warned. "Stay away from her."

"And let you handle her? Can you?"

Gerard opened his mouth to speak, his face getting hotter and redder by the second. Then he closed his mouth, swerved away and moved to the door of The Ladder.

Brad eyed him speculatively. He had never liked Gerard, which was really unfortunate. Working with the guy was a necessity, but the man just had no people skills, no sense of fun.

Besides, Natalie was *his* new toy, Brad thought, and he didn't like Neil making a stink about it. He always tried to spoil everything.

The evening had been a strain, and Natalie hadn't found out much other than when Brad had told her that some of his clients were older and needed a lot of hand-holding. She had told him that she used to work in a retirement home, which was a lie, and she had entertained him with one or two made-up anecdotes, hoping he would reciprocate. Instead he had asked her personal questions. He'd asked for her phone number.

She'd considered giving him nothing, but there was always the possibility that he might tell her things on the phone that he would never say in person. Some people were that way. In the end, they had traded cell numbers.

"How did you all start coming here?" she asked Neil after she had returned from the ladies' room and found him sitting in his usual corner.

"I don't know," he said. "People were coming here before I ever began at Starson."

She nodded. "So you haven't been there very long."

He picked up a coaster and twisted it between his fingers. "I didn't say that."

"No, but The Ladder only opened a couple of years ago." She smiled reassuringly, hoping she hadn't embarrassed him.

She had. He blushed again. "Yeah, I guess I knew that," he said. "Why are you talking to me?"

Natalie blinked. "Pardon me?"

"Women don't. Usually."

"Oh, well, maybe most women don't look beneath the surface."

"And you do?" He twisted the coaster again. It bent a little.

Natalie noticed that his hands were small, without the long, lean fingers Vincent had. Immediately, she felt angry at herself for having noticed Vincent's hands. "I'm interested in a lot of things," she said, managing a smile, "and people are almost always more interesting once you get to know them. Appearances don't count for much."

"So when men tell you you're pretty…"

She squirmed slightly. Having Neil compliment her wasn't

like having Brad compliment her. Neil was painfully shy. She didn't like taking advantage or making him think she felt something she didn't feel.

"I don't pay much attention. I'm not interested in being anything more than friends with any man."

He frowned at that and continued twisting the coaster. Damn, she had probably blown this chance.

Then Neil smiled, just a bit.

"What?" she asked.

"I guess you're not going to go to bed with Brad Herron, are you?" For a second, she thought she saw something orgasmic in Neil's eyes, but then he quickly shrugged. "Never mind. He's just a bit of a jerk. I don't like to see him take advantage."

"That's not going to happen."

"Want to play some pool?" he asked.

"Sure." Maybe once he relaxed enough, he would tell her something of what she needed to know.

It didn't happen. She had to cheat to keep from beating him at pool. Her brothers had taught her too well.

"You let me win," he told her when they were done.

Uh-oh. She opened her mouth.

He surprised her by smiling. "I like that. I like a girl who knows how important it is for a man to win. I almost never win. Girls never even give me their phone numbers."

So for the second time that night Natalie handed out her cell number. She really needed to move this along, because things were getting messy, so when an older man came into the bar, she seized on the moment.

"You don't have any older people who work at Starson, do you? At least, none that come here."

"We have a few. They don't come here. And no, the company's not an older person's world. Too much pressure."

She nodded. "I understand. I have friends who are older. People take advantage of them at times."

"Must be tough to be old. I'd hate for anyone to take advantage of my mother."

"What would you do if you thought someone was?"

"I don't know. I'd be angry. I'd want to do something. Why? What happened to your friends?"

She debated answering, but then, why shouldn't she answer? He either knew something or he didn't. He'd either tell her or he wouldn't. She was getting nowhere fast this way.

"They lost a lot of their money in investments."

He nodded. "I see." She figured that he did. "I'm sorry I don't know anything that could help your friends. Investments are tricky. Sometimes people lose. It happens every day."

"I know." She couldn't keep the wistfulness from her voice. "I just wish I could work a miracle for them, find some loophole, some way out, some way of salvaging things."

He reached out and touched her hand. His fingers were sweaty. She looked up to see that his face was fiery red. "I doubt that's going to happen," he told her. "Old people make bad decisions at times. It's just the way things happen. I guess this means you're not in the mood to talk to me anymore tonight."

She wasn't. Her friends hadn't just made bad decisions. Someone had taken advantage of them.

But she smiled at Neil and talked for a few more minutes. When he tried to touch her hand again, she couldn't help herself. She pulled away, and she looked up and saw that Vincent was rising from his chair.

Her eyes met his as she reclaimed her fingers and he sat back down in his chair.

Ten minutes later, she bid Neil a good-night and walked out the door of The Ladder.

When she finally got home and Vincent came in behind her and shut the door, she looked up at him and wanted nothing more than to throw herself into his arms and have him kiss away the memory of Neil telling her that Mrs. Morgensen was just an old person who had made unfortunate decisions.

"This isn't working," she said.

"I know. I'm sorry," Vincent said. "So sorry." He touched her hair.

"I'm a bad person, aren't I?" she asked.

"Why?" His voice was low and compelling.

"I'm playing a game, pretending to be something I'm not."

"You're doing it for a good cause. Have you made any promises, suggested that you want more than you've given?"

She shook her head violently. "I've been as honest as I can be. I've told them both that I'm not interested in more than friendship."

"Good girl." He reached out and stroked her cheek, and she wanted to lean into him. Which was just so stupid. Hadn't he already let her know that he couldn't have a relationship with her? She had to concentrate on helping her friends. Only...

"I haven't been able to find out anything much of value," she said. "I thought I could play the femme fatale and get some Starson secrets, but I just can't play up to a man when it's not real. What kind of a disastrous reporter am I?" Her voice was weaker than she liked. She looked up at Vincent. "You should be yelling at me. I've dragged you to that bar too many times, and I haven't found out much of anything."

"Shh," he said, and he raked one long, lean finger down her jaw. She trembled beneath his touch. "Don't insult yourself," he said gently. "Don't apologize for daring to be honest, for refusing to lead a man on to get him to tell you his secrets. I respect you for that."

"Well, that makes one of us. I can't help but feel that some other woman wouldn't have made such a mess out of this. Some other woman would have seduced Brad Herron's secrets right out of him."

"But you didn't, because it wasn't honest."

She nodded and swallowed. "That wasn't the only reason."

"Tell me the rest," Vincent whispered, and he tipped her head up so that she was staring straight into his dark gray eyes.

Natalie swallowed. She didn't want to tell him the truth, but there was something about Vincent. She couldn't tell him any less. "Brad makes my skin crawl. I don't want him to touch me. Neil, either. See, I'm not much of an investigative reporter. I can't even get past my personal hang-ups."

Vincent's fingers were resting on her jaw. Natalie was very aware that she had no personal reservations about being touched by him.

"Natalie?"

She nodded, and his fingers slid higher. She almost moaned with need.

"You'd tell me if I scared you when I touch you, wouldn't you?"

"I'd tell you if I didn't want you to touch me," she whispered.

But she didn't ask him to stop. Indeed, she didn't know quite how it happened, but Natalie stepped closer so that her body was only inches away from Vincent's now. She reached up and touched his chest.

"Natalie, this isn't smart," he said.

She swallowed. "I know." But in these past few weeks, so little good had happened. She still woke up at times remembering Melissa Wilkes's dead body and Jason Jamison's face after he'd killed her. She remembered that dark ride when she had run and then the frightening prospect of returning to turn Jason in. She thought of the notes that threatened death and Mrs. Morgensen giving away her husband's book because she had so little left to give. She thought of how ineffectual her efforts to save her friends had been and how Vincent was standing by her all the way, going beyond the call of duty when he helped her friends and comforted her. "I shouldn't touch you," she agreed, but she rose up on her toes and kissed his chin.

"Damn it, Natalie," Vincent growled, and he hauled her up against his body, curling his arms around her, his mouth crushing hers.

She pressed closer, closing her mind to everything but Vincent's touch. She wanted more of him, all of him. She wanted something she had never known, how it felt to be with a man who truly respected her.

"I can't touch you, Natalie. It's wrong for me to do this when I'm supposed to be protecting you."

"I know. That's why I'm the one doing the touching," she said against his lips.

"That's it, then," he said when she came up for air. "You and me, right here." He slid his hands down her back, curling his palms around her buttocks. When her body came up against his, she could feel the hard evidence of his arousal.

"You make me insane," he told her. "You make me forget who I am and what I should be doing." There was need in his voice, desire and anguish. She was driving him to the brink of breaking that code of honor he held so dear. Did she want to do that? Would he wake up in the morning and regret touching her?

Of course he would. He had as much as told her so. To push him over the edge…

With the greatest of effort, Natalie planted both palms on Vincent's chest and pushed lightly.

He let her slide down his body slowly. He let her go, his breathing ragged and labored. "I'm sorry," he said.

She closed her eyes, crossed her arms and tapped one foot on the floor, struggling for control, trying with all she was worth to stop the silent scream of protest that welled up inside her. She had wanted him beyond all reason, and he was correct. Doing this would have been so wrong, but it would have felt so very right.

"If you're implying that you started this, I'm going to be very angry. I pushed you to it. And if you're implying that you're sorry we had to stop, well, you told me so in the first place. I started it and I stopped it, and you don't have a thing to be sorry for."

"Nat, I practically begged for you to touch me. That's how much I wanted you. I couldn't have stopped on my own."

She nodded. "I guess we'll leave it at that." She turned to go. Then she turned back. "For the record, thank you."

He frowned.

"I was feeling pretty low. Now I'm just feeling frustrated."

He managed a laugh. "Frustrated doesn't even begin to describe how I feel right now."

She nodded. "I'm sorry I was acting crazy and that I started something we couldn't finish."

"We were both acting crazy, but we'll get through it. You're allowed to feel crazy. I'm assuming it's because you didn't get any information tonight."

"Not much, anyway. Just a few tiny nuggets and an exchange of phone numbers."

"Phone numbers?" Vincent's eyes turned dark and lethal. He slammed his fist against the wall.

"My cell, not my home phone," she said. "I'm not giving out any links to my address."

"But you plan to see them both again."

"I don't want to, but I might have to."

"Natalie—"

"I know, I know. I'm trying to move things along and get this over with quickly."

"Me, too," he said. "We're looking for Jamison all the time. But I'll tell you this much. I'm not leaving you until everything is concluded. I don't like the way Brad Herron looks at your behind. He covets it."

"He's not getting near it."

"Some men don't ask. They take. I'm not letting any man take advantage of you."

He walked away. For a second, she thought she heard him say, "And that includes me." But that was probably only her imagination.

Nevertheless, she had pushed him too far tonight, and she knew that if she pushed him, she would be the one getting hurt. Vincent didn't want a relationship, and she could never have one with a man who needed to be the leader, the protector.

Frustration rose up in her like hot lava. She couldn't have Vincent.

But knowing that didn't make her want him any less. Relationships were just too darned complicated.

Eleven

Relationships were just too darned complicated, Ryan thought one day later. He had told Lily about Linda Faraday a month ago, but his wife was still wearing that fragile, brave look. It had to be a blow to realize that your husband had kept a secret from you for more than ten years. If the tables had been reversed, how would he have felt about hearing there had been a man in Lily's life she hadn't told him about, even if she'd had a good reason for keeping that man secret?

"I would have been in a jealous rage," he admitted. Lily deserved better. She needed to meet Linda and see for herself that there was nothing other than family responsibility and friendship between Linda and himself.

He picked up the phone and made a few calls. Three hours later, he handed Lily into his car. "I'm sorry I waited so long to do this," he said, kissing her behind the ear. "I thought I was doing the right thing. My only excuse is that, as a Treasury agent, Linda needed secrecy. Her position, combined with the fact that Cameron's blood alcohol level was well above the limit when he nearly killed her in that car wreck, would have attracted attention. Add to that the facts that she had given birth and spent ten years in a semi-conscious state, and the story would have made national news. In these past few months since Linda has reawakened, she's been trying to get her life back together. Her son spent ten years being raised by the Armstrongs, a couple I met through my work with MADD, and she and Ricky are virtual strangers to each other."

He shrugged. "They need privacy. Moreover, I didn't want anyone to know what Cameron had become, not even you, and I—"

"You thought I would tell?" Lily's soft voice was wounded. Ryan hated thinking that he had hurt her.

"Of course not," he said. "But there was a helpless woman involved, and a child, Lily. You wouldn't have been able to stay away, to keep from helping. I wouldn't have wanted to ask you to slip around. Honesty is in your blood."

She gazed at him with troubled eyes. "Ryan, I'm your wife. I want to help you."

"You do help me, Lily. So much, every day. Just knowing you love me makes me feel ten times bigger than I am."

"I just wish you had trusted me."

"I know. I love being a Fortune, but sometimes I hate being the head of the Fortunes."

Lily leaned over and kissed him. "You have too much responsibility. It weighs on you. You look tired."

For a moment, he felt an overwhelming need to tell her about his illness, but he loved her too much. Instead, he drew her to him and kissed her gently. "Today we're just going to meet Linda, but soon I'll introduce you to Ricky, too. He's a pistol."

Lily smiled. "If he's anything like his uncle, I'm going to

adore him." She kept her hand on Ryan's knee while he drove to the rehab center.

Linda was expecting them. She was a pretty blonde, very slender, and she nodded when Ryan told her who Lily was. "Mrs. Fortune. Yes. Ryan...well, he's been good to me." She clutched a book with a blue cover tightly, as if it were a child she was trying to protect. The fact that she had a real child, one who didn't live with her, made the gesture even sadder.

Lily's eyes misted over. She looked at her husband, then back to Linda. "I'm glad Ryan's been there for you. You've gone through a lot."

A tiny, pained look in Linda's eyes was her only response. "I don't remember much," she said haltingly.

"Ryan tells me you have a son," Lily said.

Linda looked at Ryan and then to the side. "Yes," was all she said, her voice wispy.

Instantly Lily's heart went out to her. This woman had been strong, she had been in a position of responsibility and danger. Now she was like a lost child.

"Ryan tells me that you see Ricky now and then."

Linda nodded. "Sometimes we go to his house."

"I'd like to go with you next time, if you don't mind," Lily said gently.

Linda blinked. She looked at Ryan, who nodded. "All right," was all she said.

Watching this wounded woman, Lily felt her heart nearly break in two. Linda had been a good agent, Ryan had said. She was an intelligent woman, and life had kicked her around in some pretty horrifying ways. Now she looked scared and confused.

"Could I see a picture of your child?" Lily asked. "That is, if you have one?"

Linda clutched her book more tightly. Ryan walked over to a small bulletin board and removed a picture tacked there.

"Yes, that's him," Linda said in a weak voice.

The boy in the picture had blond hair and blue eyes just like Linda's. He wasn't exactly smiling, but he didn't look unhappy, either, and Lily knew that ten-year-old boys didn't always like to smile for the camera. She assumed that the happy man and woman flanking him were his foster parents. Together with Ricky, they looked like a family.

"He's handsome," Lily offered.

Linda didn't respond, but she looked confused. Immediately, Lily went to her and looked at her. When she gazed into Linda's eyes, she saw a lost woman, one who was probably frightened a great deal of the time. She couldn't imagine what it would be like to almost lose your life, to live in a void for ten years and then to awake to a different world, a world where you had a child you didn't even know.

"Thank you for agreeing to meet me," Lily said gently and she carefully touched Linda's arm. When Linda didn't jerk away, Lily gave her a little hug.

"I think you and I are going to be friends," she told the younger woman, her voice soft.

Linda didn't respond, but she gazed at Lily with a hint of interest.

Ryan watched his wife, and knew that he had done the right thing in bringing her here. Lily had been born to nurture. Lately he'd given her nothing but trouble and worry, and there was surely more worry to come. He knew the fact that Jason Jamison was on the loose and that the man resented the Fortunes, particularly the head of the Fortune family, troubled her deeply and kept her awake at night.

He didn't even want to think how devastated she would be when she found out about the cancer that was killing him, but for this moment she had something good to concentrate on, and she was in her element.

"Perhaps I can arrange a visit with Ricky soon," he suggested to Linda.

She hesitated, twisting her fingers. "All right."

It was the best he could hope for, he knew. He and Lily said their goodbyes, and he led Lily back to the car.

Linda had once been a fighter. Now she was fragile. He was sorry for that, even though he knew that it would awaken the mothering instinct in Lily.

Once he had started the car and they were moving down the road, Lily proved him right.

"You didn't tell me just how damaged she was, but I suppose I should have expected it," she said. "Now, the question is, how can we help her?"

Ryan grinned. "I'm sure you'll find some way."

"I'm sure I will." At last there was a hopeful glow in Lily's eyes, one that hadn't been there for quite a while. He'd be damned if he let anyone threaten to put out that light.

Another day had passed. Vincent watched Natalie as she sat at her computer, lost in thought, her fingers flying over the keyboard.

She had long fingers, he thought, and long legs. Dancer's legs, legs to wrap around a man in the night.

His chest felt tight, and he got up, needing action.

She glanced up, her eyes still dazed as if she was focusing on a dream world rather than the here and now. Vincent barely suppressed a groan.

"You done?" he asked.

"For now." She raised her hands over her head, lacing her fingers and stretching.

He tried to concentrate on the newspaper he was holding. Not that he was succeeding. It was all he could do to keep from marching over there and kneading her shoulders, slipping his hands down over her breasts.

The paper crumpled beneath his hands.

"Looks like someone needs to get out of the house," Natalie commented.

He considered the risks, a frown creasing his forehead.

"We don't know where he is, do we?" she asked softly, and he could see that she wasn't completely indifferent to her danger.

"No. All the leads have turned into dead ends."

"And that could go on for a long time. I can't stay inside hiding," she said, giving him a wide-eyed look.

He chuckled. "As if you have. I've had to chase you down at The Ladder twice. You've damn near killed me worrying about you."

"I know. That's why I'm telling you that I'm going to do something."

Instantly he was alert. "What are you going to do?"

She shook her head. "You don't want to know. I just don't want you to worry, and I can tell you this much. I'll be completely safe."

"Natalie—"

"Vincent," she whispered, "don't make me a prisoner in my house. Don't take away my work and the things that make life worth living."

"I'm not doing that. I would never want to hurt you," he said, gazing directly into her eyes.

"I know that. He's the one who wants to hurt me. Jason. And right now he's succeeding, because he has me hiding behind closed doors. In the meantime, I can see Mrs. Morgensen flutter in fear every time the mail arrives or the landlord comes to call. She's afraid she's going to end up in a pauper's grave. That wouldn't happen, of course. I wouldn't let it, but, this situation is killing her soul, you know? The elderly give up so much of their dignity as they get older, and then this happened and made her feel as if she had lost everything precious, and I don't mean money. I mean self-worth. She's afraid she'll look foolish or unintelligent, an easy target. I've got to take things to the next level. I have to help." She swiped at her cheek, and Vincent knew that a tear had slipped down. She didn't seem real happy about that.

"All right, you help, then," he told her. "But only on the condition that I go with you."

She opened her mouth to protest.

He stood and walked to her, reaching out to take her by her forearms and lift her to her feet, so that they were only inches apart. "I go with you," he repeated.

"Will you stay outside?"

"Depends on where you're going."

"It's a place with lots of security. No one's going to be able to take a shot at me while I'm inside."

"All right, you might as well tell me where if I'm going with you."

She shrugged and he thought he saw a spot of color tinge her cheeks. "Starson," she said in a low voice.

He glared at her.

"I'm not going in there to see Brad or Neil," she told him. "I just want to get some of my questions answered."

"And if you don't?"

She looked to the side. "I have to believe that I can do it. If I start out believing I'll fail, then I will."

Vincent noticed she said that as if she had experience with such situations. He wondered how many times her parents or brothers had told her that she wouldn't be able to do something in an effort to protect her. He understood their dilemma, as it was now his, but he wasn't going to let anyone crush Natalie's spirit.

"All right, I'll take you to Starson," he promised.

"Will you agree to wait outside? Your presence is distracting and disruptive to being able to get good information."

"I'll wait for a while."

"Two hours," she said.

"Forty-five minutes." He crossed his arms.

She crossed hers, too. "An hour and a half."

"Forget it, Natalie. I'll give you an hour, and that's being generous. And if anything happens that makes me think you're in trouble, you're out of there in five. And you're carrying a radio. I want to be able to reach you if I need to."

She leaned forward and kissed his cheek. His cheek, damn it, when she knew he wanted her lips. "Thank you, Vincent," she said. "I promise not to get in trouble."

But he was beginning to think that maybe her parents and brothers had had good reason to worry about her. Natalie was trouble, pure and simple. Unfortunately for him, she was trouble that he couldn't have.

He just knew he was going to regret his decision to let her go forward with this plan. Who in hell at Starson was just going to let her walk in there and start asking questions about whether the company had committed illegal acts?

And anyone who suggested that such a thing might have happened was going to be less than welcome.

Vincent cursed himself for promising to give her an hour. That had been a huge mistake. Of course, agreeing to be Natalie's bodyguard had been a big mistake, too.

The woman drove him nuts.

A short time later, he drove her to Starson's. It was almost closing time. He wondered what she thought she would accomplish at this late an hour.

Briefcase in hand, Natalie walked in the front door, asked to speak to someone in Personnel, asked a question about employment and was given the sorry-we're-not-interested treatment, as she had known she would. Especially when she told the woman that she had majored in art appreciation. She thanked the woman, wandered to the side entrance of the building, checked herself out, confessing that she had come in the front, and then left the building through a different door than the one she had entered.

She hated doing this, because it was lying to Vincent, but there was no way she could get the information she needed by simply asking. She needed to gain access to the building by other means, means that wouldn't involve asking questions, and she couldn't have Vincent see what she was up to.

"Darn," she whispered, looking at her watch. Ten minutes had already passed. She slipped into a building next door, went to the restroom and donned the skirt and blouse that she carried in the briefcase. The clothes that resembled those worn by the cleaning ladies in the Starson building. She'd watched and seen them days ago, and she hoped this would work. Ten minutes later, workers streamed out of the office building, and cleaning personnel shuffled in through the back door, Natalie in their midst.

Walking purposefully, she took the elevator to the eighth floor where the directory she'd read earlier had indicated Brad Herron had his office. It didn't take her long to figure out which space was Brad's. A photo of several long-legged women flanking him was on the corner of his desk.

She flipped on his computer, not sure what she was looking for.

Thirty-five minutes had already passed. Twenty-five more and Vincent would be radioing her and storming the place. Maybe twenty. She had a feeling that Vincent wasn't picky about the details when justice was on his side and he felt a woman was in possible distress.

For several seconds, she wished he was here with her. His presence made her feel stronger, she had begun to realize. But this wasn't his quest. It was hers, and she had to make at least an attempt to find out something that would help her friends.

Clicking through the documents, Natalie found her way barred in most cases. No client files were available. That wasn't exactly a surprise. But in the few times she had met Brad, she had realized that he was a little sloppy, and it was sloppy that she was looking for now.

Natalie looked at her watch. Only ten minutes left. Damn! She couldn't leave now, but she couldn't stay, either.

A file marked Memos caught her eye. She double-clicked on it.

Nothing much here. No, wait. What was that one? A file with the subject line Senior Study. The memo itself didn't say much, just something about a journal article that suggested that some seniors might develop difficulty multitasking when instructions were given in rapid succession. Nothing more. It didn't mean a thing, but beneath it was a messily scrawled list of names, addresses and phone numbers, and—

Natalie glanced at her watch. Damn, damn, damn. Any minute now, Vincent would be tearing down the walls demanding to know where she was.

She hit the Print button, grabbed the paper, closed everything and made sure the desk looked as untouched as it had when she had come in, and flew down the hall. The *squeak-squeak* of a bucket on wheels came to her, and she frantically glanced around, looking for someplace to hide. No doors were open.

Natalie slipped off her shoes and sprinted in the opposite direction, running on her toes on the tiled hallway. Thank goodness for all those workouts at the club. She rounded the corner and plastered herself against the wall.

The squeaking grew louder. Natalie could hear her own breathing loud in her ears.

She didn't even want to think about the passing of time and that Vincent might be ready to muscle his way into the building.

She tried to squeeze herself more tightly, make herself smaller and more invisible.

The squeaking grew more faint. The worker must have turned the corner. Natalie held her breath and waited until the noise had almost disappeared down the hall.

Then she quietly and as quickly as possible retraced her steps. She put her shoes on and left via the same entrance she had come in, rounding the building and heading toward where Vincent had parked his car.

When she reached the car, no one was there.

Her heart started to thud frantically. Had he gone inside looking for her?

Or had Jason Jamison decided to take out another person who was standing in his way? If Vincent had had all his attention trained on the building, he would have been an easy target.

Natalie's heart thudded in her chest. Fear rose inside her. Pressing her fingertips to her lips, she tried to think, but thought was impossible. Where was Vincent?

Panic clawed at her. She struggled to retrieve the radio Vincent had given her from her pocket.

A shoe scraped behind her. She whirled, nearly stumbling.

"Looking for someone, Natalie?"

Tears of relief misted her eyes. Her breath came back in a whoosh, and she launched herself at Vincent and threw her arms around him. "Where were you?" she demanded. "I was worried."

When she looked up at him, she almost thought he was going to smile, and she was prepared to slug him if he made fun of her for worrying about a guy who looked as if he could bring down a tank if he had to.

"I was worried, too," he said, his voice a harsh rasp as his hands settled on her waist. "And I was here the whole time. I only slipped out of sight when I heard footsteps. Where were *you*, damn it? And what in hell were you doing?" He looked down at her, and she remembered that she was wearing different clothes, clothing that couldn't be mistaken for anything other than what it was.

She bit her lip, her mind racing fast. Then she opened her mouth.

He shook his head. "No, never mind," he whispered in a ragged voice. "You're here now. It's probably not a good idea for me to know what you've been up to, especially if it wasn't strictly legal or ethical."

Yeah, there was that, wasn't there? Natalie was surprised to discover that she was disappointed about not being able to tell him everything. For some reason, she wanted him to know, to share in what she had found, to ask him what he thought that memo might mean, but telling him would put him in an uncomfortable predicament. He was sworn to protect, not to encourage people to break into corporate buildings under false pretenses.

Unable to share her find, she said the next thing that came to mind. "I'm really glad to see you."

He raised an eyebrow. "Were you really worried that something had happened to me?"

"I'm a target," she said simply. "That makes you a target. I don't want you to choose my life over yours. I don't ever want to put you in a position of danger." Which was probably pretty stupid, given his profession, but there it was, and she couldn't pretend she felt differently. "I don't want anything bad to happen to you because you're protecting me. I won't let you do that."

"You don't get to decide about that," he said, "and I'm sorry if that sounds too much like your overprotective family. You know, you might be more like your family than you want to believe."

She blinked. He was right. She had been on the verge of doing her darnedest to protect him from his chosen profession.

She flounced around to the other side of the car. "I hate knowing that, but you may be right."

"It's not a sin to worry about someone, Natalie, and…"

When he didn't finish his sentence, she looked up at him. "And…?" she whispered into the gathering darkness.

"And frankly you're a hard woman to guard. You're—"

"Trouble," she supplied.

"Determined," he substituted, and she laughed.

"You, Vincent, are a diplomat," she told him, "because I *am* trouble, and you're the unfortunate person who has to deal with me."

"Don't worry, I'll deal with you."

She certainly hoped so.

Twelve

Vincent paced the living room the next morning, unspent energy and anger coursing through him. In spite of the night that had passed since the incident at Starson, he still felt like putting his fist through a wall. He had smiled when Natalie had finally emerged from that building, he had even joked with her, but that had been a front. He didn't even want to think about reliving those moments when he had stood outside Starson waiting for Natalie to reappear. It had been all he could do not to go running into the building and renege on his promise to wait for her or to risk compromising her position by calling her on the radio. He had wanted to inflict some serious damage on someone.

Like his father had done on a regular basis. There had been so much rage inside that man.

Vincent knew that kind of frustrating anger. He didn't want to admit to it. He'd fought it all his life, but there it was.

Things bothered him, and he had to battle like a bear to keep from striking out.

What if someday he failed to hold the anger at bay? What if someone like Natalie was in his path when that happened?

He closed his eyes, refusing to allow himself to continue that train of thought. Instead, he breathed deeply, concentrating only on breathing until the moment had passed.

She had come back. She was safe, no thanks to him. He remembered the moment when she had reappeared all too well.

Her body had been soft and pliant beneath his hands. Her arms had wrapped around his neck—

"Damn, don't go there, either, Fortune," he whispered to himself. With Natalie, he was damned anyway he turned. It didn't matter if he allowed his anger about her situation to dominate or if he allowed himself to think about her when she wasn't in danger, when she was magic beneath his fingertips and lips.

Vincent groaned. He paced the room again, scrubbing his hands back through his short hair.

"Vincent?"

He turned to see Natalie standing in the doorway to her bedroom. She wore a pair of faded jeans and a soft white shirt that hugged her curves. Her feet were bare. She was beautiful, but her eyes were worried.

Vincent simply stared at her.

Natalie bit her lip. He tried not to let that affect him, but heat spiraled through him nonetheless. "I just wanted to say that I'm sorry I've been such a pain to watch over," she said. "I'll bet your other clients don't give you such trouble."

They didn't. Most people were simply grateful for the protection. In fact, most of them pretty much stopped noticing he was there after a few days.

Vincent looked into Natalie's pretty green eyes, and he

knew that she was always aware of him. She didn't like having a bodyguard and so she never forgot that he was there.

And there was one more thing, he noted as he continued to stare at her and her eyelids flickered.

She knew he was a man who wanted her. That certainly made things more difficult. And that was entirely his fault.

He made a slashing motion with his hand. "I'm not regretting this job, Natalie," he said. To his surprise he realized that he wasn't lying. She might disturb him on many levels, he might be losing tons of sleep over her, but to trust her safety to anyone else?

It wasn't going to happen. He wanted her safe and alive. When this was over and he walked away, he needed to know that she would have no more reason to fear and that she would start every day with a smile.

Even if she was the client he never forgot.

She firmed her chin. "You're not regretting this job, Vincent? Well, you should be. I certainly haven't been very helpful, and I've been thinking about what you said. You're right about my family. I *am* more like them than I want to admit. What's more, I'm willing to concede that I've probably given them reason to worry over the years. And just for the record, I absolutely hate admitting that."

She sounded so forlorn, Vincent couldn't help but smile.

"Don't laugh, it's true," she said. "I was always a difficult child. My brothers were all older than I was, but I never let that stop me from trying to do everything they did or even doing a few things they wouldn't have considered doing. Like riding my bike down a hill far too steep to control the speed, or trying to break up a fight between two people bigger than I was. When I was ten, I decided I wanted to join the circus and tried to walk across my mother's clothesline."

Vincent raised one brow. "Did you make it?"

The fact that Vincent had expressed interest rather than

immediately telling her how reckless she had been, as her family would have done, made Natalie blink. She couldn't help but grin. "I made it more than halfway there. Of course, I broke my arm when I fell and just missed cracking my head open, but it was fun while it lasted."

"And you never tried it again, did you?" Vincent crossed his arms. Natalie could swear he was trying to keep from smiling.

She shrugged sheepishly. "Only two more times."

His laugh seemed to come from deep in his chest. It was a low, masculine sound that made Natalie's breath halt somewhere between her lungs and her throat. "I noticed you didn't condemn me," she ventured.

"That's because I didn't have to watch you. You obviously survived it and are here to tell the tale, so I can appreciate your sense of adventure."

"But if you'd been there…"

"I would have tied you up before I let you risk injury again."

She frowned. "Has anyone ever told you that you're a bit of a bully?"

Vincent's expression froze. "I've been told I'm a bit heavy-handed, yes," he said, his voice emotionless.

But she remembered that he had kept his promise not to follow her into the Starson building even though she knew that it was the last thing he had wanted to promise.

"I'm sorry. I didn't mean that the way it sounded," she said. "I'll bet you were the kid everyone turned to for protection when you were young."

"I wouldn't exactly say that," he answered, and then he didn't say anything more. It was clear that he wasn't going to tell her any stories of his childhood. Perhaps she had offended him by seeming to pry.

But later, when she walked over to a window and partially

pulled the shade up, Vincent gently closed his hand over hers and nudged her away from the exposed glass.

"I'm sorry," he said, and she heard genuine regret in his voice.

Without thought, she turned away from the window. She marveled that she didn't feel suffocated by his protective gestures when she had always hated having anyone suggest that she be more careful or less headstrong. No doubt that feeling would return full force if she allowed herself to think about it long enough, because there was no way she could ever be a woman who would allow herself to be led by someone else.

Maybe she hadn't minded Vincent's gesture because he had sounded so apologetic. For that reason, she needed to let him off the hook.

"It's okay. I realize you have to do it, but I do hate being so cooped up," she said wistfully.

He studied her for a minute. "I know." And then he picked up the phone and made a call. Fifteen minutes later, there was a knock at the door.

Vincent answered it, took a package from the small man standing on the threshold, thanked him and shut the door behind him.

"I thought we might do something terribly rash and incredibly headstrong," Vincent said, walking toward her. "Something reckless." His voice sounded like that of a man about to make love to a woman.

Natalie swallowed. Parts of her body she had been unaware of seconds ago came to full, tingling life.

"You're mocking me," she said, "because you know how often I've been called those things."

Slowly he shook his head as he kept advancing. "Not at all, Natalie. I understand how stressful this situation is for you. We've been several places recently but most of them have been inside a building where I have some control over watching the entrances and exits. Your tightrope story showed me how much you probably miss the outdoors. I thought we might go outside for a short time." He handed her the package.

She peered inside. A pair of loose men's overalls, a flannel shirt, a jacket and a cap were inside. She smiled. "For me? Where are we going?"

"Someplace where you can have a few moments of freedom."

He smiled, and Natalie wanted nothing more than to move into his arms, to ask him to kiss her. But as she gazed at him, he came no closer. She remembered the bleak look in his eyes when she had tried to get him to talk about his childhood.

Vincent had secrets, ones he wouldn't share with her, and it was more than just the reporter in her who wanted to know those secrets, to understand this man. It was also the woman. That was a dangerous thought. So instead of asking questions or standing on her toes and kissing Vincent, she hugged the package close. "I'll just get changed," she said, and she rushed back to her room.

When she came out, she looked like a skinny boy in loose clothing. "Well?" she asked.

Vincent grinned. "All right, nice disguise. Now let's go find some hills."

Natalie shook her head in confusion, but she understood when she stepped outside and saw two bicycles sitting next to a tree. Derek Seefer sat in his car on the street.

"Sorry," Vincent told her. "You're too exposed on a bike for me to feel that I'm covering your back as well as I should. Derek will leave some distance, but I don't want anyone to think they can slip up on us."

Vincent's gray eyes were so filled with concern that Natalie couldn't help herself. She stepped forward, rose on her toes and kissed his cheek. His beard was rough beneath her lips, his skin warm. He went rigid at her touch, and she wanted nothing more than to step closer, but she didn't dare.

"It doesn't matter," she whispered, before she stepped back. "What matters is that you and I are going to ride bikes! And I'm going to fly down a hill," she said with a grin.

Then she turned toward Derek's car, waved and blew a kiss. "I hope you can follow me," she called out.

But she never knew whether Derek followed or not, because all she was aware of was Vincent behind her as she hopped on the bike and rode. When she swerved, he swerved. If she turned a corner, he was right on her wheel. If she climbed a hill, he kept right up with her. And when she flew down an even bigger hill, she hit a small rock, losing control of her bike, he flew right after her and was off his bike and at her side almost before she had time to get herself untangled from her bicycle.

She sat up on her elbows.

"Lie down," he ordered her.

She started to protest. He gave her a look that promised instant death if she didn't obey.

"I'm fine," she told him.

"Maybe. Let me make that determination," he told her. "For once, Natalie, could you please follow an order?"

He scrubbed his hand back through his hair, and because he sounded so exasperated and worried and because he had given her this gift, she did as he said and lay back on the ground.

Vincent's hands roamed gently down her arms, down her sides, his touch firm and warm.

She sucked in her breath as heat sizzled through her.

"Does that hurt?" he asked.

"No," she gasped out.

He stopped touching her and stared at her. "Don't lie to me, Natalie."

She shook her head from side to side. "I'm not. It doesn't hurt at all."

Vincent stared at her for a minute and he continued running his hands down her legs. She held her breath.

"Natalie?"

This time, she glared at him. "Vincent, imagine you trying to lie perfectly still while an attractive woman ran her hands over you. I'm not hurt. I'm…"

He gave her a slow grin. "Burning?" he suggested.

She glared. "I'm mildly intrigued by you."

He gave a whoop.

She sat up and started to struggle to her knees.

His hands clamped down on her arms.

"Let me up."

"I will, but first I want you to promise me you're really okay and that you're telling me the truth."

She looked up into his eyes then, nearly losing herself in those serious gray depths. "I'm really fine," she told him. "I'm just a little embarrassed. A lot embarrassed. I fell off my bike. I admitted to liking your touch. I let you tell me to lie down."

He might have grinned again, and she wouldn't have blamed him. He definitely had the upper edge. Instead, he shook his head slowly. He lifted one hand and ran his thumb over her lips. "You were magnificent," he told her. "So alive on that bicycle. People who never ride down hills never fall, but they never fly, either. And if you think I'm going to gloat over you admitting to liking my touch when I'm fighting to keep my hands off you every minute of every day…well, I'm not gloating, Natalie. I'm the one burning. You've got nothing to be embarrassed about. And by the way…"

"Yes?" She waited.

"Thank you for agreeing to lie down while I made sure you were all right. I half expected you to run. If I had been the cause of you hurting yourself, I wouldn't have forgiven myself."

"You're welcome," she said as he helped her to her feet. "What do you think Derek thought of all this?"

"He probably thought he should start looking for a new boss. If he ever let a client do this, I'd probably fire his butt."

She touched his arm. "Maybe you're good at what you do because you're responsive to the needs of your clients."

"My clients need to stay alive."

"There's more to being alive than just being free from danger." She gazed up at him, and his fierce expression held her enthralled. She couldn't even think of looking away, even though she was playing with something more explosive than dynamite could ever be. This was not a man to toy with, and she was not a woman who could ever get involved with a man like him, no matter how much he made her long for dark nights, a soft bed and the weight of his body against hers.

She gave herself a slight shake, trying to rid herself of the feelings coursing through her.

"Thank you for giving me this day. I needed it," she whispered. "I needed a few hours of feeling like a normal person again, like the woman I was before I saw Jason Jamison kill that woman."

She forced herself to throw the darkness back into the conversation, and it finally accomplished what nothing else could. It broke the erotic spell that bound her to Vincent.

He took a deep breath. "You'll understand, though, if we pitch the bikes and ride back with Derek?"

She nodded. "I've had my recess. Life awaits."

But she couldn't help wondering what kind of a life she would have when this was all over. And she wondered what a life without Vincent around would be like. Would she miss him?

"Idiot," she told herself later. Of course she wouldn't miss the damned infuriating, bossy man.

But she was a reporter, and she knew a lie when she heard one. She wanted the threatening notes to stop, she wanted her life to be the way it had been. But she couldn't kid herself that life would really be the same as it had been before. It would be a long time before she forgot Vincent Fortune. He had changed her, and she would spend a long time recovering.

The Fortune men certainly had a way of changing a woman's life, Lily couldn't help thinking as she, Ryan and Linda Faraday rode over to the Armstrongs' house to visit Ricky the next day.

She could barely remember her life before Ryan. He filled her world. And Linda?

Lily took a deep breath. The woman's experience with Cameron Fortune had deprived her of ten years of her life! Lily wondered if Linda hated Cameron or if the fact that he had given her a son would ever make up for any of what he had done.

She hoped this day with Ricky went well. Linda's face looked pinched and drawn. Sitting in the back seat of the car with Linda, Lily reached over and patted the other woman's hand.

"He's a little boy," she whispered.

Linda turned, distress on her face. "I don't know him. He doesn't know me. We don't…fit."

Lily's eyes met her husband's concerned gaze in the rearview mirror. Love filled her heart. Ryan worried about her. And he trusted her. That was why he had asked her to help with Linda. That meant everything to her.

She turned back to Linda. "This won't be a long visit," she said soothingly. "I just want to meet him."

Lily couldn't blame Linda for being distressed. Developing a relationship with her son after ten years was going to be difficult. Linda was clutching her book more tightly than ever.

Lily patted the younger woman's other hand and was surprised when Linda clasped Lily's tightly for a second.

When they pulled up to the house and the Armstrongs came out with Ricky beside them, Lily couldn't help smiling at him. He looked so serious, his blond hair sticking up in one spot. "What a fine young man you are," she said. "I'm Lily."

He eyed her warily, his eyes darting to his mother for a second, then quickly moving away. He mumbled a quick hello.

"Well, this is going to be a bit awkward," Lily confided. "Most first meetings are, but that's okay. We'll just talk about some stuff and the next time we all meet, it will be easier. Okay?"

Ricky gave a stiff nod.

Lily smiled. "All right. Let's start with the basic stuff so we can get to know you. Do you like sports?"

He blinked, then shrugged, his body still tense. "Some."

"To watch or to play?"

"Both. I race at school."

Lily gave him a regal nod of approval. "I always loved to run when I was young. I'll bet you're fast."

He studied her with those solemn eyes. "I'm not too bad."

She grinned at him. "Not too bad is good. Is it all right if we stay outside for a bit?" she asked Nancy Armstrong.

"As long as you like," Nancy said with a smile. "I'll see all of you later." Then she retreated back into the house.

"It's a perfect day for being outside," Lily declared, smiling at Ricky and Linda, even though neither of them were smiling or talking. She sat down on the stoop, and Linda made a small noise.

"Your dress," Linda said, her eyes suddenly intensely worried and darting from side to side. But Lily just shook her head.

"Dresses can be cleaned. You two come sit here beside me. We've got lots of sunshine today. Let's share it. Come on. I don't want to sit here alone."

She didn't suggest that they sit next to each other. It was clear that they both were uncomfortable being around each other. What they needed was a mediator, a friend.

Lily looked up at her husband. He was smiling at her, and

he mouthed the words *I love you* to her. Lily's heart soared. It was amazing how that man could still make her feel like a young girl after all these years.

Linda gazed at her son, her eyes bleak, as if she wasn't sure what to make of him. She glanced back toward the house where Nancy had gone. It was clear that Linda felt like an outsider, but after a moment she sat down.

Ricky sat down on Lily's other side, and she could feel the tension in his thin little body. Both Linda and Ricky looked at her as if she were their lifeline in this trying moment.

"Let's just enjoy the lovely weather today, shall we, all of us? Tell us some things, Ricky. Like what do you think the best name would be for a pet hamster?"

He gave her a sideways look. "You have a hamster?"

Lily laughed. "No, but who knows? I might have one someday. A woman needs to be ready."

Ricky studied her with some confusion. "You're just saying that. You're not going to get a hamster."

She lifted her shoulders in good-natured defeat. "You're probably right. You don't have to answer. You don't even have to talk if you don't want to."

He shrugged. "Okay, then." He sat in silence for a few minutes.

"If you ever did get a hamster, I could think of a name then," he suddenly said.

"We'll wait, then," Lily said. She nodded at him, and he seemed to relax a little, just sitting there with her and his mother as the lemony sunshine poured down on them. And after a few minutes when nothing much had happened, Linda sagged a bit herself, as if she'd been holding her breath until then.

The conversation never really did get started. Somewhere along the way, Linda looked at her son when he wasn't looking at her. There was no longing in her eyes. She watched him as if she didn't know what to make of him.

Lily quietly asked Ricky questions about school. She let Linda sit in the sun, but patted her hand now and then, and Linda seemed to be fine with the human contact, but she never let go of her blue notebook.

When everyone finally had said their goodbyes and Ryan and Lily had dropped Linda off and returned home, he put his hands on Lily's shoulder and kissed her.

"You're a good woman, Lily, my love," he told her.

"It's sad," she said. "They've been robbed of so much."

"It's going to take time," he agreed.

"More than time," she said, shaking her head. "Thank you for taking me to meet them. I'm sorry I doubted you. I didn't understand then but I do now. If the newspapers got hold of their story…it just wouldn't do." She leaned against him and was grateful when his arms closed around her.

Lily closed her eyes and gave a little prayer of thanks for having Ryan. Her life was so blessed while others had experienced such tragedy. She really was a very lucky woman.

Thirteen

Vincent was walking Natalie to the car outside work two nights later when she wheeled and headed back toward the door. "I forgot my notes on the Peacock Festival story," she called back, running for the door and fumbling for her keys. "I won't be more than a minute."

He turned to follow and saw a figure standing half-hidden behind some bushes not twenty feet from Natalie. The darkness obscured the man's face, but it was obvious that he had spotted Vincent. The man turned and ran, knocking over a garbage can.

"Freeze, you piece of scum," Vincent yelled, barreling toward the man. The guy picked up speed, racing toward the center of town.

He ducked and wove, trying to put space between himself and Vincent, but Vincent was running on anger. Adrenaline, hot and thick, pumped through his body. This snake had been spying on Natalie. Maybe he was even the one who wanted to hurt her.

The very thought made Vincent run faster. Rage consumed him as he charged. He was nearly on the guy's back now, could hear the rat panting with the exertion of trying to stay ahead.

"Not going to happen," Vincent snarled as he ran. "I'm on you, buddy."

Suddenly the man reached in his pocket, brought his hand back in a low, scooping motion and opened his palm. Loose change clattered on the ground beneath Vincent's feet and he slipped, but managed to stay upright.

The move to stay balanced, however, gave his prey a chance to gain some distance. The worm darted around the corner and into heavy traffic.

"Hell!" Vincent bellowed as cars came between him and the man who might give him the answers he needed, a man he wanted to pummel until he spilled his secrets and promised that Natalie would be safe.

Vincent pulled up short. In the rush of anger and his urgency to stop this guy, he'd left her alone. He could pursue the man, possibly still catch him once the guy thought he was safe, but what if the guy wasn't working alone?

Not even bothering to debate the issue with himself, Vincent sprinted back toward the newspaper office.

She was there, leaning against the car, waiting, her eyes big in her narrow face. The fear was still with Vincent, his heart practically exploding, it was hammering so hard.

He jogged up beside her. "He got away," he said, his breathing ragged.

Dismay filled her eyes.

"I'm sorry," he told her. And he was. Sorry he had not managed to snag the guy, sorry for more. "I should never have deserted you."

She shook her head. "I don't care about that." Concern blossomed in her eyes. "You're hurt." Natalie reached up and lightly touched his cheek.

Vincent briefly remembered skidding around a corner and scraping up against a brick building in this mad rush to catch the jerk who had dared to spy on Natalie.

"I'm fine." He had to chase the concern from her eyes.

"No, you're not." Her voice came out weakly, not like Natalie at all.

So he did the only thing he could do. He gathered her into his arms and held her. "See, the old heart's still beating."

"Don't joke," she said, placing her hands against his chest. "I hate to think that it would have been my fault if that guy shot at you or something."

That was all it took. He pulled back and gazed into her eyes. "None of this is your fault. Not one bit of it."

"I guess I know that, but—"

Vincent shook his head. "This is my job, Natalie. It's what I do. I just wish I had done it a bit better tonight."

She frowned. "You did. If you hadn't been there with me..."

He didn't want her to even think about that. He didn't want to think about it, either. What he wanted was to wrap himself around her and keep her from all harm, to protect her with his own bone and blood and resolve. But he hadn't lied when he told her that every part of him was working fine. Taking Natalie into his arms again wasn't an option, because given the heightened state of his emotions, if he touched her again, he would kiss her. And if he kissed her, then—

Damn his uncontrollable emotions! He was a man who felt too powerfully, and lust and anger weren't that far apart. He wouldn't subject Natalie to either.

Vincent took a deep breath. He looked down into Natalie's pretty green eyes. "Let's just consider ourselves lucky that everything worked out tonight," he said thickly. "Come on. I'll get you home. There's nothing more to worry about tonight."

* * *

Natalie worried that she was going to be the first client to drive Vincent nuts. Her mother had always told her that she was headstrong, and that was probably true.

Things would be simpler if she would agree to stick to writing about the Peacock Festivals and chili fests that the newspaper wanted her to. All of those events took place in very public areas, and usually they took place in the bright sunshine. A woman wasn't likely to be stalked by a potential murderer in such circumstances.

Her heart nearly flipped out of her chest when she realized what might have happened the other night if Vincent hadn't been with her to chase away the guy who was outside the newspaper office waiting for her. She hated the fact that Vincent was beating himself up for leaving her alone. Didn't he know that she knew he had to go after the bad guys of the world? It was his nature, as much a part of him as his gray eyes or his sexy grin. And having the scumbags know that she had a protector who could chase them down and beat them to a pulp made her feel so much safer.

Who was she kidding? Just being in Vincent's presence made her feel safe. It also made her feel dangerous, because when he had come back from that chase and she had finally realized that he was okay and the world had righted itself, she had felt such a rush of desire. All she had wanted to do was to burrow into his skin, to taste him, to touch her lips to the hard muscles of his chest. She had wanted his arms around her, his naked body against hers….

"Agh!" She threw down the piece of paper she was holding.

Vincent strode in from the next room. When he looked around and didn't find any intruders, he raised one brow. "Problem?"

Only that she wanted to make love with her bodyguard. Oh no, that wasn't a problem. That was proof that she was certifiably insane because if ever two people didn't belong together, it was Vincent the Protector of Women and Natalie the Woman Who Would Not Be Protected.

She took a deep breath, dared a look into those gray eyes that haunted her nights. "I need to go interview some of the people on this list. I didn't exactly obtain it legally, or at least not ethically, and I don't want to drag you into a situation where you'd be compromised."

He gave her a long, assessing look that melted her bones, and crossed his arms over that impressive chest of his. "You're not putting your toe outside the door without me beside you, and if you feel that you have to speak to a few of those people on that list in order to be happy and satisfied, then I'm with you."

Would interviewing these people satisfy her? Hardly, when she was denying herself the right to touch Vincent. But at least conducting these interviews might bring her closer to being able to help her friends, and it might keep her mind occupied for a few hours.

"Let's go, then," she said. She led the way out of the building.

Thirty minutes later, she and Vincent knocked on the door of one Henry Dallford. Mr. Dallford came to the door using a walker, and he looked frightened when he opened the door and saw two strangers.

For the first time, Natalie wondered if she was doing the right thing.

"I'm from the *San Antonio Express-News*," Natalie began to say, whipping out her ID and waiting for the man to study it. "I wonder if I might ask you a few questions for a story I'm planning."

Mr. Dallford backed away slightly.

"Maybe you'd like to see an example of Ms. McCabe's work first, Mr. Dallford," Vincent suggested. He pulled a newspaper out of his back pocket and showed the man a copy of an article Natalie had written on a children's after-school program.

She gave Vincent a confused look.

He smiled. "I snagged it on the way out the door just in case we needed it."

"Who are you?" Mr. Dallford barked, craning his neck to see all of Vincent.

"I'm her bodyguard."

Natalie's eyes widened. If they wanted to make the man feel safe, telling him that he was talking to a woman who needed a bodyguard probably wasn't the way to do it.

Mr. Dallford's eyebrows were in danger of climbing right off his head, they were raised that high. "Think I'm a danger to her, do you?" Mr. Dallford gave Vincent a knowing look.

Vincent held out his hands in a gesture of helplessness. "I can't be too careful with her safety, Henry. How do I know that walker isn't a ruse?"

Henry gave a raspy chuckle. "A woman with a bodyguard wanting to interview me. That just about beats it all. You want to come in?"

Instantly Natalie wanted to reach out and protect Henry. "Maybe we could talk out in the garden I saw when we came in. There are some tables, and it didn't look as if anyone would come by and disturb us."

"That's because everyone here is too old to appreciate a nice day. 'Cept me, of course. A bodyguard," he said again, smiling and shaking his head. "Let's go."

Natalie started to reach out and help Henry, but Vincent put his hand on her arm and stopped her.

Henry instantly stood taller. "He's right. I'm not too old to get around yet. A man does what he can for as long as he can, ain't that right, Mr. Bodyguard?"

"Absolutely the gospel truth, Henry. And you can call me Vincent."

"Well, Vincent, this bodyguard stuff…do you ever get to kiss her?"

Instantly, Vincent froze, but he quickly recovered. "Not as often as I'd like to."

At first, Natalie thought Henry was choking, but then she realized that he was laughing.

"Men," she said, and both men laughed again.

They finally made it out to the tables, and Natalie prepared to take notes. "I've been speaking to a group of seniors in the area who have invested some of their money and have not been happy with the results. I know this is a very personal area, but I was wondering if you've had any recent experiences with Starson Investments."

Henry sat up straighter. "I might have," he said reluctantly.

"You wouldn't happen to have dealt with Brad Herron, would you?"

It was as if all the air went out of the old man. He slumped in his chair and covered his forehead with one shaky hand. But when he finally pulled his hand away and revealed his face again, it was Vincent he turned toward. "A man saves his whole life to leave his kids and his grandkids something, you know?"

"That's what a man does," Vincent agreed, his voice filled with understanding.

"You don't want to get old. You don't want your grandkids to remember you as old. You want them to look up to you, to think that you did something with your life, something good."

"A man who feels that way has already done something good," Vincent commented.

Henry made a slashing motion with his fragile, bony hand. "It's not enough. I want to go out feeling like a man. You know what that's like, don't you?"

"Women don't understand that sometimes," Vincent commented.

Natalie frowned, but she didn't interfere when Henry nodded and suddenly looked tougher. "Exactly. The nurses that come to see me...some of them just think of me as a patient.

They think I should be happy just because I'm getting enough fiber or because I managed to eat all my oatmeal without dropping any on my shirt. They don't see me as a man anymore." He cast an angry look Natalie's way.

"She's not like that," Vincent said. "She cares. She knows a lot of people in the same situation as you, if your situation is what I think it is. She's going to try to do something about it. To give you and the others back your dignity. If she succeeds, you'll get justice, maybe even vengeance. If I were you, that's what I'd want."

"Damn straight," Henry said, banging his hand on the patio table so hard that Natalie was afraid he might break something. But she refused to show her concern. Vincent was right. Henry needed to feel like a man, and she needed to give him that gift if she could.

"Tell me what happened with you and Brad Herron," she said.

"I'll tell you what happened with me," Henry told her. "I wasn't in my right mind after my wife died. Lorelei was everything to me. So when Herron came and offered to make things easier, to take over all the decision-making about my investments, I let him do it. I don't know what happened. I know that there was a lot of back and forth, trades and such, but I didn't handle any of it. Maybe I said yes to some things. I don't really know. I wasn't paying much attention at the time. When it was over…" He covered his eyes with his hand again.

"Your money was gone," Natalie said gently.

"Almost all of it. By the time I'm done living, there won't be one good thing to leave my grandkids."

"Except the knowledge that you fought back and you fought hard," Vincent suggested.

Henry looked up, his eyes filled with tears he tried to blink away. Natalie tried not to look. She didn't want to embarrass him, but she couldn't escape the look that passed between him and Vincent. It was the look of men who burned to see justice done, no matter the cost.

"Do it if you can," Henry told her. "I'll tell you what little I know. Not that anyone will listen. People just think that an old man like me is stupid. Once you're past a certain age, you become easy to ignore. Invisible."

"People like that make me want to kick them in the teeth," Vincent said. He and Henry exchanged a look. Then Henry turned to Natalie.

"I wouldn't mind seeing Brad Herron kicked in the teeth."

Natalie gave him a half smile. "I'm only a reporter, Henry, but if he's done something wrong, I'll see what I can do about kicking him around with words."

Henry shrugged. "It's better than nothing." And he took a deep breath to begin his story.

When they finally left Henry at his door, Natalie didn't have much more information, but she had a glimmer of a suspicion starting to gather speed, one that had taken root some time ago and had gained a little more credibility after she found that file on Brad's computer. Now she was pretty certain she was on the right track.

And Henry was standing a bit taller, his handshake firm.

"Don't let her get hurt," he told Vincent. "She's got important things to do. And she's not bad-looking, either," Henry added with just a hint of a twinkle in his eye.

"She's worth protecting on a number of levels," Vincent agreed.

"Hope you get to kiss her again soon."

Vincent grinned. "You're a devil, Henry."

"Used to be."

"Still are," Natalie said with a pained expression. "Men."

Both Henry and Vincent laughed. Natalie was glad Vincent had helped Henry regain some of his dignity. The more she saw of him, the more she was forced to admit that Vincent Fortune really was a remarkable man.

But there was one thing bothering her. When Henry had prompted Vincent to kiss her, he hadn't said that he would.

And he hadn't said that he wouldn't, either.

Fourteen

Natalie had been wonderful with Henry, Vincent thought. She really had a talent for getting people to talk about themselves.

It was because she cared so much, he realized. To Natalie, the people she interviewed weren't subjects. They were real people with hopes and dreams and disappointments, and she worried about them.

"I don't know for sure what Brad Herron did, but I know that he did something bad," she said when they were back in her apartment. "To think that anyone would take advantage of an old man right after he had lost his wife of sixty years. That weasel! He cares so much about looking good and scoring, but I'll bet he doesn't even remember Henry's name. I've got to find out the whole story and write about it, Vincent." She had paced up and down the room and had stopped right in front of him, her head tipped up, her green eyes flashing with passion.

Vincent took a deep breath. He tried to think logically instead of thinking about the way Natalie looked right now, as if she would turn to flame in a man's arms.

He shook his head. She was looking as if she wanted to march off right now and slay dragons, or, at the very least, kick Brad Herron.

"I'm with you one hundred percent, Natalie, but be careful about backing a man like Herron into a corner. Rats tend to attack when they have nowhere to run."

She took a deep breath and nodded, crossing her arms over her chest. "Don't worry. I'm not going to back him into a corner. At least, not yet."

Without thought, Vincent cupped his palms around Natalie's shoulders. "You make me crazy. You know that?"

She looked up into his eyes. "I…" she began, but he wasn't through with her.

"And what was that about Herron only caring about looking good and scoring? What exactly *has* he said to you?"

"Nothing I wanted to hear," she whispered as Vincent leaned close. "Not from him, anyway."

Vincent fought for control when there was none to be had. "Natalie…"

"You think I want a man like Brad trying to paw me? A man without a shred of honor or decency?"

"A man with a sense of honor and decency wouldn't touch you when he knew that he had nothing to offer you," he said, fighting the desire that threatened to overpower him.

"Maybe I don't want that much tonight. Maybe all you need to offer is—"

"Natalie?" Vincent gazed into her eyes.

"I was never any good at this kind of thing," she suddenly whispered. "I spend my days getting people to tell me things they don't always want to tell me. I don't want to convince you to do something you don't want to do."

"Who says I don't want to kiss you?"

She shivered in his grasp. "Were we talking about kissing?"

"I was," he said, even though he had been thinking about doing a whole lot more. He really wasn't sure that he could stop once he'd started something with Natalie.

It was as if the air went right out of Natalie. "I was talking about kissing, too," she confessed. And as if to make her point, she suddenly rose up on her toes, curled her arms around his neck and pressed her lips to his.

Vincent's senses exploded. He gathered her to him and tasted her. He slid his hands up beneath her shirt and slicked his palms over the clean, velvet planes of her back. She was honey and sunshine and passion that drove him to the edge.

He nipped at her lips, licked them, his tongue finding hers. Her body was taut against his, her breasts against his chest, and he wanted to slick her out of those soft jeans and expose her even softer skin. He wanted to devour her, to lay her down and feast on every inch of her.

"You make me crazy, too, you know?" she whispered against his lips, her voice husky. A tremor ran through her and he started to carry her to the nearest flat surface and take this thing to its logical conclusion. To hell with tomorrow. To hell with the fact that he had to go back to being the man who kept her safe in the days to come.

"It's a good thing we're only going to be together short-term," she said. "You make me feel weak."

She made him feel weak, too, at a time when he had to keep his senses about him. He couldn't keep her safe if he was obsessed with making love to her. Not that he wasn't already burning to have her, but Vincent was pretty damn sure that once they actually made love he would think of her night and day. He might make mistakes. She might pay the price.

It was never a good idea for a bodyguard to get involved with his client...or for a man to let his emotions run rampant.

He kissed her once more, gently. He slid his hands away and patted her clothing back into place.

"You're not weak," he told her. "You're the strongest woman I know. And you're right about the short-term. We'd probably kill each other if we had to spend too long together. You'd always want to lead and so would I."

Even as he said the words, he hated himself for saying them. Natalie's eyes registered a glimmer of pain at his withdrawal.

He wanted to punch something hard, hit something with his fists. But mostly he wanted to kick himself. If he hurt her or let her get hurt in any way, there would be hell to pay, and he would be the man who would be administering the punishment.

"Tomorrow we'll both be happy we didn't do this," he said, half to himself.

Natalie nodded. "You're right. I'm glad we didn't go through with it. It was just that emotional encounter with Henry that caused us to need some kind of release."

She was talking nonsense just as he had been, and both of them knew it. Vincent only hoped that by tomorrow, the heat would have died down.

He hoped like hell that tomorrow was an easier day.

Lily had just left Ryan's office the next morning when his secretary knocked on the door. "Excuse me, Mr. Fortune, but I was just opening the mail and this—" She held out one hand in a helpless gesture, staring with fearful eyes at the piece of paper in her other hand.

Unease shifted in Ryan's chest, but then he dismissed the emotion. In his position, lots of bad news as well as good came over the transom. And nothing in a piece of paper could be as bad as the news he carried in his heart, the knowledge that he was dying.

Reaching for the paper, he read the note. Carefully controlling his expression, he thanked his secretary and asked her to locate Patrick and Blake. He needed to see them right away.

Within the hour, the men arrived, both wearing troubled expressions.

"Look at this," Ryan said. He held out the missive with its dark type cut and pasted crudely in position.

Watch out. I remember everything, and I'll never forget or forgive.

For a moment there was silence. Then Patrick looked at Blake. "Do you think it's from Jason?"

Blake ran a shaking, weary hand through his hair. "It could be. My son killed his own brother, he killed twice more, and the second transporter is still in the hospital. I—I don't really even know him. It could be him."

"It could be anyone," Ryan insisted. "Do you think Jamison is still in the area?"

"Maybe not, but this isn't something we can ignore," Patrick argued.

"All right, let's decide what needs to be done," Ryan said, "but I don't want Lily to know. She was just here before the note was delivered. If she had seen it… Well, that's my one request."

The truth was that a threat didn't mean much to him right now. He'd lived through his share, and death was going to come to him soon, anyway. If it weren't for the fact that Lily would be frightened by such tactics, and the fact that Natalie McCabe had also received another note and was still in danger, Ryan might have ignored it.

"I don't know what needs to be done, what the legal procedure should be," Blake said quietly. "But I know what I'm going to do."

Patrick and Ryan turned to him and waited.

"I'm going to go find my son. Emmett. Whoever sent this note has declared himself your enemy, which makes him my enemy now. I've grown to know you, and I can't just sit by and let someone threaten you if there's any chance I can stop it. No one seems to have a clue where Jason is. Emmett might be able to help."

"And you know where Emmett is?" Patrick asked.

Blake blew out a long, audible breath. "Wish I did. I do have a few ideas, though. Emmett's a loner, but he's a good man. At least, he was the last time I saw him. I don't know his state of mind. I definitely don't know if he'll agree to try to track down his brother, but it's the only thing I can think of to do."

Blake's shoulders sagged as he spoke, and Ryan knew what this was costing him. He had lost two sons, one to murder and one to madness. Now he was pinning his hopes on Emmett, and he was afraid that he might lose him, too.

"You're a good man, Blake," Ryan said, his voice rough. "I wish we'd had more years to know each other."

"So do I," Blake said in a croaking voice. "As for the good-man part, thank you, but I don't buy that. I'm a man who neglected a son and let him become a murderer, but I intend to do my best to stop him from killing again. It's all I can do."

Patrick walked over and shook his hand. "I hope you find Emmett."

"I'll find him," Blake promised, but as Ryan took his hand and the two men stared into each other's eyes, Ryan knew that he might be gone before Blake fulfilled his mission.

"See you around," Ryan promised.

"Absolutely," Blake agreed, but Ryan saw the regret in Blake's expression. This very well might be a final goodbye.

He hoped that he was wrong, but who knew? For the first time in his life, events were simply spinning out of control.

Another day had passed, and Natalie was getting antsy. The holiday season only served to emphasize what her friends had lost. She needed more information on what Brad had been up to. She'd done plenty of research on the Internet and knew what the possibilities for corruption in this case might be, but that wasn't good enough. There had to be concrete evidence, proof. When she remembered Henry Dallford's face, the face of a man who had been beaten up by life, or, more specifically, by a corrupt broker, she knew she had to do something. The thought that one of Brad's victims might die of old age or heartache before justice was done ate at her. Pacing the floor, she dredged up ideas, then tossed them aside.

"I wish…" she whispered to herself, and automatically she realized that she had been using that phrase a lot lately, not just in relationship to this case, either. Vincent brought out the most inappropriate of her wishes. The memory of his lips on hers crept in no matter how hard she tried to ignore them. The taste of him was still with her even though it had been a full day since he had kissed her.

"You're an idiot, Natalie," she told herself. Here she was lusting after Vincent when she had serious work to do.

But where to start? There were gaps in her information. What was she going to do in order to fill in those gaps?

The most obvious solution was to go to the source, to see Brad one more time. But Brad would just try to grab her again, and right now she didn't think she could take Brad's wandering hands when the only person whose hands she wanted on her were Vincent's.

She would have to talk to Neil. He didn't seem to like Brad very much. Maybe he would be willing to tell her something. Visiting The Ladder again wasn't a prospect she was looking forward to, but there didn't seem to be any alternative.

"Can't go without protection, though," she said. And that was where she stalled. Vincent was in the spare bedroom doing paperwork for his business. She was pretty sure he didn't usually spend this many hours on one client, and even though she knew he would consider it his duty and responsibility to escort her around the clock, she didn't want to disturb him.

Besides, there was the "Vincent" factor. When he was sitting near, observing her and Neil, she just knew she wouldn't be able to keep one hundred percent of her attention on her subject. But she needed protection. Vincent wouldn't let her leave alone.

"Okay, okay," she muttered, and making a quick decision, she dialed a number. "Marty?" she said when her brother picked up. "I need a big favor and I don't want to do a lot of explaining. Let's just say that I need you to give me a ride, and it has to do with work."

As if she wasn't going to have to offer a thousand explanations later.

Nevertheless, Marty promised to be there in ten minutes. When she heard the car pull up in the drive, she was ready. Quickly, she moved to the spare bedroom doorway.

"I'm sorry, Vincent, but I have to go to The Ladder. Don't worry, though. My brother Marty is giving me a lift. I guarantee that he won't let anything happen to me. I'll call when I'm ready to come home."

Vincent gave her a startled look. He got to his feet.

She turned and moved toward the door.

"It's not going to happen that way, Natalie."

"Vincent, you have work to do," she said, and she kept walking.

"I most certainly do. You're it." His voice was like steel. She turned and looked at him and saw that his eyes were just as cold.

She glared at him. "All right, follow me if you have to, but I'm still going with Marty. He's already here, and I don't want to have to explain who you are. He doesn't know that I have any reason to have a bodyguard. I don't want him to know."

Hustling outside, with Vincent right behind her, she climbed into Marty's car. Vincent got into his own vehicle.

"Who's that guy, Nat?" Marty asked.

"A friend," she said, fastening her seat belt.

Marty raised his brows as she told him where she was going. "Looks like one pretty pissed-off friend. He your boy-friend? You guys have a fight?"

What was she supposed to say? His guess was the easiest thing to explain.

"Something like that," she said.

"Looks big. Looks mad. Not that I don't understand that. You have a way of ticking guys off. Still, you're my sister. I'm allowed to be mad at you. He's not. I can beat him up for you if you like."

Natalie gave him a get-real look, which he missed since he was driving pretty fast. Marty had always liked to drive fast.

"Don't touch him," she commanded, because even though she was sure Vincent could best Marty in a fight, she wasn't sure he could handle all three of her brothers at once. She didn't want him hurt. She just wanted to stop lusting over him when she was supposed to be working. And Neil was so shy, she was afraid Vincent would scare him away if he got too close and Neil suspected they were together. She just needed a few minutes alone with Neil.

"I could lose him for you," Marty added.

Just a few minutes, she thought. Was that such an impossible thing? She had once had a normal life where she came and went as she pleased, where there wasn't a man like Vincent who was in her thoughts all the time, making her want things that just couldn't be. She couldn't be near him anymore today.

"Do that. Lose him," she said.

He did. Marty twisted and turned. He veered and took side streets and drove through alleys Natalie had never seen. It took them an hour to get to The Ladder when it normally only took minutes. By now, she was beginning to get worried and re-think her position. She felt perfectly safe with Marty, but she knew that Vincent wouldn't feel that way. He considered her his personal responsibility. No doubt he was going crazy wondering where she was. Probably he had already left The Ladder and had had the police issue an APB on her.

She had better get this interview with Neil over with quickly. "I'll call you when I'm ready to go home," she told Marty as she got out of the car.

"You do that, and when your work here is done, I'm going to want some answers."

As if she hadn't expected that. Weakly, she promised to give him a full rundown on what was going on in her life. Then she stepped into The Ladder.

Vincent tried to still the thudding of his heart. Where was she? And how had that guy lost him? Was he really her brother?

"Yeah, looked like her," he muttered, which made him feel only slightly better. The guy would try to take care of her, but then big brother didn't know what he was up against. He didn't understand the real danger Natalie was in. Did she?

Vincent rounded another corner. Might as well go back to The Ladder. Sooner or later, she would show up there. And yes, he was pretty sure Natalie understood what she was up against in Jason Jamison. No one understood better than her, considering the fact that she had been there right when he'd killed Melissa, when he'd looked her straight in the eyes. She had read the notes.

Pretending she was too tough to care, trying to go on as if life had not changed wouldn't minimize the danger, but that was what she was doing. He understood why. It was how strong people went on.

Natalie wasn't the kind to give up and give in when adversity stared her in the face. He knew that, had thought about that part of her a lot. Hell, he'd just thought of *her* a lot. She was always on his mind. The taste and feel of her were always with him. And the concern, the thought that someone might someday slip past him and get to her or that she might walk into danger without realizing it…

Like tonight, for instance.

Fear slammed into him. Where the hell was she, damn it?

He rounded a corner, his tires squealing and protesting the speed and his reckless maneuver.

Reckless? Reckless didn't even begin to describe how he felt right now.

And when he found Natalie? *If* he found Natalie?

"Don't even think that," he whispered. He would find her, and when he did, there would be hell to pay.

Fifteen

The Ladder was just as it had been the last time she had been here, Natalie thought. Same white holiday lights, almost the same people seated at the bar. The billiard tables were busy. Neil was getting ready to toss a few darts. There was no hint of Brad, but she was sure he would show up sooner or later.

Natalie took a deep breath and plunged into the room. She made a beeline toward Neil. The time for being coy was over.

"Hey there," she said when he turned to look at her. "Good to see you."

He gave her a strange, angry look. "You haven't been here for a while."

She shrugged. "Life got a bit busy. You know?"

He didn't smile, but he nodded. "That happens."

"Besides, I was getting tired of bars."

He frowned. "But you're here."

"Yes, well…" She looked at him.

"Would you like some dinner?" he asked suddenly. "There's a restaurant two doors down that I go to sometimes."

Good. They could talk there without her having to worry about Brad showing up and interrupting. Natalie was glad that she hadn't been forced to waste too much time. She wanted to get this information, but she also wanted to get this over with as soon as possible.

"That sounds fine," she agreed. She followed Neil out the door of The Ladder and down the street two doors to a restaurant with a big plate glass window.

"Josie, a seat near the window, all right?" Neil asked when they went inside.

"Like always, Mr. Gerard," the waitress said. She sat them in a green plaid booth looking out on the dark street.

"I like to be able to see what's going on," he said, even though Natalie hadn't asked about his preference.

"It's a nice view," she agreed, even though it wasn't.

Neil drummed his fingers on the table. He looked distinctly uncomfortable. "I suppose you really came looking for Brad," he finally said.

Uh-oh. "No," she said uneasily. "I didn't. Brad's a little forward for me."

Neil leaned across the table as if he was suddenly much more interested in the conversation and in her. Natalie fought the urge to lean back and away from him. She glanced out the window and her heart dropped to her shoes.

Vincent's car was driving past. No doubt he was on the way to The Ladder, but his headlights caught her in its glare. He stopped the car right there and suddenly swerved into a parking space. When he exited the car, there was murder in his eyes.

She almost got up to go meet him, to try to explain what couldn't possibly be explained. At least not to his liking. She had essentially slipped out on him again, followed her story, changed the rules. It didn't matter that she felt bad about it. And she did feel bad, and yet…

Natalie turned back to Neil. Surely the man knew something that would help people like Mrs. Morgensen, even if he didn't know all the details of how Brad handled his clients.

"Natalie?" Neil asked, and she realized that she hadn't even been looking at Neil.

She turned back to him just as Vincent came in the door, looking like a giant storm cloud. He didn't look her way but instead asked the waitress to seat him in a booth not six feet away from her and Neil.

Natalie practically squirmed in her seat. She stared at Neil, hoping to get her information and get out of here quickly. "Yes?" she said.

"How come you were hanging around with Brad if you didn't really like him?" Neil was asking, a frown between his eyes. "What was that about?"

Natalie tried to concentrate on Neil even though she wanted very badly to turn and look at Vincent, to explain what she was doing. "It's hard to know a person until you've spoken with them several times," she said to Neil, spinning what she hoped was a credible rationale. "Sometimes men pretend to be players when they're really unsure of themselves. I thought maybe Brad was someone like that. Do you think that's possible?"

Neil leaned forward even farther, and Natalie almost thought she heard a growl emanating from Vincent. Of course, she was wrong. She could see him from the corner of her eye, and he hadn't moved. He was drinking coffee and appeared to be reading a newspaper.

She wished she could forget that he was sitting there, and that he was probably fuming, but no matter what his mood or how invisible he was to everyone else, she just could never be unaware of Vincent. Her heart was pounding ridiculously hard.

"I think Brad is just what he seems," Neil said.

Natalie struggled to tune Vincent out and pay more attention to Neil. She nodded at Neil encouragingly. "So you've worked with him long enough to know him pretty well."

Neil's expression darkened. "We don't talk all that much. I'm not much of a talker."

"But you're an account manager." She looked at him as if being an account manager was something she deeply admired. For a second, she thought she heard Vincent's paper rustle.

"Yes, I am." Neil gave her a tight smile. "An account manager doesn't always have to be a talker. As long as the job gets done, that's all that matters."

"And I take it you get the job done." She smiled at him even though she could practically feel heat radiating off Vincent.

Neil smiled but didn't say anything.

"So Brad is the one who visits the clients?" she prodded.

"Mostly, yes." He handed her a menu. "You like a man who can talk to people?" His voice sounded somewhat resentful.

Natalie looked up. "I'm not sure that's always an asset. Someone like Brad could hurt people if they believed everything he said. I mean, how would you feel if Brad took advantage of one of your clients the way he takes advantage of women?"

Instantly, Neil was alert. Concern warmed his usual shy demeanor. He slid one hand across the table even though he didn't touch her. "Are we talking about Brad and you?"

She shook her head, almost more aware of Vincent's charged silence than Neil's apparent concern.

"No, it's just that he seems to be in a position where he could hurt people if he wanted to. That bothers me."

"You're talking about women." Neil's normally soft voice turned hard. He frowned. "Brad forgets himself at times. He says things he shouldn't, goes too far, does dumb things."

"I'm not talking about women, really. I don't think that

most of the women Brad dates are the kind looking for forever," she said, trying to smile and keep things light. But it was difficult to feign lightheartedness when she was so concerned about what was happening between herself and Vincent. Vincent was upset with her, but he hadn't said a word. He was waiting things out, even though she wouldn't have blamed him if he had made a fuss. His job wasn't to make sure she got her story but to make sure she stayed alive, and she had crossed him at every turn. The guilt of causing him a moment's worry ate at her. She realized that she cherished his good opinion and she didn't want to be a person like Brad, a liar who hurt people.

"Are you different from Brad's women? Are you looking for forever?"

Natalie blinked and stared at Neil. She felt as if both men were completely focused on her. She never had been looking for forever, but lately, with Vincent, she wanted—

"No," she said more forcefully than she had intended. She was supposed to be working, to be paying complete attention to Neil, not wishing she were at a table with Vincent who could never offer forever and who was so very wrong for her.

Natalie sighed. "I'm sorry I brought you out tonight to talk about Brad," she said to Neil and realized that she was telling the truth. "It's just that I know people he may have hurt. Senior citizens he may have lied to. I thought you might be concerned since Starson is also your company."

Neil was frowning. "You're right. This is bad. I *am* concerned. So you think Brad might be scamming people?"

"I don't know that. I think he may be doing what he seems good at, leading them to do things they're not ready for."

"And you thought I might help?"

She hesitated. "Yes, I thought you might."

He smiled. "Why exactly did you think that?"

She shrugged. "Maybe just because you seem to be different from Brad. You haven't tried anything with me. You accept the fact that I might prefer playing darts and billiards to being fed fake compliments."

He nodded slowly. "I don't think Brad has hurt anyone, but now that I know you're concerned, I'll keep my eyes and ears open. Do you have any names you could give me?"

She looked at him. The names were there in her mind.

"No," she said. She wasn't willing to do that. "The stories aren't mine to share." She rose and said goodbye, and Neil smiled at her.

Natalie felt Vincent watching her as she walked away. She wanted to turn around and tell him that she was sorry, but of course she couldn't do that.

Exiting the building, she quickly punched in Marty's number. He must have been waiting around the corner, because he appeared almost instantly. Not a surprise.

She waited until Vincent had left the building before she got in the car.

"All right, we talk now," Marty said.

She couldn't. Vincent hadn't even looked at her when he walked out of The Ladder. She couldn't wait to get home and explain everything to him. She had disappointed him and lied. No wonder Vincent didn't want a woman like her.

Pain sliced through her. She realized that Vincent's good opinion was beginning to matter too much to her. She was starting to care too much.

Turning to Marty, she gave her head a tight shake. "I can't tonight, Marty, please. Vincent and I have to talk. You understand. You've been there before." Marty had had a steady string of girlfriends ever since he was in his teens.

He hesitated. Then he nodded. "All right, but if you don't spill everything soon, sis—"

"I will. I promise." At least she would tell him as much as she could.

They drove home quickly. She thanked him and gave him a hug and went into the building, aware of the moment Vincent walked in behind her.

Fishing out her keys, she walked up to her apartment door. And stopped dead in her tracks.

"Oh, no. Please," she said, as she looked at the splintered lock.

The door was still open a crack. She started to push on it.

"Leave it," a hard voice commanded behind her.

She turned to see Vincent striding down the hallway. His mouth was set in a thin line, his gray eyes filled with rage. Every muscle radiated hot steel. Anger.

"We'll talk," he said, his voice cold and clipped. "In a minute. Wait here."

And then he quietly slipped inside.

Vincent fought to control his emotions as he made his way through Natalie's apartment. The place was eerily quiet but appeared to be untouched. He looked behind doors, in closets, in the shower, anywhere a man could possibly hide, but whoever had been there was already gone.

That didn't matter. The fact that someone had dared to come in here at all brought rage rushing to the forefront. Natalie's actions of late, the fact that she had so little regard for her own well-being, brought all the feelings he'd suppressed rushing to the surface.

He stalked to the door, drew her inside. Once she was inside, he shoved the door closed and turned to her, trying not to think that if not for chance and dumb luck, those beautiful green eyes might be sightless right now. "Talk, Natalie. Now. What in hell were you thinking tonight?" The words came out cold and rough.

She winced, those green eyes huge. She opened her mouth.

"Hell, no, don't even bother answering, because we both

already know the answer, don't we?" he yelled. "Do you realize what could have happened to you if I hadn't seen you in that restaurant? You were completely without protection during that time. Do you always just jump into danger without knowing or caring what you're getting into? You're a witness to a murder. There's a man out there on the loose who doesn't want you to testify. If he finds you, if I can't stop him from getting to you—" He broke off, knowing he would completely lose it if he envisioned her maimed or worse.

She stood there for a moment, not saying a thing. Then she pulled her shoulders back and stood taller. "I'm sorry," she said, holding her head high.

Her apology released a floodgate of feelings he could no longer hold back. "Sorry doesn't make it right, Natalie." He looked at the door, at the broken lock. "Damn it, Natalie, you saw that last note, you see this door. He's close. He's watching you. What if—"

"I know. Do you think I don't know?" Her voice quivered.

"No, I don't think you do. You say you know, but tomorrow, given the chance, you would do it again. You charge ahead without thought to how that affects your personal safety. You don't care about anything except getting your damned story."

He whirled and savagely slammed his hand into the wall, standing there breathing in great, heaving gulps. "You make me totally nuts, Natalie. Do you know that?"

"I guess I do," she admitted.

That was it. He whirled, shoving closer into her face. "No!" he roared. "You don't know a thing." He balled his hands into fists, struggling for control. "Come on, pack your stuff."

"What?"

He frowned. "Pack a bag, Natalie. You're not staying here. I'm taking you to a hotel."

Natalie's brows furrowed. "No, I—"

"Yes. Someone knows where you are and now they've breached your door. You're not safe here."

"I'm fine." But she looked at the useless broken lock, and for a moment, Vincent thought she was going to faint. He almost moved forward and drew her into his arms. He wanted nothing more than to stroke her hair and tell her that everything would be okay. But she was too smart for that. The truth was he didn't know if everything would be okay. He didn't know if he could protect her completely.

The very thought scalded him. To find her missing again…to find that someone had gotten to her when he hadn't been there to save her…

"To hell with your need for control, Natalie. I don't care how much you want to stay. I don't care how much trouble you are or how angry it makes you. Your feelings don't count in this case, because the end result is that I'm taking you somewhere safe. If that means I have to throw you over my shoulder to do it, it's happening. Live with that. To hell with your need to control the situation. Your way isn't safe, so it's not happening. Just get your stuff."

For two seconds, he saw the pain in her eyes before she closed them. Her body swayed and he reached out, but then he drew back.

Anger at her, at himself, seared his soul.

"Get your stuff now, Natalie, or I'll pack for you."

She opened her eyes and looked up at him. She tilted her head back and gave him a small nod. And then she made her way to a closet and pulled out a suitcase. Her shoulders sagged, and Vincent realized that he had finally succeeded in breaking her spirit, in damaging the part of her that made her who she was.

He cursed himself, but he didn't back down.

Sixteen

The hotel was a bit nicer than most of the ones she'd stayed in before, Natalie realized as she walked into the beige-and-jade suite and noticed the plush carpeting, the array of sofas and occasional tables sporting crystal and silver. None of that mattered.

She had damaged Vincent's trust in her. She had abused her position. He was right about those things, but...

Vincent had spoken to her as if he disliked her, as if she were a burden. The memory of a long-ago day when her mother had castigated her in front of her friends for staying out ten minutes late crept in. She had been twenty-three. It hadn't mattered. Her pride hadn't mattered one whit. And it didn't matter to Vincent.

Pain choked her. She picked up her bag that Vincent had carried in and took it into the bedroom. Slowly, she began to unpack.

It was obvious that Vincent wished he could end this job quickly. Her parents had often felt the same way.

Natalie wrestled with her pride. She fought the tears that threatened to clog her throat. She continued unpacking, fighting to stay strong and upright. Wishing she didn't care what Vincent thought.

But she did care. He was right about some things, after all.

He had hurt her. Damn him for a loud, heavy-handed, blundering male. Yes, she had behaved recklessly, Vincent thought, but she *had* at least called her brother, a person she had always trusted to protect her. Wouldn't any person be spitting mad if they had a jailer all the time the way she did? And wasn't it her spirit and her bravery and her need to pursue justice that he admired? Didn't he love the way she stood up to him and demanded her place?

Wouldn't he confront any man who tried to crush her enthusiasm for all things good and right? And wasn't he really mad at himself for not realizing that someone had discovered where she lived?

Was he a total jerk or what?

"So what the hell are you still doing standing in here when she's in there?" he muttered.

He stared around him at the lavish empty room and realized that it held no appeal for him when Natalie was in the next room.

In three long steps, he made it to the door she had shut behind her. He knocked, half expecting her to tell him to go to hell. Heck, he wouldn't blame her if she did.

"Come in," she called, her voice thick.

He looked at the door as if it were the enemy keeping him from her. Turning the knob, he stared at her.

She was standing by the bed, holding a blouse she had been ready to put on a hanger. The piece of cloth was like a shield protecting her from him.

Her eyes were pools of unhappiness.

He swore.

She held up one hand. "If you've come to continue telling me how reckless I am—"

"I haven't."

Natalie jerked, the blouse almost slipping from her hands. She looked to the side. "Well then, if you've come to remind me that I did something stupid, I—"

"No," he said.

She turned back. "It *was* stupid. *I* was stupid," she said, her voice not much more than a breath, but her chin was lifted defiantly. She looked as if she wished she could find some sharp object to hurl at him. If he hadn't been so afraid that she would order him out the door and out of her life, he would have smiled.

"I'm sorry, Natalie," he said. "You weren't stupid. I never thought that. I admire you. I respect you."

She dropped the blouse, blinking hard. "I realize that I handled the situation all wrong, Vincent. You were right to be angry with me, and I'm sorry if I scared you. The truth is that I was a little bit frightened too, once I thought of the ramifications of my actions. Marty might have been hurt. But I'm sorry. I just won't put up with being yelled at and treated like a child."

"No, you're not a child," he agreed.

She looked directly at him, and now her eyes were clear and aware.

"And yes, you scared me," he said, his voice low. "You don't know how scared I was when I couldn't find you."

He moved forward.

"I'm sorry," she said again, but he placed his fingertips over her lips.

"Shhh, I'm the one who's sorry for being such an ass. Half my anger was at myself, but I took all of it out on you." And then he couldn't help himself. He slid his fingers down her throat, placed one hand at her waist and stepped close enough so that his body touched hers. Then he brought his lips down on hers. He tasted her, assured himself that she was alive, safe, his for the moment.

She angled her head and pressed closer. Yes, for this moment she was his if he wanted to take her.

He did. He took what she was offering, his lips nibbling at hers, his tongue stroking inside, his mouth claiming what he had wanted for so long.

She pulled back slightly, her eyes dazed, her mouth rosy. "I can't be what you want me to be, Vincent."

Slowly he shook his head. "You're wrong. Right now you're everything I want you to be."

Natalie smiled at him. She rose on her toes, pressed her body against his, and then, placing her hands on his chest, she pushed slightly, sending him slipping back onto the bed.

Climbing up beside him, she eyed him. "You've probably had a lot of women," she suddenly said, her voice less sure.

He gazed into her eyes. "I've never had a woman like you."

"You mean one who's trouble?" she asked with a grin.

"Exactly." And he reached up and snaked his hand around the nape of her neck and pulled her down on top of him. "Right now, I'm in the mood for trouble."

"That's good. I'm in the mood to give you trouble." She reached for the hem of his black T-shirt and pulled it over his head, throwing it behind her. Her palms rested on his bare chest.

Vincent's heart began to thud painfully. He wanted her with a dangerous amount of passion. He wanted to grab, but he didn't want to scare her or offend her again.

With great difficulty, he lay still as she ran her hands over him, every stroke igniting tiny fires beneath his skin.

"That guy in the restaurant, the one you've met before at the bar…"

"Neil," she said, and she leaned forward and nipped at his skin. Vincent bucked against her, warning himself to stay still, not to act like a Neanderthal and rip off her clothing.

"Yes," he whispered, his voice becoming a growl as tension made its way through his body, turning him tight and hungry.

"What about Neil?" Her lips found his right nipple and he groaned, fought for breath and sanity.

"I wanted to hit him. He was looking at you as if you were a lollipop and he'd been deprived of candy all his life." Vincent closed his eyes, hoping that would help him regain control. It didn't.

He opened them again and found her looking at him, her body astride his.

"Vincent?"

He rose up on his elbows, so that his eyes were gazing directly into hers. "Yes?"

"I don't want Neil. I want you, and I'm not afraid. You can touch me."

"*I'm* afraid," he managed to say through gritted teeth. "You don't know how much I want you. I don't want to be rough. I don't want to hurt or scare you."

And then she gave him a long, slow smile. "You won't."

She didn't know that.

"I want you, Vincent. Desperately," she said, and then she peeled away her blouse. She wasn't wearing a bra, and her small perfect breasts sprang free. Within reach of his hands, of his mouth.

"Aw, hell, Natalie. How am I going to keep my hands off you now?"

"I'm hoping you aren't." She reached for the zipper on her jeans.

That was it. He was lost. Rolling with her, Vincent tucked her beneath him. He shoved her hands aside, freed the zipper and slicked her jeans down her legs and aside. She lay before him clad in wispy white panties that sucked the breath right out of his chest.

"You're damn right, I'm not keeping my hands off you,"

he told her, and he slipped his thumbs inside her panties and pulled them off her in one swift move.

Now she was naked. His. For tonight, he could indulge the passion that had surged between them from the word go.

"You want me?" he asked, staring down into her eyes as she sprawled pink and white and beautiful beneath him.

"Like mad," she said, and she unfastened his pants, slipped her hands inside and slid his pants and his boxers away, her hands stroking and burning his flesh all the way down.

"You do drive me mad," she whispered, rising up to plunge her fingers into his hair.

He caught her lips with his, he stroked one hand down her shoulder. Moving farther still, he found one delicate breast, his thumb grazing the sensitive tip over and over.

She arched and cried out as the tender bud tightened beneath his caress.

"Vincent," she gasped, and he lowered his head and suckled her, his hands framing her slender waist as he tasted what he had wanted to taste ever since he had met her.

His body tightened, arousal ran thick and hot. He needed her, but he wouldn't rush her. Not in any way.

With the greatest of care, he kissed first one breast and then the other. She moved restlessly beneath him, and he returned to her lips, breathing in the minty taste of her, sliding his tongue against hers as his body strained with the need to hold back.

"Don't hold back," she said as if she had read his thoughts. "Don't wait."

But still he waited. He kissed his way down her body, licking her navel, nipping at her belly. Then he kissed his way lower, holding her still for his touch.

"Vincent, no." She reached down to stop him.

He kissed her hand, then returned to his pleasure, licking deep inside her.

Her body quivered in his grasp, and he held her as she cried out and the tremors began. He stroked her until the explosion was over, and then he covered her with his body.

She gazed into his eyes. "Yes," she whispered as he joined his body to hers. Her legs came up around him, and he surged inside her. He filled her, barely able to hold back, wanting to take her with him.

He rocked his body against hers.

"Now," she said.

"No," he answered on a groan. She wasn't far enough along. He wanted her with him.

An anguished cry burst from her. "Vincent, now."

"Almost." He could see her struggling for completion. He was going out of his mind, but he reached down and gently stroked the softest part of her.

She arched and twisted. "Vincent, please, yes," she said again, "oh, yes," and he lost the battle for control. Heat suffused his body, pleasure overtook him. He filled her with one more deep thrust, and she called out his name as her body took over.

Together, they fell back to the bed, and he rolled to keep from crushing her, tucking her in against his side.

That was where she belonged for now, he thought.

Natalie rested on one elbow, watching Vincent breathe. Watching the magnificent muscles of his chest rising and falling, she wanted to lean forward and kiss his skin again, but that would only wake him up.

Instead, she sighed and got up, searching for a robe.

"Take my shirt," a voice offered, and she jumped, turning to find him watching her, a slow smile lifting those clever lips.

Suddenly shy now that the passion had passed, she reached down, found the black shirt and pulled it over her head. He lounged back against the bed, apparently completely at ease with his nakedness.

"You seem nervous. Did I hurt you? Was I rough?" he asked suddenly, sitting up.

Natalie glanced up. "Vincent, no. You didn't hurt me. You wouldn't."

He didn't answer.

She climbed up on the bed, kneeling beside him. "What's bothering you?"

"I lost control there for a minute. I didn't even know what I was doing."

She smiled. "I consider that a compliment."

But Vincent didn't smile. He gently touched her cheek. "A man like me, one as big as I am, can't ever lose control, Natalie."

Natalie leaned into his touch. "You're telling me that you're always completely in control?"

He shrugged. "I work at it. It's important." His dark eyes looked pained.

"I'm fine, Vincent. Better than fine. Have you…hurt anyone before?"

The pained look turned to horror. "Never, but my father…"

Ah. Leonard Fortune. She'd heard of him. He'd been a successful banker, another successful Fortune male. "What did your father do?" she asked.

"He hurt people." Vincent's voice was flat.

"You?"

"Sometimes. Mostly my mother. He had a temper, a devil of a temper, and when he drank he had even more of a temper. She was tiny. A feather. And he was a big and physically powerful man. He hit her. And then he would go into a rage and hit her again. Sometimes I think he might have raped her."

His voice was an aching whisper. Natalie started to touch him, but he evaded her touch.

"Did he hit your siblings?"

"Not once I got old enough to knock him around." Vincent's voice was flat. "I only hit him when he meted out punishment to my mother or tried to get at my brother and sisters, but…"

Vincent stared straight into Natalie's eyes. She could tell he was remembering something very unpleasant. Something terrifying.

"What?"

He swallowed. "When I hit him, I felt good about it. When I heard that my parents had been in a car accident, and I wondered if he had been drunk again, I wanted to kill him for taking her life, but he was already dead."

"Vincent, you're not like that," Natalie said gently.

"I lost control, Natalie. Maybe I didn't hurt you this time, but I could have. Easily. You're so slender. A man could hurt you without even thinking. I don't want to be that man."

As he rose from the bed and headed for the shower, Natalie watched him go with a sense of longing and regret. She understood now why he needed to be a protector, and she had to admit that, given her volatile, stubborn nature, he had been very restrained with her. Life with a woman like her, one who crossed him at every turn, would be hell for a man like Vincent.

He needed to keep people safe, to know he would never hurt the woman he cared for, and she was a woman who drove him up the wall. To constantly have to check his emotions at the door? What would that be like?

It would be awful. It would be the worst thing in the world for him, his most terrible nightmare, she admitted.

And that was heartrending. Because, she realized as she heard him moving around the next room and wished she had the courage to push past his reservations and join him there, she had fallen for him.

She was in love with Vincent Fortune, a man who wanted her in his bed but would never surrender his heart to a woman like her. And would she want him to, knowing she would only bring him pain, have him watching his every move to keep from throttling her?

No. She wanted him to be able to give his heart unconditionally, without reservations, to find joy in love.

And she could never be different. She couldn't ever bring him joy. Natalie closed her eyes. "Life is just so tough sometimes," she whispered to the empty room.

Seventeen

Life is just so tough. The phrase ran through Emmett Jamison's head as he tipped back his chair and stared out the crooked window of his house. Not that it was a true house. More like a tumbledown shack, and even that was being kind.

Not that it mattered. He hadn't chosen this location for its charm, but for its complete lack of other people. He didn't handle human contact well anymore. Had he ever?

I have no clue, he thought. All he knew was that he didn't want to deal with the niceties of interacting with people right now. Maybe he never would.

"Too much trouble," he muttered. But he knew that what he really meant was too much pain. Get involved with people and a man was bound to get burned…or do something he would regret for the rest of his life.

"Hell." He said the word in a voice devoid of emotion as memories coursed through him. Maybe he couldn't outrun his demons here, but he could keep trying. Sooner or later, something might stick. He wasn't certain of that, but there was one thing he was sure of. He wasn't going back to civilization anytime soon. It was nice not knowing or caring what was going on in the world. He intended to keep things that way.

"Do you think Blake will find Emmett?" Patrick asked Ryan when more than a week had passed and they still hadn't heard from him.

"I hope so," Ryan said. "For Blake's sake."

"So that Emmett can help locate Jason?"

Ryan shrugged. "Partly because Blake needs family. He needs more than the bond he's forged with you and me, and Emmett is the only true son he has left. But yes, I'm also hoping that Emmett might be a bridge to Jason."

"Still no sign of Jason?"

Ryan shook his head. "No, and the second transporter isn't yet recovered enough to talk. I'm worried."

"Because of the notes."

"Yes, and because I talked to Vincent on the phone yesterday. His voice was strained. I'm afraid Vincent is starting to become attached to Natalie McCabe. It's not like him to mix work with his private life, but he sounded like a man who was doing just that. And you know as well as I do that Jason is crafty. He's killed already. If he managed to get to Natalie, I'm not sure what that would do to Vincent."

"And what would it do to you?"

Ryan ran a hand over his brow. "I'm the one who supported Jason, even promoted him. I let the fox loose in the henhouse. And Natalie is an admirable and brave woman. I want her safe."

"Well, if anyone can keep her that way, it's Vincent."

Ryan nodded. "Yes, but the question is can anyone truly keep her safe when we don't have a clue where Jason is or what he's up to. Someone wants her scared. If someone also wants her dead, that someone might just succeed. And if my nephew tries to stand in his way, Vincent might end up dead, too. I hope someone catches Jason soon. I don't want to think of a world without Natalie and Vincent."

What would life be like without Vincent, Natalie thought as she and Vincent cruised through the grocery store on another shopping venture the next day. She was sure he had suggested the trip to stock their hotel kitchenette more as an excuse to give her a chance to get out of the hotel and take her mind off her situation than it was for a real need for food.

"I'll get that," Vincent said as Natalie reached for a heavy case of water.

She crossed her arms. "Vincent, I am more than capable of doing my own grocery shopping."

He gave a lopsided grin. "I'm not so sure. You bought artichokes."

"You don't like artichokes?" She raised an eyebrow.

"I don't like eating leaves," he agreed.

She laughed. "Any other complaints?"

He studied the cart. "No, you've done a pretty darn good job. Maybe you are capable of buying your own groceries," he teased. "But I still get to lift the heavy stuff. I'm sure you could do it," he added hastily when Natalie frowned, "but why should you risk hurting your back when I'm here and more than willing to help out?"

"My own personal muscle?" she asked with a chuckle.

"If that's what you want to call me, you go right ahead. Just don't hurt my poor bruised, masculine feelings by making me trail after you while you do all the work. It just makes sense to divide the labor."

She nodded. "All right, you win. It does make sense. As long as you're not suggesting that I'm weak and incapable."

Vincent gave her a long look. "I've seen you in action. Have I ever questioned your ability or your courage?"

He hadn't, she had to admit. He had gotten angry with her when she had skipped out on him and put herself in danger, but he had never questioned her work, her worth or her ability.

"Thank you," she said, and her voice broke a little. As if he knew that she was embarrassed for showing her emotions, he glanced down at the grocery cart.

"Artichokes," he said in disgust. "Let's get some ice cream, and maybe some berries. Something a man can eat out of a woman's navel."

She almost shrieked, but she caught herself as he took her hand and led her back toward the produce section, just as if they were a real couple.

The thought hit Natalie just as they cut through the ice cream aisle. Alisha Hart was leaning over into one of the cases, her long wavy red hair trailing down her back.

Alisha was a public defender Natalie had met once at a charity function she was covering. Natalie called out a greeting, and the woman turned, flashing a warm smile. As they chatted, Natalie realized that Alisha was buying a pint of ice cream. Ice cream for one.

Because she was a woman alone, Natalie knew. By choice? Natalie didn't know. Alisha was pretty, with her blue eyes and slender, curvy figure. She was also a strong, capable woman, but for whatever reason, she moved through her life unaccompanied. *Like me,* Natalie thought, as the vision of herself and Vincent being a couple evaporated. They were not a couple. Vincent was her bodyguard, she was his client. Soon, all of that would end.

"It was so good seeing you," Alisha said, walking away.

"And you," Natalie said. *How polite we are,* she thought when Alisha had gone. *We smile, we chat and then we go back to our homes where we sleep alone.*

Natalie tried not to acknowledge the pain that seared her at that thought. She couldn't be a couple with Vincent. She wasn't meant for him or him for her. They couldn't be together.

At least, not for long.

And the longer she stayed with him, the more it was going to hurt when they said goodbye. Waiting for the other shoe to drop and not knowing when it would do so was killing her.

Ending it now would be the smartest thing she could do. If she let go now, maybe her heart wouldn't be too damaged. Maybe she could pretend she wasn't falling in love with Vincent, and she could start to get over him.

Suddenly Natalie wished she could come out of hiding and stop looking over her shoulder, stop having Vincent worry about her, stop worrying that Jason might hurt or kill Vincent to get to her. She wanted Jason to show his face right now. The police had been looking for him for weeks, to no avail. She wished she had some way to draw him out into the open.

That was something she would have to think about, but for tonight…for tonight she would hold on to what little of Vincent she was allowed to have.

Natalie was quiet this evening, Vincent noticed, and he couldn't keep from worrying about her. Not that he would tell her. She would only point out to him that she was a strong, independent and capable woman. He smiled, because she was all those things, and he didn't feel his masculinity threatened one bit. In fact, if anything, her openness and forward ways only made him desire her more. And yes, he still wanted to do serious damage to anyone who would dare touch her or threaten her, but he admired her so much for being put in this position and still pursuing her life and her work.

Anyone else who had lived through what Natalie had— practically witnessing a murder, having that murderer escape and then being sent dark and dangerous threats—would probably climb in his bed and pull the covers up until the murderer was caught. And who could blame him?

But that wasn't Natalie's way. She had people she cared about, and she wasn't about to let the injustice that had been done to her friends go unpunished, even if seeking the truth meant that she had to walk into danger every day.

How could a man not cheer for a woman like that? How could he hold his passion in check? How could he not feel more than he had ever felt for another woman?

Vincent tried to sidestep that thought. He watched Natalie gracefully traversing the small kitchen area, putting things away. When she grabbed two cartons of ice cream in her hands and started toward the freezer, he almost thought she licked her lips a little.

"You are irresistible, did you know that?" he asked her, striding across the kitchen. How could a man not burn for a woman who was so passionate about even something as ordinary as ice cream?

Natalie looked up at him, clearly caught off guard. "Irresistible? Not me. Now chocolate swirl is irresistible," she teased, her voice a whisper that promised the kind of delights most men only dreamed about.

"Is it?" Vincent asked, taking the container from her. "Let's see." He grabbed a spoon from a nearby drawer, popped the top of the ice cream container and then, holding both spoon and ice cream in one hand, advanced on Natalie.

Her green eyes widened. "Vincent, what are you doing?"

"Being sinful," he told her, and he took a spoonful of ice cream and fed it to her. Then he moved close and, without touching her, leaned close and took her mouth with his own. The cold and chocolate and Natalie all joined, filling him with an intoxicating rush.

"Irresistible," he said again.

"Yes," she said breathlessly, leaning against him. She

plunged her fingers into the container of ice cream, ate a bite and slowly licked her fingers one by one, her tongue tantalizing him. He let out a groan.

Then he reached out and undid the buttons of her blouse, tearing one loose in his haste. She took a deep and audible breath, her breasts rising and falling and making him wild to have her.

Following her lead, he slipped his fingers into the container of ice cream and scooped up a small amount. Then he gave her a wicked smile.

"What are you planning, Vincent?" she asked, her voice a husky whisper.

"A trip to paradise," he said, and he reached out and gently smeared the cold ice cream on the enticing curve of one of her breasts. Then he leaned forward, slid one hand around her waist and brought his lips to her breast. His tongue found the ice cream, his mouth devoured it and her, tasting, licking, sucking.

She gasped and threaded her fingers through his hair.

He dropped the container of ice cream into the small sink and lunged for her. They dropped to their knees as his lips found hers, as his arms threaded around her.

"You are amazing," he said on a groan. "I have to have you right now, but this floor is hard."

"There's carpeting a few feet away by the living area. I'm not sure I can make it that far, though," she said on a gasp.

"I'll help." Then he lifted her, walking on his knees the short distance to the carpeted part of the room.

"Thank you," she managed to say before she tugged his head back down to hers. "I want to be on top this time."

He smiled against her mouth. "I'll bet you say that a lot."

Instantly she pulled back. Her eyes looked wounded.

He wanted to kick himself, to take back what he had said.

"I don't do this very much," she said. "I— Men and I don't work well together."

"That's because they're all fools. Me, too."

She shook her head and kissed him again. "Not you."

"When you're around, I behave very foolishly."

"I like that," she said suddenly. "Let's be foolish together."

"Let's be naked together," he countered. In what seemed like seconds, they were both undressed. She tilted her head and looked at him, one hand resting on her lovely, pale hip.

"You don't mind that I'm a bit aggressive?" she asked. "I know you don't like it when I act impulsively."

"When you put yourself in danger, I don't like it," he said, swallowing hard as she reached out and touched his chest, her fingers slipping down his side. "But otherwise?" He lay back on the carpeting. "Be impulsive," he dared her.

Natalie gave him a sly smile and slid her body over his, her arms resting on his chest. "You'll lie still, won't you?" she asked, threading her fingers through the hair on his chest and wiggling as if to get more comfortable.

He was already fully aroused, and her movements made him ache to flip her over and thrust into her depths. With great difficulty, Vincent resisted.

"Natalie," he warned, "I want to let you lead, but I have to tell you I'm very near the edge."

In answer, she dipped her head and lapped at his nipple. His entire body bucked as the sharp edge of desire knifed through him.

"I'm near the edge, too," she said, her voice ragged. "Kiss me."

As he raised himself slightly and captured her lips, she rose above him and impaled herself on his erection.

He gripped at the carpeting, his hands closing on empty air. He wanted her to have it her way, wanted her to call the shots. No matter how much it killed him.

"Touch me," she said, and he brought his hands to her

breasts. He suckled at one small, perfect breast, and desire clutched at him.

Natalie cried out his name. She shifted, turning, and he rolled her beneath him, taking over the rhythm she had begun. As they moved together, the heat intensified, the need grew until he could barely breathe.

Then she raked her fingernails over his buttocks. He reached down between them, sliding his fingertips over her slick, wet nub.

She cried out, tremors rocked him simultaneously. He wrapped his arms around her tightly and held on.

Slowly, very slowly, the world came back into focus. Vincent gazed down at Natalie, at her pretty thick lashes resting on her cheekbones.

"Let's try strawberry next time," she said, and she smiled. But the smile was tempered with sadness.

Their lovemaking had been fierce and quick, and now it was over. Time was ticking. Surely Jason would show up one day soon, and then Vincent would have to let her go. She wasn't the kind of woman who wanted a man to hold her forever.

But for now...Vincent leaned over and kissed her bare shoulder. Then he pulled her back into his arms and held on.

He had her for now. Someday would have to wait.

Eighteen

Vincent was in the bathroom showering, and Natalie was lying in bed enjoying the memory of last night, when the familiar tones of her cell phone ringing in the next room sent her scurrying to answer it.

"Who is this?" she asked. The digital clock on her nightstand only read 6 a.m.

"Natalie?" The sound of Neil's quiet voice coming through her cell was eerie. For some reason, she felt exposed even though she was in a high-rise hotel room.

"Neil? What is it?"

"I know…that is, I realize it's early, Natalie, but I think I've found what you're looking for. You were right about Brad. Those old people are being bilked out of their money, and it's only going to get worse. He's got another list, more people. It's not going to stop, is it?"

Her heart leapt. Here was her proof. "Neil, where are you?"

"I'm at Starson. I've been here all night scanning Brad's

files, because…well, you know, because of what you said, and because it was the only time I could check his files. Maybe I shouldn't have called this early," he said hesitantly. "You probably don't want to see this stuff right now, do you?"

When things were getting worse for her friends with each passing day? She and Vincent had just gone to see Mrs. Morgensen yesterday and when her friend had answered the door, it was clear she had been crying and was trying to hide it.

"Just a bit of dust in my eye, Natalie," she had said. "I'm really fine."

But the mere fact that Mrs. Morgensen wasn't even discussing her problems anymore pointed to their increased severity. How could Natalie walk away without trying to help? Her heart was breaking for her friend.

"I guess we can wait on this," he suggested.

"No, I want to see what you have now," Natalie said calmly, but she wasn't going to break Vincent's trust again. If she met with Neil, it would have to be here. "I'm en route to a breakfast at the Delarosa Hotel," she lied, knowing Vincent wouldn't be happy if she confessed that she was actually living at the hotel. "Can you meet me in the lobby?"

"I…Natalie, I don't want to be seen handing you the paperwork."

And she couldn't leave the building without betraying Vincent's trust again. "The lobby will be pretty deserted at six in the morning," she reasoned.

He hesitated. "All right," he finally said. "Five minutes."

"Done."

But it wasn't completely done, Natalie thought. She couldn't show up with Vincent in tow, but there wasn't any way she was going to simply slip downstairs leaving him in the dark, either. He needed to know that she was around and safe.

Hastily, she scribbled a note, threw on some clothes and sprinted for the elevator.

When she reached the cavernous lobby with its fountains and multiple seating areas, it was, as she had predicted, empty except for one lone clerk at the distant desk.

She found a spot near a window and prepared to wait, but she had barely positioned herself when Neil came up beside her. He must have come in the entrance by the restaurant.

"You have the papers?" she asked, eager to get this over with and get back upstairs before Vincent began to worry. She hoped he would find her note.

"I have them," Neil said.

She held out her hand, and he smiled. "Eager, aren't you?" he asked.

Natalie blinked at his tone. "I thought you wanted to make things right, to make sure Brad got his comeuppance for abusing his position."

"I do want to make things right," he said, and he smiled again. It wasn't a nice smile, Natalie noted, and his voice wasn't shy or hesitant any longer. What's more, he hadn't produced any papers, even though he had seemed very eager to get them to her only moments ago. The sense that something was very wrong rushed through her, but she had scarcely had time to register that thought when Neil slipped one arm around her and grasped her opposite arm in what would have looked like a romantic gesture to anyone watching. Except his grip was very tight.

And he was shoving something hard into her side with his other hand.

"I really do want to make things right, Natalie," Neil said in a conspiratorial voice. "And I intend to. If you attempt to run or call out, I'm sorry, but I'm just going to be forced to put a bullet through you. And then I'm going to have to shoot the desk clerk. I'm sure you don't want me to do that."

Panic kicked in. Natalie fought for breath and sanity. She

glanced at the desk clerk, a woman so young she had barely had time to begin living.

"Coming with me?" he asked.

"Yes." Somehow she would have to find a way out of this, because she couldn't risk the life of a total innocent. The urge to look back over her shoulder toward the bank of elevators was intense, but Natalie resisted. If Vincent came down, he wouldn't know that Neil had a gun, and that would make him a target as well.

Instead, she moved more quickly, hoping to get out of sight before she dragged Vincent into this.

Her last thought was that he would think she had lied and ditched him again. If she survived this, he would never trust her again.

Vincent felt the quiet as soon as he exited the bathroom. He scanned the bedroom. Empty. Rushing into the next room, he found no one there, either.

"Natalie?" he called, but already he knew there wouldn't be any response.

Hot, ugly fear slammed into his chest. He started toward the door, then paused when his body's movement sent a piece of paper fluttering from the table to the floor. It fell face up.

Neil Gerard has info on Starson scam. Am meeting him in the lobby to pick up documentation. Be right back. Natalie.

A string of curses flew from his mouth. He flew down the hall and down the stairs, his untucked shirt flying out behind him. Flinging open the door to the lobby, he saw Gerard shuffling Natalie toward the door, one palm locked around her arm, the other hand tucked in against her side. Was that a gun he was holding on her? She was looking toward the elevators, her face pinched and anxious.

As Gerard walked her toward the door, she looked wildly to the side.

Vincent rushed forward. He vaulted over a couch in his way and flew toward the opposite doors, only to see a car pulling away with Natalie at the wheel and Gerard in the passenger seat.

"That's the woman I love, Gerard," Vincent whispered. "You are such a dead man." And then he ran for his own car.

Natalie had been driving for what seemed like a long time, a gun pointed at her, when Neil finally ordered her to stop. The graveled road ended here, and he shoved her toward a narrow path overgrown with weeds.

For the twentieth time, she asked him where he was taking her, but this time he didn't just yell at her to shut up and drive.

"Well, I know how you like a good story, Ms. Reporter, so I'm going to give you tomorrow's headlines. Get this: Reporter's Body Found At Bottom Of Lake."

Natalie stifled a gasp.

"Did you think I wouldn't figure out who you were eventually? All those snoopy questions? Hanging around Brad when it was clear you weren't interested in him? That story about the old people? You're the witness in that Jason Jamison case. Good thing that your buddy couldn't follow you this time."

Natalie looked at him. "What do you mean?"

Neil laughed. "You know who I'm talking about. That guy who escorts you wherever you go and looks daggers at anyone who dares to so much as give you a glance. If he were here, I'd have to dump him in the lake, too. Could get crowded."

Nausea threatened to overcome Natalie. What if she had brought Vincent downstairs with her? He might be dead now. He might still be dead if Neil started thinking that Vincent was a danger.

"Why are you doing this?" she asked. Surely Neil had a weak spot. If she could just find it…

She turned, trying to stare into his face.

A hand clamped down on her arm. "I wouldn't think about

moving around too much. I might get nervous and shoot before I'm ready." His voice was chillingly calm.

Breathe, think, she told herself as she forced herself to be still. Okay, that talk about her being a reporter. She had made a mistake, and now he thought she was dumb. That could work to her advantage if she let it.

"So, you're telling me you don't have any real information about Brad Herron?" she asked incredulously, stalling for time, taking in her surroundings, looking for a likely source of cover if she could get free.

Neil sneered and squeezed her arm hard. "Herron is an idiot. I can tell you that much."

"Why? What did he do?"

Neil's laugh was cold and humorless, maybe even a little mad. It sent a chill through her. Had she really ever thought of him as shy?

"Listen, this is great," he said as he nudged her closer to the water that lay ahead. "He did everything you think he did. He coerced senior citizens into granting him discretionary trading power. Then he made excessive trades, trading solely for the purpose of generating a commission. It's called churning."

"Which is illegal?" she asked as if she didn't already know the answer to that.

"Oh, yes." In spite of the way Neil's voice dropped to a near reverent whisper, his fingers were clamped on her like a vise. Fear made Natalie's heart gallop, but she fought it, trying to surreptitiously take stock of her captor. He was about her height, she realized for the first time. That was good to know, so she could locate his vulnerable spots as her self-defense instructor had taught her. All her training came back, all the tactics she was to use if she was ever in a situation where her safety was at risk.

Natalie's heart dropped as she thought about how Vincent had been brought in because her safety had been at risk. She tried not to think of what he was going through now. Her heart ripped in two when she realized that she would never get the chance to tell him how much she loved him.

"So you're interested in churning?" Neil asked, snagging Natalie's attention. A strange new note had entered his voice, a note very much like sexual excitement.

She braced herself against the acidic bite of fear that immediately slid through her. "Just a little," she lied, even though she had thoroughly researched the practice. "A fascinating subject."

Fighting to keep the quiver from her voice as Neil gave her a hard shove and pushed her closer still to the water, she noted a small stand of trees not too far from the water. Probably not much use to hide in. "But there's something I don't understand," she coaxed, stalling for time. "If Brad is the culprit, why am I here like this?"

She moved her arm to indicate the hold he had on her, and Neil jerked her back against him hard, squeezing her arm tighter, stroking his gun down her throat, across her breast.

"Because you're too nosy. You talk too much, and you ask too many questions, and sooner or later, Brad, who likes to drink to excess, was going to mess up and spill something to you. I thought you would give up and go away, but you kept coming back." Revulsion filled her as she realized he was getting a thrill out of holding her captive this way.

"And it wasn't just Brad who was involved, was it? You had to sign off on the trades," she accused. If Neil was going to succeed in killing her, she wanted him to know just how contemptible she thought he was.

"Oh yes," he said as that orgasmic tone returned to his voice. "It doesn't work otherwise. Besides, do you think Brad has what it takes to engineer something like this? I told him what kind of clients we were looking for. In some cases, I cruised the obituaries looking for widows or widowers. Do you think Herron would think of the details like that? He's got the teeth for the smile, but he needs to be led."

"So you led him."

"It was so easy. Herron doesn't even know that much about the business, but he knows how to get signatures. He was glad to have someone who could help hide his incompetence. He would do anything I wanted, as long as he got all that pretty money."

"And then I came along."

"You did." He slipped the gun back down to her side and prodded her with it. "It was obvious you were going to screw everything up. You kept coming around, sniffing around Brad, who wanted you far too much to be smart. What's more, you brought your boyfriend with you to watch your back. Well, guess what? He's not here today."

No, he wasn't, Natalie thought. She wondered if Vincent would ever forgive her for this day. Somehow she didn't think he would. Not again.

"You think Brad would have talked eventually, then?" she asked, eyeing the empty horizon. There wasn't another soul around at this hour in the morning.

Neil snorted. "You've seen how Herron works. He was doing fine until you came along, but Brad is a sucker for a nice set of tits and legs. Without your interference, none of those people would ever have figured out on their own how they lost all that money. They're old, they're confused, they're used to thinking of themselves as victims. No one listens to them. Old people get scammed all the time because they're too trusting or they're not thinking straight."

"You preyed on people who were in mourning, people who were already scared."

"They were greedy."

"No, they weren't. They were trusting. You were greedy."

"Aw, Natalie, you wound me. Why do you care about them

so much, anyway? They're not going to need that money very long. They're all going to die soon."

Hot, dark anger swirled through Natalie. Her anger must have made her move, because Neil dug his fingers into her. He prodded the gun deep into her skin.

"And you, Natalie, are here alone with me, the man you weren't ever the tiniest bit interested in. Now I'll be the most important man in your life, and you'll die alone without ever telling anyone your story."

The thought nearly brought her to her knees, because Vincent would find her body. He would blame himself, when he was blameless. It was her fault. She was headstrong, just as her parents had always said.

"Of course, maybe you told your boyfriend about your suspicions," he said suddenly. "Probably you did."

Fear froze Natalie in place. She and Neil were at the water's edge now. She could see he had laid out weighted shackles there in anticipation of this moment. Her body would not resurface. No one would know what had happened to her. Vincent would never find her. And then after she was gone, Neil would start thinking about Vincent. He would decide Vincent knew too much…and he would kill him.

"I'm really fortunate that everyone thinks Jason Jamison is going to kill you, you know," Neil said, as horror filled Natalie's soul and she realized that Neil wouldn't even be a suspect. Even Vincent might think that Jamison had caught her while she was out on her own.

Her immediate instinct was to twist away, to try to run. She had to do all she could to save herself. If she died, so did Vincent.

Stop. Think. Be patient. Choose the right moment, the right movement, she ordered herself just as every self-defense instructor she'd ever had had taught her.

But the right moment might never come…

Nineteen

Vincent came to the end of the gravel road and saw Gerard's car parked there.

It wasn't the first time Vincent had been to this lake, and he knew there was nothing at the end of this path but water. If Gerard had brought Natalie here…

His breath was trapped in his chest and blackness threatened to overwhelm him. He had to move fast…but he had to move silently.

Carefully, he picked his way down the trail. Muffled voices became intelligible sounds. Natalie talking, then Neil, now Natalie, Neil.

"I'm really fortunate that everyone thinks Jason Jamison is going to kill you, you know." Gerard's voice was evil. Vincent got a good view of them now. Gerard had his gun buried in Natalie's side. He had a look on his face that Vincent had seen before—the look of a man who enjoyed inflicting pain and was about to inflict more.

He was going to kill Natalie. Now.

No! Shoot me, you bastard, Vincent thought as he opened his mouth to shout, to draw Gerard's attention from Natalie and to himself.

But at that moment Natalie erupted in a whirl of arms and legs, ramming her elbow into Neil's gut and simultaneously dropping to crush her foot square into his groin.

Vincent was on the run as Gerard dropped to the ground, screaming and clutching at himself, and the gun fell to the grass.

Natalie turned to pick up the gun and glanced up right into Vincent's eyes.

Immediately, tears filled her eyes. She ran at him full tilt and launched herself into his arms.

Vincent caught her to him tightly. He kissed her eyes, her nose, her lips.

"I'm so sorry. I'm so, so sorry, Vincent," she cried, but he only held her and rocked.

"Shh, love, don't. Don't." He kissed her again. Then he gently disentangled himself from her and went over and picked up Gerard's gun. The man was beginning to stir.

"I wouldn't get up if I were you," Vincent said. "Because if you move, I'm just going to have to put a nice, neat hole in you."

Neil lay very still. "I—I didn't really hurt her."

Vincent swore. "Only because she outsmarted you and got the best of you, you bastard. For the record, if you had hurt her, you'd already be dead."

As sirens sounded in the distance, Natalie came up behind Vincent and wrapped her arms around his waist. She rested her cheek on his back. "Did you call the police?"

"I called everyone I could find. Did you think I would let my pride get in the way when your life was at stake?"

"Your pride?" she murmured, her lips hot against the cotton of his shirt.

"Mmm, love. I failed you. I was supposed to be the one saving your skin."

"You *did* save my skin. You're the reason I'm alive."

"Natalie, you're wrong. One hundred percent wrong. And I'm never going to forgive myself for that."

The sirens grew louder until several squad cars pulled up. When the officers got out, Vincent went over and handed them the weapon.

One of them looked at Natalie. "Is this the young woman Gerard kidnapped? We'll need her for questioning."

"She's the one," Vincent said, and he knew that the words meant something more to him than they did to the police officer. Natalie was the one who held his heart. But he was the wrong man for her.

"Keep her safe," he told the officer as he explained about Jason Jamison.

It was what Daniel had told him, but he hadn't done a very good job of keeping Natalie safe, had he?

"Vincent," Natalie said, and she started toward him.

He smiled at her. "You need to talk to the police," he told her, "and write your story. It's important. Remember?"

She nodded, but he thought he saw tears in her eyes. "Will you be waiting for me when I'm done?" she asked.

"I'll be stepping up the surveillance on you," he said. "I have four men, including Derek. They're all excellent bodyguards."

Natalie bit her lip. "You're going to leave me to them, aren't you?"

"Four is better than one," he said. It was what he should have done already, in fact. He wouldn't be selfish and leave Natalie to his solitary care ever again. The truth was pounding painfully in his chest. He had risked her safety because he was in love with her. Maybe he had loved her from the start. Because he had cared for her so much and hated to risk her spirit, he'd allowed her liberties, such as those days at The

Ladder, that had put her at risk. The truth was if he had been standing guard around the clock instead of making love to Natalie, Gerard would never have gotten to her.

A responsible bodyguard would have taken himself off the case as soon as he realized he was falling for his client. Any other man wouldn't have been so blind.

It was time to step away.

"Have a good life, Natalie. Stay strong. Be safe. I'll look for you in the newspapers."

"Vincent, don't do this." Her voice broke on his name. "I'm never going to forgive you if you leave me."

And he would never forgive himself if he stayed and she got hurt.

When he didn't answer, she finally turned back to the police officers, her head held regally high. "Let's do this quickly."

They led her away, and Vincent walked back to his car. He called Derek, Jeremy, Adam and Lewis. He had never assigned four guards to one woman, but Natalie was no ordinary woman. As soon as Derek's car pulled up and the four men emerged, Vincent gave them their orders, asked for reports on the hour and then drove away.

But he knew he would never be through with Natalie. Not really.

Natalie turned in her story and then turned to her four bodyguards. Pain, panic and a sense of fear and loss that she had never known flowed through her heart in long, aching waves.

She had lost him. Finally, she had pushed him too far. His work was his life, but she had only thought of her own needs, her own impulses. Now he was gone.

"Where is he?" she asked Derek.

"I don't have that information."

She glared at the stoic Derek. "I'll bet you could get it if you wanted to."

"Mr. Fortune has taken himself off the case," Derek said, crossing his arms.

Natalie knew that. And she knew why Vincent had taken himself off the case. Because he thought he had failed her.

She wanted to scream, to make amends, to tell him that she loved him.

Well, he didn't want her love and never had, she reminded herself, trying to ignore the tears that threatened to start flowing. She couldn't have him, but she could at least tell him the truth about her escape from Neil.

"I want you to take me to Vincent," she said.

"I'm afraid that isn't possible." Obviously Vincent had given his orders, but she knew one thing about him. He would never place orders before her safety.

"I'm really sorry about this," she told Derek. "You're a very good man." She ducked under his arm and bolted for the door. He was fast, but she was lighter on her feet and she had taken plenty of fitness classes. Derek's body was made for wrestling, not running.

Rushing down the stairs, she came out the downstairs door where Jeremy and Adam were waiting.

Damn! They must have taken the elevator.

Wheeling, she headed for the opposite door, made it through, ran down the street looking back over her shoulder. If she could just keep ahead of them…if she could just keep this up long enough…

"Escaping your captors again?" a deep, low voice asked.

Natalie turned and skidded straight into Vincent's chest. The door to his car was still open, the engine still running.

She bit her lip and tears filled her eyes, but she didn't touch him.

"Natalie," he said, his voice harsh. "Please don't cry."

"I never cry," she said stubbornly. "I'd certainly never cry over a man."

"I know that," he said, and he swiped his thumb over an errant tear that had slipped down her cheek.

She looked up at him and knew her heart was in her eyes. She had spent all her life hiding her heart. Now she didn't care. "You left me," she accused.

He cupped her cheek with his big palm. "I explained that."

Natalie nodded. "I know. You think you let me get kidnapped, but you didn't let me explain."

"It doesn't matter that you left while I was in the shower. I could have prevented you from leaving. If I hadn't been so selfish, I would have had another man watching. It would never have happened."

She tried to laugh. "Vincent, I just evaded four of your best men."

He grimaced. "I know. They're going to catch hell for it, too."

"You know that when I'm determined there's no stopping me. I was doomed the minute I betrayed myself to Neil by questioning him. It was my own fault, Vincent."

He crossed his arms stubbornly. She placed her hands on his arms and rose on her toes so that she could look him more fully in the face. "You saved my life, Vincent."

"Damn it, Natalie, would you stop saying that? I know who saved your life. You did it yourself." His voice was so anguished, she couldn't keep herself from leaning forward and kissing him lightly on the lips.

"I was a dead woman, Vincent. I was so afraid I couldn't do anything but keep talking. I couldn't figure out the first thing about how to get away. He was going to kill me, and he would have. But then he told me that he was going to kill you, too."

Vincent closed his eyes tightly. "You were never a dead woman, Natalie. I couldn't have borne it if he'd hurt you, even a little."

"You were going to draw his fire away, weren't you?"

"I didn't have to. You did a good job of taking him down. You were magnificent."

She tried to smile. "I was a woman in love, Vincent. I was too afraid to save myself, but I didn't want you to find my body. I didn't want you to feel guilty, and most of all, I couldn't stand letting him try to kill you. Loving you is what saved me."

He opened his arms and pulled her tight against him. "Natalie—"

"No." She placed her palm across his lips. "I know what you're going to say. You think you're like your father, that you might get angry at me one day and take out your anger against me, maybe hurt me. But, Vincent, look at all I've done. I've been the worst kind of client. I've been sneaky and bossy and irresponsible, and I've nearly gotten both of us killed, and you've been just wonderful."

"Shh, love," he whispered, taking her lips with his own. "You say I saved you. Well, you've saved me from myself. I would have gone to the grave thinking I couldn't love like this, but…you sneak out on me, and I get so angry that I just have to kiss you. You make my men look bad, and I think what a strong, admirable woman you are. You're the only woman who has ever stood up to me, Natalie, the only woman strong enough and brave enough and good enough to break through my defenses."

"You don't ever have to worry about hurting me, Vincent. I'm the one who keeps walking into danger, and you keep forgiving me."

"I'm just so grateful each time I find you safe," he explained.

"Are you going to call your men off and go back to guarding me yourself?"

Instantly, his brow furrowed. "I would do almost anything for you, Natalie, but…he's still out there. And you distract me too much. It's safer the way it's been the past couple of days."

"You could completely confine me to quarters."

Slowly, he shook his head. "I wouldn't try to do that to you. It would kill your spirit."

She ran her hand down the side of his face. "Not being with you will kill my heart, Vincent. I love you. You love me, too."

"Yes," he said, his voice thick. "There is…one possibility."

"Tell me."

"An island. It belongs to the family, very private, very secluded. The Fortunes think of it as a good place for a honeymoon."

"Take me there, Vincent. We could have a very long honeymoon…."

"One day they'll catch Jamison. But it could be a long time."

"Oh, that's all right," Natalie said. "I'll be with you. And if we stay there long enough, I might even be pregnant by the time they find him."

"We'll have one of those five hundred babies that you want." He ran one hand down her side and rested it where one day a baby would grow.

Natalie shivered. "Oh yes, we'll have everything," she whispered.

Everything you love about romance...
and more!

Please turn the page for Signature Select™
Bonus Features.

Bonus Features:

BONUS FEATURES

Keeping Her Safe

A conversation with
MYRNA MACKENZIE

A former teacher and college recruiter, Myrna Mackenzie's work has won the Holt Medallion for outstanding fiction, and she has been a finalist for the Romantic Times Reviewer's Choice Award, the Orange Rose, the Reader's Choice and WisRWA's Write Touch. Recently, she chatted with us as she took a break from writing her latest book.

Tell us a bit about how you began your writing career.

If it weren't for two encouraging teachers (one in high school and one in college) I would never even have thought of writing for a living. Both of these instructors told me that they thought I had talent and that I should consider pursuing that talent.

I didn't do what they suggested, however. I had never even considered writing as something one did for anything other than personal enjoyment or homework, so I became a teacher.

Their words stuck in my mind, however, and just wouldn't go away. Years went by, and I began to write snippets of stories and hide them away for fear that someone would see them. The urge to write grew stronger every time I tried, and eventually, while I was still teaching I decided to take a class. I began seriously thinking of writing as a profession, and was determined to keep at it until something good happened. Fortunately for me, something did.

Was there a particular person, place or thing that inspired this story?
My heroes and heroines tend to be conglomerations of my ideals (heroes tend to be protectors and females tend to be strong-willed nurturers) and the flaws I most relate to, whether they be male or female. I make a serious effort not to base my characters on anyone I have actually known. That hits a little too close to home for me.

What's your writing routine?
I have a daily schedule which involves a lot of getting up and walking around (i.e., looks like goofing off, but isn't—yet my sons could never get away with this line of reasoning with me). I begin about an hour after everyone leaves the house and work on some less demanding aspect of writing (titles, brainstorming, things that don't require tons of discipline). Afterward, I edit yesterday's work and then begin on the new

scene. About every hour or so I get up and pace, do some small mindless task or...if the weather is right, I might even take a short walk around the block. I do this because it's not good for a writer to sit and pound the keys for too long, but mostly because it keeps the ideas flowing. If I'm really stuck for a idea, I take a shower or go to the grocery store. Don't ask. There's something magical about the produce section—fear of vegetables or maybe fear of cooking?—that often seems to trigger an epiphany and sends me back to the computer with an aha! idea.

How do you research your stories?
I work on an "as needed" basis, which means that my fingers may be flying across the keys one minute and in the next I may be on the Internet searching for information on arson investigations. One would think that would be an efficient way to gather information; however, I inevitably end up with tons of information that I never actually put in the book. That doesn't mean it doesn't make a difference in the book. Almost everything a writer reads ends up being used in some way, even if it's only in the writer's attitude toward her subject matter. Although I travel every year, I tend to set most of my books in the Midwest, the area I know best. It's a comfort level thing. I don't want to concentrate on the setting but on the characters. Now and then, however, it's fun to try a new setting. I've spent a lot of

time in Maine and set a couple of books there. I'm sure I'll do that again, since it's one of my favorite places, and I keep promising myself that one day I really will delve into the soul of Chicago and use the setting to full advantage.

How do you develop your characters?
This is the heart of how I develop a book. I always begin with a character and his or her "problem," after which I set up an opposing character. Backgrounds grow from this brief beginning and other characters are pulled in to serve as ways to emphasize the hero and heroine's difficulties (or to ease the tension now and then). Every secondary character in the book must serve a purpose relating to the hero and heroine. I'm not always aware that that's what I'm doing, but it's the end result. If a character isn't doing his or her job, then that person doesn't belong in the book, no matter how much I like that person (and if I like them well enough, they may get their own book down the road).

When you're not writing, what are your favorite activities?
I always want to invent something very cool and exciting here (such as admitting to a fondness for skydiving in a thong/bikini/clown suit or alligator wrestling), but my chief pursuits tend to be reading, taking long walks (which gets called hiking if I'm on a trail on vacation) and traveling whenever possible. I'm not particularly

adventurous, but my husband tends to be, so I've rafted rivers, climbed mountains and had the occasional bear or moose encounter. Oh, and people watching is another favorite hobby, a quiet but guilty pleasure and one which every writer (at least the honest ones) admits to engaging in. There are loads of other things I'd like to pursue (playing the piano, knitting something someone could actually wear as opposed to something the person has to hide in the back of their closet, learning how to decorate a cake that would make people swoon, growing roses, juggling, being in good enough shape to actually run a race), but all those things take buckets of time and if I took that kind of time I wouldn't be able to write books, something I love doing.

If you don't mind, could you tell us a bit about your family?
Sure. I didn't get married until I was twenty-eight, but when I did, I married my high school sweetheart. We have two sons. They're both runners and both musically inclined. No pets, but I once had a dog and I love to "imagine" having pets (so much less mess and allergen free and you can change breeds as frequently as you like), so animals tend to show up now and then in my books.

What are your favorite kinds of vacations? Where do you like to travel?

I've spent many trips setting up tents, and I do tend toward vacations that concentrate on the great outdoors and the national wonders of the world, but I also love museums and simply seeing how other people live. England is a favorite as are the Canadian Rockies and Bar Harbor, Maine. Utah has some beautiful areas, and who can deny that California offers a host of different kinds of terrain, lovely cities and the ocean, of course? But there are so many places I'd still like to see (Australia, Ireland, the Netherlands...the list goes on). Isn't variety great?

Do you have a favorite book or film?

Not the dreaded "a" which means I have to choose! This could take pages, years, even decades. But only one? All right. *Jane Eyre*. It was my first favorite and has great sentimental value for me.

Any last words to your readers?

Yes, thank you for the companionship of loving books as much as I do. No one understands a reader the way another reader does, that thrill of holding a single small paperback in one's hands and realizing that an entire world resides inside. May all of you keep discovering new and wonderful worlds and stories!

Author's Journal
Ten Ways to Conceal the Identity of Your Bodyguard
by Myrna MacKenzie

1. Go jogging with him. Tell everyone you were *never* going to fit back into that size-six dress for your next high school reunion without a personal trainer, and yours has been accommodating enough to make himself available whenever you have a "doughnut attack," which is pretty much around-the-clock occurrence.

2. Teach him some foreign phrases. When in the presence of others, converse only in your language of choice. Tell your friends that you're planning a trip abroad and need to immerse yourself in the language. Your "personal tutor" is here to help in any way he can.

3. Along those lines, have your bodyguard speak to you only in foreign endearments (*Je t'adore, Te quiero* or *Ti amo* are all good). Tell everyone he is your long-lost pen pal and now that you have "found" each other you may never speak English again.

4. Set him to washing windows, painting the house or whatever suits your fancy, preferably sans shirt. Your female neighbors will enjoy the show of watching your handsome, muscular handyman so much that they won't ask any questions (other than how much does he charge?), and you'll get the double benefit of having a bodyguard *and* a man who knows how to handle a hammer.

5. Suggest that he's your ex-boyfriend here to take part in a new reality show titled *My Former (Worthless) Lover*. The two of you have to live together until one of you runs screaming into the night (in which case, the remaining person wins $25,000) or until you end up in bed (in

which case no one wins anything...but
neither of you cares).

6. Ask him to wear a cowboy hat and boots
(chaps might be pushing it) and spread
the word that he used to be your cousin's
friend from Montana, but now he's your
own personal cowboy. Women will envy
you; men will want to steal you away
(because any woman who rates a cowboy
must be worth having).

7. Kissing cousins. Need I say more?

8. Dress him in black and have him answer
the door. Haven't you always wanted to
have a hunky butler to do your bidding?
Do not miss this opportunity!

9. Tell everyone he is your bodyguard. Is
anyone *really* going to believe that? (And
if they do, wouldn't that be the coolest
thing?)

10. Marry him. Now he's your husband,
your knight in shining armor, the
future father of your children, the man
of your dreams, your soul mate
and...oh yes, your bodyguard, as well

(but what's one teensy little title amongst all the others—as if anyone would ever notice that big gun he carries when most of the time they're watching the way he gazes into your eyes). Sigh.

Author's Journal
Getting Away in
Outdoor San Antonio
by Myrna MacKenzie

After being cooped up in her house, Natalie McCabe was more than ready to get out, but her sexy bodyguard, Vincent Fortune, refused to put her at risk. If they were going to go out, it would have to be to a more secluded area, something outdoors. Finding the right place was a tough choice for Vincent, so...for anyone else who might feel the need to make a brief respite from the everyday world, here are some suggestions:

O.P. Schnabel Park, 9600 Bandera Street, San Antonio, TX 78250
Open Daily 5:00 a.m.-11:00 p.m.
A great place to get out and away from your troubles!
Once known as "the cleanest little park in Texas." O.P. Schnabel Park boasts basketball courts, a baseball and soccer field and picnic areas, as well

as several miles of trails suitable for running, biking and hiking. The trails range from gently sloping to challenging and boast some lovely oak and laurel cover.

McAllister Park, 13102 Jones Maltsberger Road, San Antonio, TX 78247
Open Daily 5:00 a.m.-11:00 p.m.
Another good place for biking, hiking, jogging and a good choice when our heroine needs to escape the tension of being in constant danger while trying to avoid falling for her bodyguard.
Located on over 900 acres of land north of the San Antonio International Airport, the park has three miles of jogging paths as well as soft surface and nature trails. Picnic areas are shaded with barbecue pits, and there are fields for baseball, soccer and softball.

Hill Country State Natural Area,
10600 Bandera Creek Road, Bandera, TX 78003
Feb-Nov open seven days a week; Dec-Jan open Fri. noon to Sun 10:30 p.m.
An excellent choice for escaping whatever troubles ail you.
The 5,400 acres here offer a grand taste of nature, including steep canyons, stands of oaks, springs and grasslands. There are thirty-six miles of trails suitable for horseback riding, backpacking and mountain biking (four miles are open only to horses and hikers). Primitive camping as well as

limited swimming, fishing and equestrian
camping are also available.

San Antonio Botanical Garden, 555 Funston Place,
San Antonio, TX 78209
Open year-round 9:00 a.m-5:00 p.m. (closed
Christmas and New Year's)
*What could be better than the solace of beautiful
gardens when our heroine needs to get out and smell
the roses?*
Founded in 1980 and occupying thirty-three acres
in the heart of San Antonio, the gardens are a
great place for birders and for letting one's spirits
soar.

16 **Dwight D. Eisenhower Natural Area Park,**
19399 NW Military Highway, San Antonio
Open seven days a week (closed Christmas and
New Year's)
*A great place for soaking up the sun, for
communing with nature and for trying to forget that
someone is trying to harm you...and that you're
falling in love with the wrong man!*
The 320 acres of Eisenhower Park offer examples
of Texas Hill Country vegetation and landscapes.
Wooded dry creek beds and rocky canyons may
be found along the five miles of trails suitable for
hiking, jogging or nature study. Trails vary from
Level 1 (handicapped accessible) to Level 4 in
difficulty. Trail Markers along four of the trails
indicate examples of Texas Hill vegetation, and

the Cedar Flats Trail leads to the highest point in the park and a lookout tower offering views of the surrounding area. Picnic facilities are available; however, no roller blades, scooters or bicycles are allowed.

Emilie & Albert Friedrich Wilderness Park,
21395 Milsa Road
Open seven days a week 7:30 a.m.-Sunset (closed Christmas and New Year's)
A few hours of fresh air, breathing in the wonderful scent of cedar and hiking up and down canyons can really help a girl get away from it all.
About fifteen miles from downtown San Antonio and situated on 233 acres, seven hiking trails (5.5 miles) ranging from Level 1 to Level 4 in difficulty offer access to ancient cedar, rare birds (the park is internationally known for bird-watching), terrestrial orchids, steep hills and canyons.

Choke Canyon State Park
Gates are open 5:00 a.m.-10:00 p.m. Seven days a week, year-round except for Public Hunts.
If a girl really needs to escape the area and her troubled thoughts...
A bit farther afield, Choke Canyon State Park is about seventy-five miles south of San Antonio near the town of Three Rivers. There are two units, the South Shore and Calliham (about ten miles west of the South Shore unit).
The Calliham Unit is located on 1100 acres in

McMullen County and the South Shore Unit is located on 385 acres in Live Oak County. Both units offer camping, picnicking, boating, hiking, wildlife viewing, birding, fishing and lake beach swimming. The Calliham Unit also has a swimming pool (open summers from 12:00 noon to 8:00 p.m.), shuffleboard, tennis, volleyball and basketball, two miles of hiking trails, a mile-long bird trail and a wildlife educational center. The South Shore unit offers baseball and volleyball areas. Wildlife in the area includes the American alligator (the westernmost occurrence), Rio Grande turkey, whitetail dear, javelina, coyote, opossum, fox squirrel, raccoon, skunk and the crested caracara (Mexican eagle).

Lost Maples State Natural Area, 37221 FM 187, Vanderpool, TX 78885
Open seven days a week year-round except during Public Hunts.
What a great romantic name for a getaway! How could our heroine resist?
About sixty miles west-northwest of San Antonio, Lost Maples covers 2,174 scenic acres north of Vanderpool on the Sabinal River. The area was once used by prehistoric peoples at times and later played host to the Apache, Lipan Apache and Comanche. The land is a combination of steep canyons, springs, grasslands, wooded slopes and clear streams. There is a large, isolated stand of Uvalde Bigtooth Maple with

beautiful fall foliage. Rare species of birds (such as the Green Kingfisher) can be seen year-round. Activities include camping, picnicking, backpacking, hiking (half-a-mile nature trail, eleven miles of hiking trails), bird-watching, fishing and swimming.

San Antonio Missions National Historic Park,
2202 Roosevelt Ave., San Antonio, TX 78210
Hours 9:00 a.m.-5:00 p.m. daily (closed Thanksgiving Day, Dec. 25, Jan 1)
Biking the trail here is sure to make our heroine feel rejuvenated and ready to face her troubles when she returns home.
Though not an outdoor area in the sense that the other places listed here are, the park boasts a 7.1 mile Mission Hike and Bike Trail that connects the four missions (Mission Concepcion, Mission San Jose, Mission San Juan Capistrano and Mission Espada), all located along the San Antonio River. A large portion of the trail runs parallel to the river with ample opportunities to see egrets, great blue herons and terns, and the missions themselves are unique.

Enjoy your days of sunshine and fresh air in the beautiful San Antonio area!

Here's a sneak peek...

The Law of Attraction
by
Kristi Gold

You won't want to miss the continuation of
THE FORTUNES OF TEXAS: REUNION, *a 12-book
continuity series featuring the powerful Fortune family.
Enjoy this excerpt of Kristi Gold's*
THE LAW OF ATTRACTION, *the eighth book in the
series—available January 2006.*

Daniel Fortune was tempting. He also qualified as a potential mistake.

When Alisha pushed out the door into the cool, misty night, that potential mistake was leaning against the lone lamppost, hands in his pockets, face illuminated by the halogen bulb. Suddenly making that mistake didn't seem like such a bad idea.

You should do him, Hart….

Alisha could not imagine that. All right, she could imagine it, and she had, several times. She certainly wasn't going to make the first move, or any kind of move, for that matter. But she faced a certain dilemma. She had to walk past him on her way to the pay-by-the-hour parking lot across the street. Of course, she could ignore him, as if that were really possible since he'd already seen her. Or she could sprint to her car with only a muttered good-night.

How silly. She could handle this situation with adult diplomacy.

This is not that difficult, Alisha.

Stepping onto the sidewalk, Alisha studied the stars and blurted out the first thing that came to mind. "A really nice night for sex." Oh, crap. She'd been paid a visit by Freud instead of Baby New Year.

Daniel pushed off the pole and narrowed his eyes. "Excuse me? What did you just say?"

Alisha felt the fire rising to her face and more than likely, she probably looked as if she'd been slapped. Someone should slap her for the questionable comment. "I said it's a nice night in Texas." *Good save, Alisha.* "Why?"

"Because I could've sworn you said something about sex."

She folded her arms beneath her breasts and prepared to lie. "I'm not surprised you thought that. I hear men think about sex about every six seconds."

"A total exaggeration. More like every ninety seconds." He topped off the comment with the most patently seductive smile she'd ever seen on a man.

"I stand corrected." Although right now standing before him made her want to drop to her knees in brazen worship as if he'd been ordained as a D.A. demigod.

I'd do him...in a heartbeat....

A round of *pop, pop, pops* from a series of firecrackers echoing through the streets yanked Alisha back into the real world, where defense attorneys and prosecutors didn't mingle, especially between the sheets. Yes, it happened, that much Alisha knew.

But not to her. She'd learned her lesson the hard way, and since that time she'd walked the professional line even though right now she wanted to walk right up and kiss the esteemed Daniel Fortune. The way she'd fantasized about kissing him for months now. She'd fantasized about a lot more than that.

He broke the silence by asking, "Why didn't you wait inside until midnight?"

She hugged her bag to her chest. "First, it's too crowded. Second, Billy Wade was singing like a wounded banshee. Third, sleep's at a premium these days and I need to get home."

"Yeah. I imagine it is with the Massey case pending."

She attempted to look appropriately incensed, very hard to do in the presence of a man who took charisma to a whole new level. "You're determined to get me to discuss that, aren't you?"

"No. Just making an observation."

And that was the reason for his attention. "You're being too polite to me, Counselor, which leads me to believe you're making nice so I'll give you a clue about my strategy."

"There's a couple of things you need to know about me, Counselor. The Massey case isn't my problem because my job is to prosecute the worst of the worst. Felonies, not misdemeanors. And I don't make nice with a woman to gain information."

"Then what do you hope to gain by making nice?"

"I don't hope to gain anything. At least not in terms of our professional relationship."

Alisha wasn't sure where this could be leading but she did know it could be down a dangerous path. "We don't have anything other than a professional relationship."

"We could."

That almost shocked Alisha right out of her vise-like heels. "I don't think that's a good idea."

"Why not?"

"Because you're a prosecutor and I'm a defense attorney."

"No reason why we can't be friendly outside of the courts."

Alisha could think of one big reason, namely she'd gotten a little too friendly with a colleague, and she'd lived to regret it. "Maybe having a personal relationship with associates might work for you, but I've never considered it to be a wise move."

"I don't know if it works for me because I've never done it before."

That was a hard one to swallow. "You're telling me that you've never fraternized with one of the many female attorneys in this town?"

"Never found one I cared to fraternize with." The look he gave her said, *Until now.* Or maybe her imagination was commandeering her brain again.

Turning the topic back to their profession seemed

wise. "By the way, I wanted to add my congratulations on your handling of the Richardson case."

"And I should congratulate you on bulldozing the new guy into taking a plea on the Langston case."

"I didn't bulldoze him. I just did some serious negotiating."

"You scared the hell out of him."

She lifted one shoulder in a shrug. "Okay, call me scary. I've been called worse."

"Such as?"

"Stubborn. Single-minded—"

"Sexy as hell?"

Ha! "Can't say that I've heard that in anyone's verbal repertoire when describing me."

"Well, it's in mine, because you are. Especially tonight."

Alisha fought the inclination to look behind her to see what other woman had arrived on the scene. She pointed toward the street. "I'm going to head home now." Before she did something totally stupid.

"Where do you live?" he asked.

"In an apartment north of town, about twenty minutes away."

"I'm a lot closer. Only a few blocks away. The new condo development."

"The one that overlooks the river? That's rather pricey. I didn't know the D.A.'s office paid so well."

"I manage. The view alone is worth it."

"I'm sure it's great."

"You should come over tonight and see for yourself."

Surely this couldn't be happening to her, a tremendously sensual man asking her over. Actually, it couldn't be happening, or it shouldn't. "Let me guess. You want me to go over your briefs."

"My briefs are in order, unless you feel the need to do a quality check."

She rolled her eyes for the second time tonight even though she had a sudden image of doing that very thing. "You're a big boy. I'm sure you're quite capable of tossing out your old underwear when necessary."

"We were talking about underwear?" His grin was teasing, and terribly tempting.

She laid a dramatic hand on her chest. "My apologies, Mr. Fortune. I guess I've confused you with all of the other male jurists who just love to throw out those clichéd legal pickup lines."

"You mean things like let's engage in a little discovery? I'll show you mine if you'll show me yours?"

"Yes, but we can't forget my personal favorite. Let's go back to my place and study the penal code."

He took a step toward her. "How about I have no statue of limitations when it comes to making you feel good?"

From the deep, compelling tone of his voice, Alisha inherently knew he was telling the truth. "I've never heard that one before."

"That's because I just made it up. I can be pretty quick on my feet."

She was surprised her feet were still holding her up. "Very creative, Counselor. And to quote another cliché, I don't want to end up as another notch on your bedpost."

He sighed, a rough one. "Why is it that women always think men have ulterior motives?"

"Probably because they do."

"Believe it or not, my reasons for inviting you over don't have anything to do with sex. What if I told you that I could just use a friend?"

She could tell him she related to that on a very personal level. "I'm sure you have plenty of friends."

"Sometimes it's hard to know who your friends are in this business."

How true, Alisha thought. "I'm not sure we can really be friends."

"Sure we can." He moved a little closer. "We have a friendly conversation, like we've been doing since the first time we met."

"Friendly? You call telling me my car was a piece of junk when I asked you about a mechanic the other day friendly?"

"And then you told me in explicit detail where I could drive it."

"True, but you deserved it."

Daniel shrugged. "I think you take everything too seriously."

"And you don't?"

"Yeah, most of the time, but not around you. Beats the hell out of me why you bring out that side of me."

"That's because I'm not like most women you know. I don't automatically swoon in your presence." It took great effort on her part not to do that.

"To be honest, I like that about you. That's why I want to spend some time with you. We can watch the fireworks from my living room window. Do you see a problem with that?"

Alisha saw a big problem, namely she was sorely tempted to climb all over him if he moved even a millimeter closer. "For all intents and purposes, we're opponents."

"We're not opposing each other on any case."

"We could in the future."

"I'm not concerned about the future. I'm only thinking about tonight."

How tempting it would be to take him up on his offer. How very, very tempting. But Daniel Fortune's status as an unflappable attorney was second only to his rep as an in-demand lover.

He took another slow step toward her. "Do you really want to spend the rest of the evening alone, Alisha?"

She didn't want to react so strongly to the way he'd said her name, but she did. "I've been alone before."

"So have I, but it's New Year's Eve. People

shouldn't spend the holiday alone if they have other options. Unless you're involved with someone."

"Not currently."

"Then I don't see any real harm in it. Nothing complicated. Just two friends seeing in the new year together."

Alisha hadn't really viewed him as a friend per se, but he wasn't a seedy stranger. After all, he'd made it his life's work putting criminals behind bars. In that regard, he was safe. His magnetism…well, that was another thing altogether.

But she truly didn't want to be alone, not tonight. She would keep a tight grasp on her control. She would go to Daniel Fortune's apartment and take her chances. She looked at him and nodded. "Do you have any champagne?"

His gorgeous grin heralded success. "Then you'll come home with me?"

"Yes. To watch the fireworks and have a drink."

"You're welcome to check out my bedpost for notches."

She didn't dare get anywhere near his bed. "No thanks."

"I wouldn't mind showing you my custom-made wet bar. Lots of shelves, and counter space."

"Room enough for two, no doubt."

"Probably so, with a little careful maneuvering."

Alisha felt as if she'd been thrust into some unknown dimension. Maybe he did want to do her.

Worse, she wanted to do him. Joe and Julie would be so proud. But caution spoke louder than carnal need. "Be careful, Counselor, or I'm going to rescind my offer."

He looked somewhat contrite. "Sorry, but you walked right into that one."

She only hoped that when she walked into his apartment, she'd keep a chokehold on her hormones. "Where's your car?"

"I'm on foot."

She pointed to the lot across the street. "Mine's over there. I'll drive us."

"Save your gas. We can walk it from here."

Maybe walking wasn't such a bad idea. Maybe then they'd be too tired to do anything that might be deemed risky. Maybe they should jog. "Okay, Counselor. Lead the way."

And with only minimal second thoughts, Alisha accompanied Daniel Fortune to his condo, feeling as if tonight she might go anywhere he cared to take her.

...NOT THE END...

Look for The Law of Attraction *by Kristi Gold in stores January 2006.*

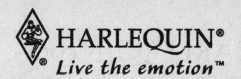

HARLEQUIN®
Live the emotion™

Upbeat,
All-American Romances

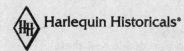
Romantic Comedy

Historical,
Romantic Adventure

INTRIGUE
Romantic Suspense

HARLEQUIN ROMANCE®
The essence of
modern romance

Seduction and passion
guaranteed

Emotional,
Exciting, Unexpected

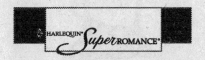
Sassy, Sexy, Seductive!

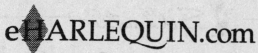

SPECIAL EDITION™

Emotional, compelling stories that capture the intensity of
living, loving and creating a family in today's world.

Desire®

Modern, passionate reads that are powerful and provocative.

INTIMATE MOMENTS™

Romances that are sparked by danger and fueled by passion.

SILHOUETTE *Romance*

From today to forever, these love stories offer
today's woman fairytale romance.

BOMBSHELL

Action-filled romances with strong, sexy, savvy women who save the day.